Conviction of the Heart

by

Alana Lorens

This is a work of fiction. Names, characters, places, and incidents are either the product of the author's imagination or are used fictitiously, and any resemblance to actual persons living or dead, business establishments, events, or locales, is entirely coincidental.

Conviction of the Heart

Contact Information: info@thewildrosepress.com

Cover Art by *Kim Mendoza*

The Wild Rose Press, Inc.
PO Box 708
Adams Basin, NY 14410-0708
Visit us at www.thewildrosepress.com

Publishing History
First Crimson Rose Edition, 2012
Print ISBN 978-1-61217-251-4
Digital ISBN 978-1-61217-252-1

Published in the United States of America

"Hey, woman! Where do you get off stealing people's kids from them? Huh?"

The shout came from behind her. There. Wachowski, the father who'd lost his case, lurking behind one of the pillars at the top of the stairs. His graying hair was rumpled, and his pale blue eyes held a wild and unpredictable look.

"Mr. Wachowski, I really shouldn't speak to you while you're represented by counsel." While ethically true, it was actually a maneuver to buy time.

"Don't need a mouthpiece to deal with you." He put his right hand in the front pocket of his suit jacket.

In a move born more of instinct than intent, Suzanne raised her solid-sided black briefcase so it blocked her torso. If he was going to take a shot—

"Suzanne!"

Running up the steps from the sidewalk, almost as though he were riding a white steed, was Nick Sansone. He ascended to the step where she stood, then one higher, so he was directly between them. His trained eyes flickered from her to the man above her, and back. "Everything all right here?" he asked.

Wachowski's eyes never released her gaze, but she saw doubt once Nick appeared. What was in Wachowski's pocket? It could be a gun, or a wallet full of family photos. She cleared a throat that had tightened beyond speech and took a deep breath. "I think everything's fine. I believe Mr. Wachowski was just leaving."

Wachowski twitched, jaw working, hand still in his pocket. Nick wasn't in uniform, but something about him conveyed an air of authority. Even Suzanne could feel it.

What was he doing here—just when she needed him?

Dedication

For the spirit and heart
of all those who empower, counsel and work
with domestic violence survivors…
Keep up the good fight.

Chapter One

Suzanne Taylor eyed her gold link watch. Six o'clock already. She'd be the last one home again.

Guilt swirled through her midsection. Her mother nagged her about leaving the girls home alone so late. *"Too many bad things they can get into out there. Predators! On Dateline last week..."*

Suzanne groaned at the thought. If she had to hear about the pervs on *Dateline* one more time, she'd consider moving out of Pittsburgh, away from her parents. Far away.

Annoyed with her life and the solo practice of family law, she grabbed her soft leather briefcase and shoved a handful of files inside. She'd have to finish at home. One file in particular that she wanted, she couldn't find in the ever-undulating stack of clutter on her heavy wooden desk. The desk she'd inherited from her grandmother's Indiana farmhouse. For the clutter, she could only blame herself.

"Eureka!" she muttered as she finally located the paperwork and put it in the case, buckled it up. Her hand hit the switch, and the book-lined office went dark. She shouldered her purse and headed through the still-lit secretary's office for the door.

As her hand hit the door handle, it twisted under her fingers, and the solid wooden door came toward her, slamming into her foot. She yelped. A gasp sounded on the other side of the door, and a tear-streaked face poked around the edge.

"Oh, I'm so sorry! Oh, my gosh, are you all right?" the woman asked.

The woman wore no makeup, and her hair was a disheveled mess, but her jacket and skirt were pricey—Suzanne had admired that set at Coldwater Creek a week before.

"I'll live," Suzanne replied wryly. "I was just leaving." She gestured to the clock, which now read six-fifteen.

"No! Please, you can't!" The slender woman seized her hand, dark eyes wild, like a panicked horse. "I don't have much time. He's going to kill me!"

"Who's going to kill you?"

"My husband. I know it sounds crazy, but I know it. I know it." The conviction in the woman's voice seeped into Suzanne's bones. She believed what she was saying. "I know it's late, but Nick said you'd help me. He said you were the best."

"Nick?"

"Nick Sansone. He's a policeman we know from the community center. I called him from a pay phone outside the grocery store, and he said you would help me."

"Oh, he did?"

Nicholas Sansone had been a witness in one of Suzanne's cases several months before. She had caught him looking at her with something that might have been attraction. And though it could have been accidental, the detective with the huge dark eyes and shoulders that looked as if they had the benefit of hours at the gym had seemed thereafter to cross her path frequently in the Courthouse corridors. He hadn't asked her out, but there had been times she thought he was going to, and she'd purposely given him "chilly." Suzanne didn't date cops. Cops had a way of landing in trouble. She didn't need trouble.

But she wouldn't hold it against this woman in obvious distress. Suzanne stepped back, inviting her in. "What makes you think he's going to kill you?"

The woman scanned the hallway with a nervous glance, then came in and closed the door behind her. "He went out of town this morning. He took his gun with him, so I couldn't hide it, but I found the number to the funeral home on his dresser. The card had my birth date and social security number." She leaned back against the door frame, one hand over her heart, breathing rapidly. "He's planning something, and I'm not meant to survive."

Suzanne glanced at the clock again and sighed. "All right, sit and I'll grab a pen—"

"No, I can't. Not now. I've got to be home by seven. He'll call." Her hand fluttered, fell back onto her chest. "If I don't answer, he'll punish me."

"Punish you?" Suzanne's brow puckered. As an attorney working in family law, she'd dealt with domestic violence cases before. After fifteen years, there was little that shocked her. Never made it easier to hear, though.

The woman struggled to rephrase what she'd said. "I mean, he'll be mad. I don't want to make him mad. Not when he..." Her voice faded and trembles wracked her body. She nearly fell.

"Come on," Suzanne said, dropping her case. The last thing she needed was a lawsuit if this woman collapsed on her doorstep. She slipped an arm around the woman's shoulders to guide her to the nearest chair, "I understand what you're saying. How can I help you?"

"I have a doctor's appointment on Friday morning. He'll expect me to be gone for two hours. Can I come back then?"

"He'll still be gone?"

"He's at some national conference in St. Louis,

not due back till Saturday afternoon. But he set people to watch me." That panicked look again. "He's very important."

Suzanne snorted. "Importance doesn't give anyone the right to terrorize their wife." She reached for a yellow pad off her secretary's perfectly organized desk. "Are there children?"

"Yes. A boy and a girl."

"Has he been violent toward them?"

A long hesitation. The woman's tongue flicked out to wet her lips before she spoke. "He broke Katie's wrist last year."

Suzanne caught her breath and made a note. "We can get you a protection order that would make him leave the house, if you want to stay there, or we can get you to a safe place with your kids. Do you want to file for divorce?"

"I…I…don't know." Those long-fingered hands fluttered again, settled in her lap, twisting against each other for comfort.

Suzanne never understood why a woman stayed with a man who had injured her child. She believed in the right of a woman to be autonomous, independent, and never forced to depend on a man for anything.

But the world didn't always work that way.

As a chunk of auburn bangs fell into her eyes, Suzanne tucked her hair behind her ear with irritation. She was due for a haircut. Somehow, she'd have to make the time. She rattled off a quick list of documents she wanted to see.

"Bring those to me Friday morning. Come as soon as you can. We'll be quick."

"God bless you," the woman said, breaking into tears of relief. She took Suzanne's hand again, and for a moment, Suzanne thought she'd actually kiss it, but she got herself under control. "God bless you!"

"What's your name?" Suzanne asked, leaning

backward over Donna's desk for her calendar.

"Maddie. Madeleine Morgan." The woman took a handful of tissues from a box on the nearby table and dabbed at her face.

"Maddie Morgan?" Suzanne nearly dropped the planner. Everyone in Pittsburgh knew that name. "You mean your husband's Gregory Morgan? The city councilman?"

The woman bit her lip.

"I'm sorry, I don't mean to sound that way." Suzanne backtracked as fast as she could. Disbelief had flooded her voice, she was sure. The Morgan name was in the papers at least once a week, usually more. She'd met Councilman Morgan half a dozen times at charity or city events. He'd always seemed so…nice.

Experience had shown, however, often those were the ones worth watching out for. Violence could lurk, well-concealed, behind a charming façade. Especially one with money and position.

The clock chimed six-thirty, and Maddie jumped to her feet with a little shriek. "I've got to go, now! He'll be calling."

"All right, all right. Friday morning. I'll be here by eight-thirty."

"Thank you, Miss Taylor. Thank you so much. Thank you!"

Her fervent words following her out the door, Madeleine Morgan was gone, light footsteps tapping down the hall to the stairs to take her down one flight to Carson Street.

Suzanne picked up her case and her purse again. This woman's story, even the brief part she'd shared so far, resonated with others in Suzanne's memory. Some of her brethren might have pooh-poohed the woman's fears, but not Suzanne. Not anymore. A cold wave of nausea washed over her. She'd lost one client to a psychotic husband already.

The murder might have been three years before, but Suzanne hadn't forgotten one detail. She hadn't believed that man was serious. He'd proved her wrong.

She wouldn't make that mistake again. She wouldn't lose another one.

She'd lay everything on the line to protect Maddie Morgan.

Chapter Two

There he was again.

Nick Sansone.

Waiting for her, in ambush, like a guerilla assault team, when she approached the elevator in Pittsburgh's City-County Building. Since she practiced family law, and he was a police detective, they weren't often in the same building. The criminal courts took place in the old red granite "castle" next to the stone former jail building. City-County was the home of the civil courts. No reason for him to be here.

But here the lanky detective stood, in the busy first floor lobby. His suit was dark gray, his tie a conservative print with maroon diamonds, and his shoes were spit-polished to a perfect shine.

"Counselor," he said with an easy grin. "Starting early today, I see."

Put him off. Don't let him engage. "Tough job being a homewrecker, but someone's got to do it," she said.

It might be corny, but it was better than the usual jokes about lawyers and sharks. Or lawyers and bottom feeders. Or lawyers and...about anything one could think of that was disgusting. Cops seemed to know them all.

"Now, I've seen you in action, Ms. Taylor. I know that's not your *modus operandi* at all."

Her cheeks flamed. "Don't try to flatter me with

your fine command of Latin phrases, Detective."

"Not flattery at all! Spoken with true admiration, I assure you. I've observed enough of my colleagues raked over the coals to know a shark when I see one. And you're not."

A tight smile was her only response as the elevator doors opened. They both walked in, along with half a dozen other people chattering, involved in their own lives. She debated bringing up Maddie Morgan, but it wasn't her habit to discuss her clients with others. If she needed information from Sansone, she could certainly ask him after the meeting on Friday.

"Who's the unlucky man today?" he asked, gaze warm with amusement.

"You assume it's a man?" Suzanne clutched the handle of her briefcase more tightly. "I don't only represent women, Sergeant."

"Lieutenant."

"I'm sorry?" She eyed him with a little frown.

"Lieutenant. I've been promoted since we last met."

The elevator doors opened at the floor below the one she wanted. Jostled by people behind her wanting to get out, she was shoved closer to him to allow them to pass. Close enough for her to get a full inhale of his aftershave, something spicy with a hint of citrus. It was her immediate new favorite. *Damn him.*

She put intentional distance between them as soon as the others left the small space, said nothing until the doors slid shut again. "Congratulations, Lieutenant. I'm sure it's well-deserved."

"I hope so. My granddad would certainly be tickled. I've been waiting to celebrate, thanks to a hellish schedule at work. Interested?"

"In celebrating with you?" She squeezed the handle tight again, so tempted. Her reaction to him was something she couldn't control; the way she expressed it certainly was. She didn't intend to allow him to see one bit of it.

Echoes of her mother nagging that she worked too much and never had any fun floated through her mind. *It's only a date. What could a date hurt?*

She shoved her mother's complaints into a dark corner of her mind. "Fun" didn't pay the bills. "Fun" didn't make it possible to survive as a single mother. Work did that.

Besides, he was a cop. Better to protect her heart.

The elevator doors opened again, the metallic "ding" announcing their arrival.

Saved by the bell. She stepped out of the car and managed a social smile. "I don't know how long I'll be today, Lieutenant. I'll have to pass."

The disappointment on his face pained her. It wasn't just some casual invitation then. He must have really meant it. The doors closed, and she turned away toward the courtroom where she was calendared to be, her throat choked with mixed feelings. She didn't forget his wounded expression for the rest of the morning.

****

Late that afternoon, Suzanne's custody case concluded, past the closing of the courthouse itself. The hallways were empty, the sun burning in through west-facing windows. Two rambunctious preschoolers, the subjects of her case, released from the prison of courtroom decorum, burst into giddy action, footsteps echoing as they twirled in the vacant corridor.

As the combatants staggered out into the hallway, her client, having been granted custody, impulsively hugged her, while the father glared from twenty feet away, conferring for a moment with his own attorney. Suzanne disentangled herself, adrenaline starting to wear thin after the day of cat and mouse, question and answers, emotions and tears. “Will you be all right getting downstairs?” she asked.

The woman smiled. “He won’t dare try anything now.”

“All right. Drive carefully. Remember to call me if you have any problems.”

She waved at the children as they skipped away with their mother, then gave a nod to the attorney on the other side, a classmate of hers from Pitt. Good friends outside the courtroom. Inside, both had acted quite reserved toward one another, even antagonistic from time to time, for the sake of their clients and their case.

She waited after they’d all left, breathing the quiet in deeply, eyes and brain not focused on anything in particular for a few moments. The only thing she worried about was that angry gleam in the eye of her client’s husband. Understandable that people got upset, even violent, when their lives were crumbling around them. Custody hearings were emotional battles, draining the combatants and counsel alike.

She took a deep breath, blew it out slowly. Her colleague had no doubt talked to the husband, calmed him down. All she needed to do now was decide what to do with her evening.

Suspecting she’d run late, she’d arranged for her girls to spend the night at her parents' house in Perrysville, several miles north of the city, so she had no concern about them being home alone.

Free at last.

Considering the possibilities, she headed for the elevator, her footsteps loud in her own ears. It wasn’t the first time she’d gotten out of court after hours. With any luck she’d avoid the worst of the early evening traffic. The ride to the lobby was quick, not interrupted by floor-by-floor tedium. She shoved open the heavy door to the outside, assailed with the noise of five o'clock traffic along Forbes Avenue. Three blocks west, her car waited in the parking garage, then she'd be on her way.

"Hey, woman! Where do you get off stealing people's kids from them? Huh?"

The shout came from behind her. She turned to see Jack Wachowski, the father from upstairs, lurking behind one of the pillars at the top of the stairs. He'd lost his overcoat and tie somewhere between the courtroom and outside. His graying hair was rumpled. He'd never been an attractive man, but the wild look in his eyes made him almost frightening.

A quick glance reminded her the doors were closed. And locked.

"Mr. Wachowski, I really shouldn't speak to you while you're represented by counsel." While ethically true, the statement was actually a maneuver to buy time.

"Don't need a mouthpiece to deal with you." He put his right hand in the front pocket of his suit jacket.

In a move born more of instinct than intent, Suzanne raised her solid-sided black briefcase so it blocked her torso. If he was going to take a shot—

"Suzanne!"

The interruption drew her attention, as well as that of Mr. Wachowski. Coming up the steps from the sidewalk, almost as though he were riding a white steed, was Nick Sansone. He ascended to the step where she stood, then took one more step, so he was almost directly between them. His trained eyes flicked between her to the man on the stairs above her and back.

"Everything all right here?" he asked.

Where had he come from?

Suzanne eyed Wachowski. His pale blue eyes never released her gaze, but she thought she saw doubt in them now. What did he have in his pocket? It could be a gun. It could be a wallet full of family photos. She cleared a throat that had tightened beyond speech and took a deep breath. "I think everything's fine. I believe Mr. Wachowski was just leaving."

Wachowski studied Sansone, jaw working as he decided what to do. Nick wasn't in uniform, but something about him conveyed an air of authority. Even Suzanne could feel it. Nick must be over six feet tall, those five or six inches' difference always forcing her to look up at him, putting her at a disadvantage.

What was he doing here—just when she needed him?

The other man coughed and took his hand out of his pocket. It was empty. "Yeah. Yeah, I was just going home. It's been a damned long day." Wachowski looked at her a long moment, then turned and walked away, taking a diagonal path away from them down the steps. He didn't look back.

Suzanne breathed a sigh of relief. Nick didn't miss it.

"So there *was* more here than met the eye," he said, scrutinizing her face. "What did he have in his pocket?"

Was there any point in ignoring him? No doubt the man was an expert interrogator. He might even be better than Suzanne herself. "Honestly? I don't know."

"Did he make any threats?"

"No." She looked down at the traffic passing by, something concrete and normal. Not like angry litigants with potential weapons. Or attractive police lieutenants.

"I can have someone investigate if—"

"It's fine," she said, an edge in her voice pitched to the end-of-discussion level. "We were in court all day. We're both tired. Can we leave it at that?"

He searched her face for more clues, apparently finding none. "All right. You know him, I don't." His alert stance relaxed, just a little, but his eyes were warm with concern for her.

Why was he worried about her? Annoyance provoked her sharp tongue. "You're here late," she said.

"So are you." His attention moved away from her, and he watched the street below them, particularly in the direction Mr. Wachowski had gone.

"Two people, after hours in the courthouse, at the same time. Heck of a coincidence." She started walking down the steps.

He followed her. "Not really. I was waiting for you."

An imaginary grasshopper twitched to life in her stomach. "You need a divorce lawyer?" she asked without turning around. She didn't want him to see her expression.

"Not at all. I was just heading down to Mama Rosa's for some lasagna," he said. "I thought you might need dinner, too. Interested in Italian tonight?"

"I was planning to go back to the office. So much to do." A tiny voice in her heart berated her for putting him off. She even had a babysitter in place. What was the harm?

"You have to walk the dog?"

"No."

"Expecting more trouble?"

"No!" She stopped and turned around to face him. "I can handle myself, Lieutenant. Thank you so much for your interest."

Then, as the traffic light at the corner changed,

the noise level diminished for just a moment, but it was long enough for both of them to hear her stomach growl like a wild tiger on the prowl. She stared at the concrete steps, wishing she could disappear right through them.

"Put my mind at ease, counselor. No hassles, I promise. Just dinner," he said softly.

She took a deep breath and surrendered to the hands of fate. "Just dinner."

Chapter Three

He couldn't believe she'd actually agreed to a date. Well, not a date. Dinner.

But he wanted to consider it a date.

He'd watched her for some time. It was more than just his natural attraction to redheads. He found something more compelling in her behavior, her demeanor. He found her different from the rest of the ambulance chasers he encountered in his work.

During their midwinter case, he witnessed her inner fire and passion for what was right, whether or not it fell squarely within the law. She never let opposing counsel walk over her. She even used humor as a tool to pry open judges' hearts to let her pleas inside.

When the case concluded, he wanted to see her—unprofessionally—but she created a distinct distance between them that dissuaded him. He tried to put her out of his mind. She kept re-appearing. Every so often, he caught a glimpse of her in the court buildings, or in her favorite lunch spot in the inner courtyard of the old castle, and those feelings would bubble up again. He couldn't forget her.

Not that he hadn't tried. Brother officers used his fascination with the standoffish attorney to rib him without mercy. A lawyer and a cop? Might as well be oil and water, one working to get bad people locked up, and the other working just as hard to set them free again. It didn't matter that she worked in a different specialty. His associates lumped them all together as a waste of educated flesh. It could never work. Just asking for trouble. Who needed trouble?

Nick wasn't convinced.

Determined, he cultivated the judge's secretaries, many of whom had a soft spot for him. If she was scheduled to appear, they let him know. He'd put himself in the way of finding her, to ask her out.

And now, she'd finally said yes.

Mama Rosa's was a cop hangout, a place with good Italian food and checkered red and white tablecloths and candles on the table after dark. He arrived first and took his usual table, chewing over whether he should have taken her somewhere fancier. She was probably used to more upscale places, restaurants with three forks in a setting. He was the kind of guy who ate with his elbows on the table.

He'd offered to drive her, but she wanted her own car. Although it appeared the man with the mysterious pocket had left the scene, he wasn't convinced it was safe to leave her. She'd finally allowed him to walk her to her car in the lot. He'd told her how to get here. But a half-hour later, she still hadn't arrived.

Maybe I should have insisted.

Maybe she wasn't coming.

He adjusted his posture, at a loss to explain why his seat wasn't as comfortable as usual. He loosened his tie, then took it off, shoving it in his pocket. He unbuttoned his top button. Perhaps she'd find the casual look appealing, looser. Maybe she'd relax. It sure as hell made him feel better.

He leaned forward on his chair, sitting on the edge, just short of a fidget. Concetta, one of the older ladies who'd been serving at Mama Rosa's as long as

Nick could remember, stopped by the table to ask if he needed anything. "You're watching the door awful close, Nicky. Your boss coming? Or a woman?" She studied him, dark birdlike eyes boring into him.

"Is it that obvious?" He allowed a laugh, finding it came with a wash of relief. Suzanne owed him nothing. If she didn't come—

Then she stepped through the door.

She'd shed her brown jacket. Her yellow dress, sleeveless, exposed more of her skin than he'd ever seen. He thought she'd lost her professional pumps, too, brown sandals on her feet instead.

More stunning was the shoulder-length red mane she'd released from whatever semi-magic pinning procedure women used to twist their locks into knots. Loose around her shoulders, her hair was beautiful.

"Oh, ho!" the waitress said. Something in her voice triggered his notice. He looked away from Suzanne, tracking Concetta's quick exit. What was she up to? She scurried off into the back. A moment later, a group of curious faces popped up at the pass-through window from the kitchen.

Great. An audience. Just what I need. Intent on his original purpose, he stood up to greet Suzanne. "Counselor. I thought perhaps you'd gotten lost. Or that your...admirer...had returned."

Her cheeks turned the faintest shade of pink. "No, Lieutenant, your directions were fine. I took the long way around so I could wind down a little."

As she sat down, he held her chair and carefully pushed it in. "I might have been here before. About a thousand times."

"A thousand? Really?"

"Maybe." He chuckled, feeling like he'd turned a police-issue flashlight on himself. "My dad was a cop, and my grandfather was a cop, and *his* father was right off the boat from Italy. So I practically grew up in this neighborhood."

She smiled, and the smile gave her whole face a warm glow, as if someone had lit a candle inside her.

Concetta brought two menus and poured icy water into short, heavy glasses. "Vito made lasagna today," she said.

Nick glanced across the table at Suzanne. "You don't want to pass up Vito's lasagna."

Her gaze flicked across the menu, then she handed it back to Concetta. "Of course not."

"Two lasagna." Concetta scribbled on her pad. "He's got fresh bread in the oven. I'll bring some out. Wine?"

"Merlot?" he asked, and Suzanne nodded.

"Got just the thing." Concetta grinned and waddled back to the kitchen. Nick glanced in that direction and caught a glimpse of all the would-be mother hens clucking up a storm in the back. They'd fussed over him since he was a boy eating meals with his grandfather; Nick was sure he remained their topic of conversation. He and Suzanne.

Fortunately, Suzanne seemed oblivious to the buzz. "So, a legacy cop," she said. "Your family must be proud you're a lieutenant."

Nick nodded. "Best day of my dad's life, I think. Even better than the day I graduated from Pitt."

"You went to Pitt? My alma mater, too."

"Not in the same class, I'm sure." Nick was forty-five; he'd always thought of Suzanne as at least ten years younger.

The fingers of her left hand ran lightly over the fork, cushioned in the folded white napkin on the table. "Well, I went for law school. We wouldn't have seen each other anyway."

"Probably not. It was twenty years ago, before I joined the force."

She looked up, surprised. "I was just finishing up. But I was sure you were older than I am." She hesitated, bit her lip. "I just turned forty."

"Not so much. I'm forty-five." There, he said it. He hated thinking about the passing of the years. So many of them, so many alone. An awkward silence between them preceded the arrival of the wine, as well as hot bread with the strong aroma of garlic and cheese. He uncorked the bottle with a well-practiced hand, then poured them each half a glass.

He suppressed the urge to ask about her love life. "Where'd you go for undergrad?" he asked instead.

"Penn State." She took a sip of the wine, holding the cool edge of the glass against her lip for a moment.

"Business major?" he guessed.

"Oh, no! Sociology. Headed for a career involving 'Would you like fries with that?'" She laughed. "Graduate school was pretty much a given."

"So you've been bent on saving the world all along."

She shrugged. "Some of it, at least."

He could understand the sentiment. "I believe that's what I do, too. God knows there isn't much other reason to be on the street some days. I want to know I'm making a difference for some man, woman or child every time I step out on the street."

He waited for her to mock him, as other women had over the years. Many women wanted to date a police officer. Some found it a ticket to an "E" ride, great benefits, good pay, the opportunity for them to hang out with the girls at the outlet malls all day and get their nails done. Some, with violent men in their pasts, thought being with a cop would protect them. Some just were cop groupies, taking the thrill and excitement of the profession by proxy.

But most denigrated his genuine need to serve as corny and fake.

Suzanne didn't poke fun. She skewered him

with a dissecting gaze. After a few silent moments, she ostensibly accepted him at face value. “Did you always want to be a cop?”

“Sure. I mean, the family history and all. Guess I never wanted to be anything else. Except an astronaut.” He grinned.

“You? Roger Ramjet? Hard to believe.” She laughed softly, and he thought the cool distance in her eyes mellowed. Maybe he had a chance with her.

“More Elroy Jetson, I think. You know, visions of the future, all of us with jetpacks to get where we wanted to go, whatever’s ‘out there.’” He gestured toward the ceiling. He saw her about to laugh and gulped some wine.

Their salads arrived, and he was grateful for the distraction. By the time they’d finished those, then the bread, and the stacked tomato, noodle and cheese bit of heaven that defined Vito’s lasagna, he’d discovered her to be an educated and interesting companion.

They’d talked their way through politics and religion. They’d danced through current events, books, movies, and a shared love of 1970s music. They’d discussed parents and the difficulties of being adult children.

Everything, essentially, except their possible feelings about each other.

Neither seemed inclined to bring that up.

All the while, he supposed she was appraising him. Her gaze perched often on his lips as he spoke, almost as warm as a touch. He imagined what they would taste like, those soft lips. He was ready. One of them had to make the first move.

As they sat over coffee and the remains of a shared tiramisu, he decided to go for it. He leaned forward, speaking quietly, almost a whisper.

“What?” she asked. When she leaned forward to hear him, he kissed her.

"Hey!" she said, pulling back. Expression alarmed, she picked up her napkin, holding it in her hand on the table before her, almost like a shield.

Damn it.

Immediately contrite, he said, "I'm sorry. I shouldn't have done that." He sat straight, and raised his hands. "Sorry. I had to get it out of my system. I've been thinking about kissing you ever since you walked in here. You look amazing."

She eyed him, retracted her hand and its napkin into her lap. "Well…thank you." Her eyes slipped away, but a smile tried to hide in the corner of her lips.

He reached for his coffee cup, fiddling with its handle. "Thank you for not slapping me."

"And risk being charged with battery on a police officer? Not likely." Suzanne took a deep breath, then let it out. "I'm a big girl, Nick. I like to make informed decisions, that's all." She stood up. "Thank you for dinner."

He awkwardly rose to his feet, too, chagrined his impulsive move had brought the evening to a close. "You're very welcome. It's been great. Suzanne, really, I'm sorry. I'd love to see you again."

"You know, I'd like that, too." She studied him a moment, then leaned down and kissed him. "Good night, Lieutenant." She headed for the door.

Off balance, he sank back into his chair. Concetta was at his elbow with a coffee carafe before he could even form a sentence.

"She's not Italian," she scolded.

"With that hair? I doubt it." He laughed.

"A Mick…What your ma would say, rest her soul." She clucked her tongue. "But, Nicky, that one is quality," she said with a smile. "The dress…those earrings. She's got money, right?"

"Huh? I guess, yeah. She's a lawyer." Nick was still mulling over her kiss, hoping it meant what he thought it did.

"A lawyer?" She turned back to the kitchen, calling out, "A lawyer!" The watching faces lit up with approval like a Christmas display.

"Concetta." He held his hand over the cup as she was about to pour. "I've had enough. Got to be up at the crack of dawn tomorrow." He gave her three twenties. "Keep the change."

Concetta grinned and patted him on the arm. "You're a good boy, Nicky. I hope this one sticks."

"Yeah. So do I." As his face twitched into a goofy smile, he wandered off toward the door.

Definitely hope this one sticks. She's worth it.

Chapter Four

When Madeleine Morgan arrived on Friday morning, she appeared every bit the pampered politician's wife. The earlier panic seemed under control. Her hair was coiffed, the blue suit expensive, and she even wore pale lipstick. But dark half-circles under her eyes and the ragged edges of her polished nails told a different story.

Donna gave her the standard intake form on a clipboard, which Madeleine filled out while clutching a large brown envelope with a dried coffee stain on the front. Suzanne hoped the envelope contained the documents she had requested. She stole a peek at Maddie, then went back to her office, pacing while she waited, the office seeming smaller the more she walked.

She'd rented the space before Carson Street emerged as one of the hottest nightlife areas in Pittsburgh, and she'd been lucky to have signed a long term lease. The office was in the back of the building's second floor, and the broad window looked out toward the Monongahela River. At one point in time, tenants might have been able to see the river from the window, but the area between Carson Street and the river had gradually built up with shops and warehouses, blocking the view.

She had four good-sized rooms, the largest of which she'd taken for her own office, its walls lined with books she hardly ever used now that most of her research was done online. Behind her grandmother's desk sat Suzanne's worn black leather chair, a hulking bit of furniture that, after ten years, molded around her bottom. A pair of upholstered loveseats with a small gray print sat diagonal to one another. That was where Suzanne preferred to interview her clients. The "family" setting seemed more intimate, and more likely to put clients at ease when discussing sensitive personal, even shameful, matters.

Two framed diplomas graced the wall. Her favorite framed art, though, made by her daughters over the years, hung across from her desk, reminding her of the reason she worked so hard.

"Thank you again for this appointment," Maddie said as Donna ushered her in.

Suzanne held out her hand for the envelope, which Maddie gave to her. "Of course. Have you heard from your husband?"

"He calls twice a day, but I never know what time each call will be. He...he doesn't suspect anything, if that's what you mean."

"Good. Are people still keeping tabs on you?"

Suzanne opened the envelope and drew out a marriage certificate, retirement documents, a deed to the house, birth certificates for Joshua, age fourteen, and Katie, ten, and Social Security cards for the family, and half a dozen other pieces of paper that would start to define the assets and debts of the Morgan family.

"His friends drive by in the evening to make sure I don't go out after dark." At Suzanne's curious look, Maddie added, "He always thinks I'm meeting another man."

"Other men only come out after dark?" Suzanne asked with a grin.

There was no answering smile. "I'm not allowed out after dark," Maddie said in a monotone.

Too soon for humor for this one, Suzanne realized. Maddie was still beaten down, subjugated. Healing would take time. She'd learn to step away from the cloistered life she was living.

"I'd be willing to bet he also controls all the money."

Maddie nodded.

"He probably hides it, or keeps you ignorant enough so you don't know the extent of the accounts."

"I have some idea. But you're right. It's been my job to make a lovely home and raise his children, not to interfere in his business."

Pretty typical. "He's always been like this?"

"Yes." Maddie's voice was flat.

"You've been married for..." She read down the intake sheet. "Sixteen years?"

Maddie nodded.

"He was like this even before you married him?" She looked Maddie in the eye. "Was he physically abusive then?"

Maddie shuffled her shoes on the carpet, eyes cast down. "Yes," she said quietly.

"Some judges might not understand this, Maddie. I mean, why you'd marry him when you already knew he was an abuser." Suzanne quit writing and looked closely at her client, whose panic seemed to flicker back to life. "You don't have to explain to me—I know many reasons why domestic violence survivors stay with abusers. At some point, we'll need to explain to the court. So, let's see if we can flesh those reasons out."

Maddie squirmed in the chair, picking at her skirt. A long few minutes passed before she answered. "He was always so good afterward. It only happened once before we were married, and he said it would never happen again. He promised." She leaned back against the cushion, but sat upright again almost immediately, her hands fretting in her lap. "The next was almost two years later. He begged me to forgive him. I did." Maddie looked out the window. "The next time, it was too late."

"How do you mean?"

"I was pregnant with Joshua."

Suzanne nodded with understanding. "And after that?"

"He made sure I was pregnant often enough so I never had the courage to get out." She looked directly at Suzanne. "He's beaten me so badly I lost four pregnancies. Only Katie and Joshua survived. I've held on as long as I can. I won't sit around now and wait for him to kill me. I can't do that to my babies."

One tear, then several more, cascaded down her cheeks. Her thin fingers picked at the expensive skirt.

"I'd recommend we file papers to keep him away from you and your children. If we file today, we'd get an immediate restraining order. He couldn't come to the house or send anyone after you. Do you have somewhere you can stay until the dust settles? Friends? Relatives?"

"He's run off all my real friends. He'll probably go after you, too. He does that. He wants to make sure no one helps me." Maddie took a long, ragged breath. "All I have left are the wives of his buddies. I can't tell them what's really been happening. Not after I've covered it up so long. No one will believe me."

Suzanne sighed. Despite Maddie's assertion that Greg Morgan would go after Suzanne, she certainly couldn't base her representation on that. Maddie would have to be able to count on her, no matter what. Suzanne could take care of herself. "How about family members?"

"My parents are dead. My sister lives in

California and isn't much help."

"Did you talk to the people at Womanspace?"

"I did, but..."

Again Suzanne saw emotion peak in her client's eyes, though she tried to throttle it back down.

"I mean, you don't know the kind of people who will be staying there. People from our neighborhood in Shadyside...you know, just don't stay there. Besides, my son is too old to share a room with his sister. They said they didn't know if they could find separate rooms."

Suzanne had encountered such protests before, mostly from those who didn't understand domestic violence stretched across all socioeconomic classes. The shelter was considered demeaning by affluent people. But it wasn't about money. It was about sanctuary.

"You must understand the risks here. I'm going to send the sheriff to his office with an envelope of papers telling him you're leaving him and taking the children after sixteen years. Do you think he's just going to come home after work looking for pot roast?"

Maddie stared at her, deer-in-the-headlights frozen. After several moments, she jerked in delayed reaction and put her hands over her face.

Suzanne tried again. "Statistics show that violence increases at time of separation. Before we do this, I want to believe you've got somewhere safe to go."

"I don't know what to do! Tell me what to do. Please," Maddie begged, a little girl lost.

"I can't. You need to decide for yourself what's best for the children, and for you. Let me give you a few minutes." She slid the documents back into the envelope and walked out to the secretary's desk.

Donna had been with Suzanne for four years, a heavy-set woman in her mid-thirties who preferred fitted suits for work. She wore sensible shoes and kept her desk immaculate. Her one fashion statement was a pair of large, square-framed tortoiseshell glasses; otherwise she was a mixture of neutrals; dishwater blonde hair, hazel eyes and office wardrobe of tans, grays and beige.

Donna looked up from the document she was typing. "Everything okay?" she asked.

Suzanne blew air up at the bangs that continued to trail over her eyebrows. "Fine. I'll need copies of all this—she can have the originals when she leaves."

"You want coffee?"

"I'll wait. This woman doesn't need any caffeine. Trust me."

Hesitating outside the door a moment, Suzanne counted to ten, then went back in. Maddie still had no answer for her. Suzanne considered the best way to approach the councilman's wife. "Maddie, tell me about the last violent incident, the one where your child's arm was broken."

The woman haltingly went through the event, how Gregory had come home late from work one afternoon, found the children's toys in his recliner, and exploded into a rage, throwing the children like stuffed animals, beating Maddie with both sides of his hands.

The stories reminded Suzanne of many others she'd heard about batterers. The way Maddie presented it, with the constant small excuses, such as "I know I should have picked up the toys before he came home," placing the blame on herself, rang true. But this man's short fuse seemed shorter than most. He didn't restrain himself to avoid legal consequences, which puzzled Suzanne, considering his stature in the community.

Batterers often understood the letter of the law and governed themselves accordingly. They could verbally abuse as much as they wanted. As long as they didn't leave marks, they could physically abuse as well, because without medical evidence, the court judged one spouse's word against the other. Even if they left bruises, by reminding the dependent spouse who controlled the financial lifelines, the harsh reality hit—no other option but to stay.

Perhaps Greg Morgan believed he was invincible.

If she remembered correctly, Morgan was part of a larger family entity that reached out to charities in the community. The Morgan benevolence included a scholarship for minority youth, substantial contributions to United Way and other local causes, and big donations to the "right" political campaigns as well.

It would be hard to convince the court Greg Morgan's public mask hid an evil underlining.

But this man broke his child's arm. Such an injury had to be treated by a doctor, who would be required by law to report the incident.

"Did you take Katie to the hospital?"

"We had to. She wouldn't stop screaming." Maddie was trembling a little in her seat, remembering.

"What did you tell the doctor?"

"That she fell off her bunk bed."

"Katie backed you up?"

"Greg was sorry by then, and he begged her to forgive him. He bought her a new dress. The pink one she'd been wanting at Kaufmann's for the last few months. He loved her up and gave her all kinds of attention. She forgave him."

Suzanne shook her head. So Gregory Morgan had created another victim, introducing her to the cycle of fight and make up, fight and make up. When little Katie grew up, and met someone just like her daddy, she'd already be familiar with the lifestyle. It would be a comfortable fit.

She brought her thoughts back to the woman before her. “Are you prepared for another scene like that?”

“No, I don't want one,” Maddie said softly.

“There's no one you can stay with? Can you access any of the bank accounts to get enough to stay in a hotel a couple of days? You can't use credit cards—they can be traced.”

Maddie shook her head.

“I don't feel right sending him these papers until I know you'll be safe afterward. Womanspace has locked doors and concrete walls. He can't get in there, no matter who he is.”

Maddie rocked slowly in her chair. “You're right. Maybe that is best.” She looked into Suzanne's eyes again, and this time Suzanne saw a spark of growing resolve.

“Do it for the children,” Suzanne urged. “They're going to be confused and scared. Counselors at the shelter can help them through this transition. You, too. If you're ready to break away for sure, I can help you do that. But you're going to have to be strong.”

“What about the children's school?”

“They may be absent a couple of days until things shake out.”

“How long will I have to stay at the shelter? If I leave the house, the children will miss their friends, their school activities.”

The boy was a teenager, and Suzanne expected he wouldn’t want to give up his friends and activities. The daughter was several years younger, but it was hard to imagine that she’d be happy about leaving a comfortable home in one of Pittsburgh’s nicer neighborhoods to move to a crowded shelter, where she’d share a room with her mother and brother, and the communal baths and living rooms with thirty other strangers.

"Probably. I won't lie to you. They'll likely be mad at you, too. They might blame you for disrupting their lives, since you're the one who took the final action, so be prepared."

Maddie shrugged. "Hopefully, they'll understand I did what I had to, for all our sakes."

"Absolutely. That's what I'm saying. Counseling will help them in the meantime."

Maddie continued to fret. "Do you want to see a picture? I have a picture." She dug in her bag and pulled out a professional family portrait—the smiling brown-haired children looking like cherubs, Maddie, stiff, frozen, and her husband, olive-skinned and dark. His face smiled, but the posed display of lips and teeth were belied by his eyes, burning and intense. He stood with one hand on his wife's arm and one on his daughter's shoulder, almost as if claiming ownership.

Suzanne shivered, wondering how she could feel threatened by a photograph. Something in Morgan's eyes...

In person, the councilman was openly expansive, big, booming voice, a hand-shaker, news footage always catching the famous grin under the beginnings of male pattern baldness. He'd held his seat for two terms and looked to be a shoo-in for a third. Had the smile ever penetrated those fiery eyes?

Who would believe this kind of madness from a city councilman?

Nick Sansone had done the right thing sending Maddie to Suzanne. Someone needed to make sure this woman survived the misinformed decisions she'd made so far. She handed the photo back to Maddie, who sat, rocking, staring at it. Her choice made, she had withdrawn again, perhaps considering all she'd have to deal with, convincing the children to leave.

"I'll get the paperwork together and call you to meet me at the courthouse, all right? Can I reach you at this cell number?"

When Maddie gave a noncommittal shrug, Suzanne leaned forward and put her hand on the thin woman's knee. "I mean it. I want to stay in touch. Call me after Greg comes home, so I can make sure you're all right."

Maddie looked up with tears in her eyes. "I can't believe I'm really doing this," she said. "I feel so free. For the first time, I feel free." The hope in her voice had an eerie quality. "Thank you so much," she whispered.

Suzanne shared a confident smile. "Try not to worry. We'll handle this guy. You need to take care of yourself."

A few minutes later, the councilman's wife pulled herself together and straightened her jacket, wiping her eyes with a tissue from the box on the table near her seat. She smiled after a deep, quivery breath. "You're prepared, I see."

"It's an emotional subject. Even men have difficulty talking about this." Suzanne stood, rolling shoulders that had grown tense. "You've been very brave. Certainly nothing to be ashamed about."

Maddie paid the consultation fee in cash, untraceable, and went on to her doctor's appointment. Suzanne hoped Maddie would learn all the little tricks of survival, much harder for a dependent spouse accustomed to using credit cards and relying on someone else's accounts to purchase even basic supplies. This case would not be an easy one.

Donna's eyes widened in amazement when Suzanne handed her the paperwork. "You know this is Councilman Morgan," she said.

Suzanne nodded. "Sure is. If he steps a foot in here, I want you to be ready to call the police."

"Police? Really." With a confused look and a little shrug, Donna took the papers and slid them into a prepared file. "If you say so."

Her mind already engaged in unraveling the dangerous situation she faced, Suzanne returned to her office, glad that Donna had learned, over the years, not to ask a lot of questions. This was going to be complicated.

Handling the private life of a public official was always challenging. Those attorneys in the county who routinely represented the upper crust had their ways around some of the messier details, keeping them out of court papers and out of the press. But Greg Morgan had pushed his luck past the borders of discretion. Suzanne would have to take him on, head to head. Was Maddie right? Would Greg strike back at Suzanne for helping his wife?

No way to know.

Her resolve returned to her convictions. The abusers, the manipulators, those who used others—they couldn't be allowed to win. People like Maddie needed someone to stand up for them. And Suzanne was one of those someones. Greg Morgan wasn't going to know what hit him.

Chapter Five

Suzanne let her maroon Toyota sedan coast up the long gravel driveway of the rehabilitated farmhouse in Indiana Township after the ten-mile drive northeast from Pittsburgh. In her mind's eye, she pictured the way she'd like to find her home when she arrived—a peaceful oasis, soft jazz playing on the stereo. The laundry would be put away, the floor swept and waxed, fresh flowers on the table.

When she stepped from the car, however, her dream was shattered by shrill teenage voices she heard when she was still at least twenty-five feet from the house.

"I hate you!"

"Bite me. You're such a baby. You're going to be living with Mom until she dies!"

Suzanne sighed as she crossed the grass to the porch, noting the white paint on the steps was beginning to peel. When she opened the door, she saw bowls on the couch, next to the full basket of laundry.

She closed the door with a thud, which immediately ended the shrieking.

Her armload of files went on her desk in her home office down the hallway to the immediate left of the front door. Then she retrieved the dirty dishes and headed to the sunny yellow kitchen. The girls whispered furiously in the hallway, then their footsteps sounded in the direction of the living room.

Suzanne washed her hands and began chopping broccoli and onions as she put on her other "hat," that of single mother to dark-haired Hope, age fifteen, and blonde Riviera, two years younger. She had raised the girls alone for thirteen years.

She'd met John Taylor in law school and finished her last year pregnant with Hope. They married only when they'd both passed the bar. He lived with her until it became clear, to him anyway, that he was not cut out for living with a small child. When she told him she was pregnant again, he left. He moved from Pittsburgh to Nevada, lived there long enough to file for divorce and proceeded without even sending notice to her. She received a copy of the final decree. He probably thought she should be grateful. He then moved from his legal Nevada address, and the Taylor family had never had contact again.

John Taylor's exit, and the subsequent behavior she'd seen by men in many of her divorce cases had convinced her she was doing the right thing by remaining single. One betrayal had been enough. She didn't intend to let herself fall in love again.

Particularly with a cop.

She chopped zucchini and snow peas, thinking about her dinner with Nick Sansone. She'd truly enjoyed the chance to kick back and talk about something that wasn't business. Just pleasure. She'd almost decided he was that rare beast, a nice guy, when he'd pulled the switch on her with that kiss. "Just dinner," he'd promised.

Yeah, so much for that.

Sure, she'd kissed him, too, but that was something under her control. Her will. Because she'd wanted to, by then. And she'd even said she'd see him again. What had she been thinking?

The girls carried the laundry down the back hall, and Suzanne sighed with relief. They'd turned out well—healthy, happy, normal siblings, responsible and anything but self-centered.

Riviera was the more outgoing, working backstage at the local community theater, twirling flags for the marching band, and singing in the City Chorus. She'd always liked performing for others. Hope, more cerebral, was a long-time Girl Scout, and a member of the National Honor Society. She also worked Sundays at a local church in the nursery for some spending money.

The reminders a warm ball of pride inside her, she scraped the vegetables off the wooden cutting board into the wok. They sizzled and danced in the olive oil as she stirred them. She hunted in the refrigerator, discovering leftover beef, which she tossed into the pan with some cooked rice, soy sauce and several cloves of garlic.

As the aromas blended and filled the small kitchen, Suzanne gathered the peels and tops to discard. In the wastebasket, she found an empty potato chip bag, a cereal box and three apple cores. She threw the garbage away and called the girls to come eat, shaking her head.

At least they had apples, she thought.

****

They ate at the dinner table, an unusual event in light of their busy schedules. Riviera laid out the plates, while Hope poured each a glass of milk. Suzanne served the main course, and the three dug in.

Settling back into her chair, Suzanne asked, "Anything I should know about happen at school?" She never believed, of course, that either girl would confess to a transgression. Asking a general question was the best way to find out from one girl what the other had done.

"No," Hope said promptly. With her long dark hair delicately French-braided, and her face scrubbed clean, she looked as angelic as she wanted her mother to believe.

"Steve Jones got the flu at lunch and puked on Mr. Racine," Riviera said, taking a huge bite of rice and vegetables. She was shorter and rounder than long-stemmed Hope, strawberry blonde hair straight to her shoulder blades, parted on the side. "It was so sick!"

"How was the geography quiz?" Suzanne asked her.

Riviera's fork hit the plate as she dropped it. "Mom, Mrs. Batt is such a jerk! She tested us on all this stuff that's in our next unit, and no one knew what she was talking about."

"Did you ask her why?"

"After she collected the papers, she walked out of class before the bell rang. You couldn't ask her anything."

"Would you like me to speak to her?"

Hope burst out laughing. "Good plan, Mom." Sarcasm coated every word.

Simultaneously, Riviera blushed and cried out, "No way!"

Suzanne looked from one to the other. "What's wrong with your mother talking to the teacher if there's a problem?"

Hope asked, "Do you remember last year, when you talked to Mrs. Weber about her math?"

Riviera covered her face with her hands, her response muffled and unintelligible.

"What about it?"

"The teachers carried on afterward for a week. They're all afraid you're going to sue them about something. Mona Rheinfeld just eats it up. She even reminds them about you all the time so she can be class suck-up."

"Fine," Suzanne said, swallowing her frustration along with her rice, preparing for a good digestive mess later. "I just thought communication might be a good thing."

"Mom, this is Mrs. Batt we're talking about. Remember my seventh grade year? She locked herself in the teacher's lounge and wouldn't come out until after school when the police came?"

Suzanne smiled. "Sounds reasonable to me. You couldn't pay me enough to do her job anyway."

One worry she didn't have—money. Even though she'd never received a dollar from the girls' father, they were okay financially. She definitely understood her clients' feelings as they traveled their own road of separation, custody and division of property. The anger, resentment, desperation and bitterness—she'd lived them all.

But she also believed her experiences made her a better advocate than some of her colleagues who had never faced a day's need in their lives. As a second year law student, she remembered eavesdropping on two young women chatting about money worries between classes. One complained she'd found shoes on sale for ninety-five dollars a pair and she couldn't buy two pair because she'd spent her allowance. At the time, Suzanne had twelve dollars and fifty cents in her pocket to cover all her living expenses for the next three weeks.

Fortunately, she didn't have those worries anymore.

Several hours later, the dishes done, daughters in bed, Suzanne retired to her office to complete the work she'd brought home. She spread her materials out on the polished oak rolltop desk, one of the prized possessions of her sanctuary.

When the farmhouse had been remodeled, Suzanne had taken great pains to make this room as comfortable as possible, because she planned to spend a lot of time in it. The southern exposure held a bay window with a seat cushion matching the sage and mustard, large-flowered chintz draperies which fell from ceiling to floor, ruffling softly at the bottom. The room's west window was filled with plants, hanging, potted, rooting, that benefited from the long hours of sunshine each day. Paintings of geraniums and other flowers hung on off-white walls. A conversation corner grouping of natural rattan with soft flowered cushions, ruffled pillows and a glass-jar lamp filled with sea shells completed the office.

Suzanne stretched out as she sat in the desk's swivel chair, trying to clear her mind and get down to the files. But she couldn't.

She kept reliving snippets of Maddie's anxious interview, her mind juxtaposing those words with remembered moments of Gregory Morgan in public, philanthropist, concerned city father. In all likelihood, Maddie hadn't shared with her the worst of the violence. Survivors seldom did at the first meeting. So the situation was worse, probably much worse, than she'd said.

She wondered, too, about Morgan's capacity to make her own life difficult. The kind of brush-up she'd nearly had with Mr. Wachowski was fairly common. Litigants in divorce and custody cases were emotionally invested down to their souls. They were difficult cases. People didn't always react well. But Greg Morgan was "connected" in a number of legal ways, and if the rumors were true, some not-so-legal ways, too. He had the potential to cause a great deal of trouble. Serious trouble.

And, perhaps this time, she wouldn't have a champion waiting to ride in for the rescue. That police lieutenant. The one she didn't want to think about.

In the years since John Taylor had abandoned her, she'd not been a celibate nun. She'd dated, very discriminately. Nothing serious. That's the way she liked it. She could focus on her career and her girls. If her practice had taught her anything, it was that no woman “needed” a man.

Something about this man, though, warned her that she could be lost, if she wasn’t careful.

The feel of his lips on hers, the two kisses—different yet the same—stayed with her like a physical contact. Without her volition, her fingers went to her mouth. She experienced the sensation again, soft skin to soft skin, gentle when he kissed her, exploratory and yielding. When she’d initiated the kiss, she’d kissed him with a little more force, intending to make a statement. But that choice only reinforced the danger.

A small electric sizzle ran through her as she let her imagination rummage through possibilities, insinuating its way as if through smoke-filled halls inside her head. The task was easy: Nick Sansone was the quintessential “mystery man” the fortune-tellers pointed out in movies, tall, dark and handsome.

She knew by the breadth of his shoulders and the smooth movement of his muscles as he walked that he was strong. That baritone resonated right through her, its warm timbre melting something long frozen in her woman parts. She imagined how his voice would sound in a whisper, lips pressed against her ear, his breath stimulating the soft skin within…

A shiver shaking her whole body as she followed that thought to its conclusion, she jerked back to the room, shoving herself away from the desk and to her feet in one fluid movement.

None of that.

She rubbed a hand over her face, feeling more like she should slap herself, get control. Nick Sansone seemed like a good man, certainly well-intentioned. If she’d been inclined to seek a relationship, he'd certainly be the kind of man she'd want. *If*. But for now she had more important areas of focus: her girls, her clients. These things mattered to her on a day-to-day basis. These people needed her special attention, and she intended to give it to them.

She surveyed the desk, concentrated on the files there, then crossed back to her seat and sat again, opening the file on top.

Ah, the Remoun matter. She'd brought home the twenty-page appraisal on the value of the personal property in the parties' large Southside home, their vacation home, and all the items the husband had recently stashed at his girlfriend's house, hoping they'd been forgotten. There was a fine example of a man.

Back on track again, Suzanne plunged into dry figures and text, letting them cloud her mind once more. This was someone else's life. Their pain was not hers. She was protected from committing errors that would cause herself trouble, as long as she kept those walls up.

With enough work, and enough discipline, she'd resist the temptation the handsome lieutenant provided.

Chapter Six

Nick Sansone scrutinized his domain just before Monday's lunch hour, satisfied with the work he and the unit officers accomplished since the shift started at seven that morning.

The fluorescent lights were too bright, the floors grimy from the mud and dirt tracked in by the detectives, and the color which dominated the main office outside the supervisor's cubicles was the slate gray of the officers' desks. The phones rang incessantly. The room smelled of sweat and other things even less pleasant. But Nick loved it.

From his youngest years, Nick dreamed of being a detective. As he'd told Suzanne, he'd watched with wide, adoring eyes when his grandfather and his father dressed in their sharply-pressed blue uniforms, their pride shining bright as the polished pins that denoted precinct and rank.

"Every man's got to give back, Nicky," his grandfather used to say. "God's given us so much. What we make of ourselves is our gift to God, our thanks."

Nick firmly believed, just like his father, and grandfather, that the opportunity to be a police officer made them the man in the white hat, the knight in shining armor. They held the lives of the public in their hands, protecting them from the bad guys.

The mission wasn't as easy as it had looked back

in the days when Nick spent his time reading superhero comic books, especially Batman. The Dark Knight didn't have any superpowers. What he accomplished, he did with the product of his own mind and hands. Like a cop. Sure, he used some fancy gizmos, but for the most part, he relied on his own inner strengths to get the job done. Nick tried hard to do the same.

Mid-morning re-assessment and assignment called for several detective teams to hit the street as assorted crime reports came in. Nick dispatched Crime Scene Investigation techs to meet his guys around the city as necessary and stacked the initial paperwork in a file basket marked "Pending," until he had more information.

He observed through the glass windows of his ten foot square office as most of the squad members he'd assigned filed out of the communal room to their endeavors. His workstation looked much like every other supervisor on the floor, furniture too old, too piled with paperwork, too small to meet in, even if he could have cleared space for more than three people to sit down.

The budget office finally allotted him the funds to install blinds on the front windows of the cubicle, but the janitorial staff hadn't found time to hang them yet. Admin forbade Nick to do it himself. So, he still waited.

He stretched weary legs, pointing toe and then heel to stimulate the circulation. Leaning down to rub off a scuff on one of his black shoes, he groaned at an ache in his back he'd first noticed earlier in the week. He was spending too much time at the supervisor's desk.

He stood up, rotating his shoulders a bit, hoping to shake the tension in them. His dark blue jacket hung on a coat rack shoved behind the door. He'd gone to shirt sleeves by ten a.m. Police work was no nine-to-five day of looking fine and chatting at the water cooler during breaks, particularly in the detective division. All his guys worked hard, worked long, and Nick didn't cut himself five minutes of slack more than they got. They deserved that much.

The overflowing basket of paperwork on his desk awaited his attention like a long-neglected wife, sullen and bound to be more trouble than it was worth. He knew officers who liked filling in the blanks, making sure all the t's were crossed at just the right angle. He wasn't one of them.

This particular trait seemed to bite him harder the farther up the promotion ladder he went. As a lieutenant, he'd discovered he now carried some responsibility for budget issues—at a time when both the federal and state funding streams were drying up faster than a flash flood in an Arizona wash.

There ought to be a penalty for hidden job descriptions, he thought. Clipping, at the least. Offensive holding. Certainly something offensive. He already didn't have enough hours in his day. And now another distraction had raised her head—attorney Suzanne Taylor.

He still couldn't believe she'd finally agreed to have dinner with him. Her decision must have had something to do with the guy with the crazy expression on the courthouse steps. Nick was sure he intended harm. But then, Nick always tended to lean toward a paranoid view. It's why he was still alive.

A smug satisfaction settled over him as he realized he'd guessed spot on about her on many counts. Not surprising, exactly, because he read people pretty well. All the same, he was pleased he'd been right this time.

He returned to his seat and reached for the offending pile with a glance at the clock. An hour until lunch. If he screwed his determination to the wheel, he might be able to clear at least half the stack. His eyes wandered away from the columns of figures in the budget report before he'd spent five minutes on them, his mind recalling the faint musky scent of Suzanne's hair. He'd never seen it loose till that night. He liked it.

What about her appealed to him so much?

He found it hard to divine an exact answer.

He'd lived on his own some twenty years. Over those years, he'd never found a woman he could marry, one to whom he felt he could pledge himself fully. Marriage, for him, meant what it had to his parents and his grandparents—a deep, thorough commitment that truly implied "forever." He didn't know Suzanne Taylor well enough to decide if she was the one. Not yet. But everything he'd seen so far whispered to him she might be.

She just might be.

She had a quick tongue, even in casual conversation, and a quick mind as well. Dinner had been a many-course delight, not on the table, but in the conversation. Unlike most attorneys he knew, she wasn't egotistical and arrogant, but warm and amiable, broad in her interests as he, and not afraid of controversy.

He wanted to know more about her family. She'd revealed she had children from a previous relationship, daughters, but said very little else. His attempts to expand that area of conversation were gently rebuffed by a change of subject, and he hadn't pushed hard. There would be time.

The ringing of his phone shook him from his daydreaming. On the second ring, he hit the speakerphone button so he could keep working.

"Lieutenant Sansone."

"Nick? That you? I can't hear you."

Police Chief Sam "Butch" Reickert's querulous

voice rattled across the speaker. Nick grimaced, knowing Reickert could hear him just fine. The chief put on the same act any time he detected use of the speakerphone, no matter who was on the other end of the line. He hated the thing.

No point in pursuing this battle. Nick picked up the receiver with a tolerant grin. He liked Reickert. A long-time friend of the family, the man mentored Nick's career since he first put on his uniform. Now, twenty years later, Reickert was Chief, and Nick was lieutenant in charge of the general detective bureau. The mutual respect had only grown, and Nick owed the man a debt of gratitude.

"Sorry, Chief. My hands were full," Nick explained. Not exactly a lie. Not like the old man could see him, anyway.

Reickert chuckled. "It's lunchtime. I'm sure you weren't that busy."

With a nervous glance for a tiny red light at the corners of his ceiling, Nick wondered, not for the first time, if Reickert had a secret video camera installed in the office. Reickert's reputation included a little paranoia, as did the mental outlook of most police officers. It certainly was possible.

"What do you need, Chief?"

"Vice is short this month, one officer out on comp and another on maternity leave. Dick asked me if we could spare any officers to fill in for a couple of weeks. Just on a temporary basis while they finish this task force to clean up the prostitutes in the east end."

Nick considered the request. Already pushed to cover current cases, the budget kept all the department heads from hiring anyone for at least another six months. "When does he need them? Now?"

"ASAP, Nick. Sooner we get this sweep wrapped up, sooner you'll have your men back."

Nick glanced over to the erasable vacation schedule tacked to his wall. Only one officer had time marked off. He could probably send one man, maybe two. As long as it was only a couple of weeks. Even as he agreed, a small cold sting poked the "should-be" in his head. It would take longer. It always did.

"I can find someone. If my guys are deep into cases, maybe I can take a couple of shifts myself just to help Vice cover."

"Good man. Get rid of that speaker, son. It annoys people."

The jovial warmth in Reickert's tone made Nick smile. "I hear you, Chief," he said before he set the receiver back in its cradle.

Somewhat fortuitous or downright creepy? He'd just been thinking he spent too much time in the office, and Reickert handed him a vice assignment. Prostitute pops provided male officers with one of two roles, johns on the hunt or backup for female officers posing as ladies of the evening. Nick was happy to do either. Street busts meant quick turnaround, the exchange of offer and acceptance in a few words between hooker and john. The city had started impounding cars used for solicitation, and that put some dollars in city coffers and won commendations.

The down side, of course, embodied risk. These patrols often took place in areas like Homewood, or along Liberty Avenue, where gang activity and heavy drug use created situations that were often volatile and dangerous.

In recent years, the department spent more time busting Internet prostitution rings spawned off Craigslist and the classified ads of the City Paper. Advertisers boldly teased their wares, believing that because they were anonymous on the Net, they couldn't get popped as fast as on a street corner. The

Pittsburgh police did their best to disabuse these criminals of their beliefs.

Either way, Nick might volunteer. A bit of the old days would be good for him.

Nick's former patrol partner, Hank Ferguson, peeked in the door. The man, who'd lost most of his hair and the paunch he'd hauled around for sixteen years on the force to a recent bout of chemotherapy, wore a brown polo shirt and slacks. Nick guessed Hank wasn't wearing a suit because he was buried in paperwork and knew he'd get no street time.

"You got thirty minutes for a bite, Nicky?"

Nick eyed his desk. He didn't. But he needed to get some air. "Sure, Hank." He grabbed his jacket from behind the door and followed him out.

Before they left the squad room, Nick caught sight of the major cloud on the office horizon. The Three Amigos, three officers in their mid-twenties. Individually, each of the three malcontents performed well as officers, properly motivated. Together, they resonated off each other, compounding their bad attitudes, steeped in inner city piss and vinegar.

Emilio Vasquez, a Puerto Rican from the Bronx, stood three inches over six feet, once firm muscle sliding over into fat, in much the same way his work ethics softened as he contemplated the options for someone not born a white middle-class male in a city like Pittsburgh.

Jojo Washington hailed from the city of Atlanta, raised up by a single mother under some of the toughest conditions a boy could face. Somehow, that education by fire produced a wiry young man who now felt the world owed him a living.

Clara Malron—pronounced the Creole way, with a long O and accent on the second syllable, she was quick to remind people—was the slender peasant-shaped daughter of Haitian immigrants, who'd worked hard to overcome economic and educational deficits. Of the three, she seemed most likely to move up like a rocket through the ranks.

Washington and Malron carried twelve months' seniority over Vasquez in the department and had worked under Nick for nearly twice that. Vasquez complained from the beginning about the assignments he received, blaming management for giving the "island boy" less than glamorous duties, and whipping up racist sentiment among those in the lower echelons. Before long, Nick started hearing similar bitches across the board.

Although he addressed the concerns immediately, in group settings as well as one-on-one, they hadn't ended. The simmering dark eyes of Jojo Washington verified their persistence as Nick and Hank left the office.

"Hey, man," Washington said. "What's up with this robbery detail?"

Nick remembered he'd assigned him to investigate a string of convenience store stick-ups, the latest one early that morning. Nick straightened his shoulders, his feet set a foot apart. Fully in command mode.

"What about it?"

"You think because I'm black that I can catch a black kid who stuck a gun in some clerk's gut?"

Looking at their three stone faces, Nick summoned patience from a place in his heart. "No, Jojo, I wasn't thinking that at all. I decided to send you because I need to know what the clerk knows before she goes off shift. I thought I should send someone to the Sheets to talk to her. That's what I do. You're the one who needs to go talk to her. That's what *you* do. You're the lucky guy."

"Man, I don't believe this shit." Washington turned away, not before Nick saw the exaggerated roll of his eyes. At the desk behind Washington,

Vasquez smirked. Malron picked up her jacket and walked off without a word.

"And, Jojo, I want that data compiled by end of shift." Nick waited a long moment for an acknowledgement that finally came as a grunt, then he went out the door with Hank. They took the stairs, six floors. Nick nearly ran down. The movement, the impact with each stair, shook Nick, jostling the irritation around his brain. He was very careful not to treat those three unfairly. Who wouldn't be, with department affirmative action lawyers breathing down his neck? Sometimes he really wondered if all the hard work he'd put into that promotion was worth the hassle of dealing with whiny crybabies.

Hank lagged back, finishing the descent two flights behind.

"What's got into you, Nick? You can't let them under your skin." Hank limped over, breathing hard. "They're just blowing smoke, like young guys do. You keep your cool, give your orders, they'll come around."

"Maybe." Nick held the door for Hank, and they walked several blocks to Peppi's.

"No maybe about it. If they don't straighten up and fly right, kick 'em to the curb," Hank scolded as they got a table. The waitress had long experience with this pair and showed up with two iced teas, no sugar, no waiting.

Hank passed up The Roethlisburger, number seven on the menu, which Nick knew he dearly loved, but the sausage and burger topped with egg and cheese was off his diet list. He ordered a salad, disappointment practically dripping off his long face. Nick took one, too, to keep Hank company. After the waitress gifted them with her flirty smile and a little flip of her skirt, she headed back to the kitchen. Hank returned to his lecture. "Have you talked to

Reickert about it?"

Nick shook his head, watching out the window for wrongdoers, his vigilance built of long habit. "What's he going to do? No sense in my complaining. I wanted to be the lieutenant, so now I've got to handle the situation."

All the same, Nick realized, Reickert might have handed him the solution to his problem. His request for extra men might separate the rabblerousers long enough to defuse the situation. Indeed it might.

He had his plan in mind before the meal hit their table.

Chapter Seven

Suzanne didn't hear from Maddie Morgan for nearly a week.

With the papers prepared and ready for signature, she'd nearly written the case off as one of those that so often resulted in reluctant reconciliation when she found a bruised and battered Maddie Morgan waiting on her office doorstep.

"What happened?" Suzanne demanded, herding Maddie inside after a quick look to make sure the assailant wasn't lurking in the hall. If Morgan had followed his wife, they could have a brawl right in her lobby before the police could ever arrive. But no one was there.

Maddie didn't speak until they were settled in Suzanne's office. She trembled as she sat in the chair, chewing on her lip, a scarf tied over hair she hadn't bothered to comb. Her blouse and slacks didn't match each other or her shoes.

"I don't care where I go," she said, her affect and tone flat. "I'm done with him." An emptiness in her eyes said more than her words.

"I was concerned when you didn't call," Suzanne said. Maddie's blotchy purple cheek, the eye nearly closed from the swelling, turned Suzanne's stomach. She could imagine the force necessary to cause such injuries, the blinding pain Maddie must have felt at the hands of a man who professed to love her.

"I'm so sorry. I should have. The first few days after he got back, he didn't bother me. He just went to the office and stayed there late. But yesterday he came home before the children got off the bus, and he was furious."

"About you? We haven't sent him the papers yet."

"Rocco saw my car when I was here the other day. Greg accused me of having an affair when he left town." Maddie began to cry, her throat choking with tears. Suzanne could barely understand her. "He took his gun out of his drawer a—and laid it on the table in front of him. He m—made me sit down at the table. God, I was scared. I knew I was going to die, and my kids would come in and see it."

Maddie's fingers shredded the worn hem of the lavender blouse. Suzanne set the box of tissues closer. Her mind clicked ahead into action. With a threat and an injury within the last twenty-four hours, she had grounds for the protection order. But first she should hear the rest of the story.

"He looked at me across the table. He just stared. His eyes were like lasers. I thought I would burst into flames. He said, 'No other man will ever have you. I'll kill you first, so you better not even think about it.'" A little whimper escaped her lips, and she covered them with her hands, as though it would keep her from telling too much. "Then he stood up and picked up the gun with his left hand. I was watching the gun, and I never saw his right hand coming at me. I went right off the chair." She looked away. "I should have left then, but the children weren't home from school. I didn't want to go without them."

"That's a wise choice," Suzanne said, "but we could always get the children later. If something happens to you first, you won't be there to care for them."

The silence stretched out, taut like a thread. Still Suzanne waited.

Maddie reached for a tissue and wiped her face, patting her injured cheek with caution. A ragged breath spurred her to continue. “Greg wouldn’t leave. He sent me to my room. When the kids were ready for dinner, Greg ordered pizza and told them I had a headache. He was Mr. Wonderful Dad and they loved it.”

“You didn't call the police?”

“Not while he was home. I would have been dead before they arrived.”

“Did you go to the hospital this morning?”

Maddie shook her head. “I just wanted to see you. I asked my neighbor to drop me on Carson Street because my battery was dead. She thinks I'm at the dentist across the street.”

“You must go to a doctor today, either yours or the emergency room, and get a medical record made of this.” Suzanne indicated Maddie's face. “I can take you now for your protection order.”

Suzanne pulled out the file, showing Maddie both the protection order request and the divorce papers she’d prepared. Maddie had to take hold of her writing hand with the other to steady it while she signed the papers, but she did it. When she was done, she stared at the black scrawl, intently, like it was a poisonous bug or something dangerous.

“Do we have to file for divorce?” she asked.

“You said you were finished, Maddie. I support your decision. We might as well make it a package,” Suzanne advised. “Let the sheriff serve him with everything, divorce and all.”

Indecision flitted across Maddie’s face, and Suzanne suggested she wash up and take a few minutes to pull herself together. When she returned, she appeared more composed, and even managed a faint smile.

"Maddie, we ought to take pictures. If you haven't already."

"Pictures?" Distress sucked blood from her face. "What for?"

"For court. We might not have a hearing for ten days. By then, you won't look like this anymore." Suzanne reached for her Blackberry. "May I?"

Stiff with shame, Madeleine Morgan pulled up her sleeves and let Suzanne photograph her from several angles. Suzanne finished as quickly as she could, feeling guilt at causing her client embarrassment. "I'll get these printed. Are you okay?"

Maddie nodded, not meeting her eyes.

"Let's go," Suzanne said, feeling like she was leading the first assault at Normandy.

The wait for the *ex-parte* order seemed endless. Suzanne wasn't worried about getting the order—Maddie's face alone showed the damage had been done. The hard part would be having the sheriff serve Mr. Civic-Minded Morgan and force him out of his house until a full hearing could take place sometime in the following ten days.

The courthouse hall echoed with the sound of voices and footsteps, the coming and going of court personnel carrying files and running errands. Examining the papers one more time, Suzanne didn't notice the man who stopped in front of them until he spoke.

"Maddie? Is everything all right?"

Suzanne glanced up at the gray-suited man, then at Maddie, who was frozen in her seat.

"Can I help you?" Suzanne asked, annoyed by his casual stare at Maddie's bruised face, even more dramatic under the unforgiving fluorescent lights.

He turned to study Suzanne a moment, then dismissed her without a word. "Maddie, tell those kids I love them," he said. "I'll be over to see them this weekend. I'll see all of you then."

As he walked away, Maddie's hand found Suzanne's and squeezed so tightly Suzanne gasped. "W—We should g—go," Maddie said through chattering teeth. She stood up and Suzanne pulled her back down.

"You need to stay here. You *need* this order. Don't let him scare you." She watched the guy vanish into the crowded hallway. "Who is that?"

"One of the guys who does Greg's dirty work. He'll call Greg."

Suzanne forced her voice to be light, to downplay the blow this dealt to their case. How powerful was Morgan really? Could he manage a phone call to the judge before they could even see him? Would it matter? "Greg would have found out within a couple of hours anyway." She patted Maddie's hand and pried it gently off hers. Danger brewed on the horizon like a summer thunderstorm. "You'll be okay, Maddie. I promise."

Judge Franken's secretary came out. "The judge will see you now."

Five minutes earlier, Suzanne thought. *Three, maybe. And Maddie's secret would have been safe for a little while longer. Long enough to get her out of the courthouse and into a safe place. Damn it.*

Maddie told Judge Franken her story and, as expected, the judge signed a restraining order removing Gregory Morgan from the house, giving Maddie temporary custody of the children. Due to the broken arm, Greg was only allowed supervised visitation. Maddie was granted temporary support of fifteen hundred dollars per month.

Suzanne took a copy of the order from the judge's chambers, along with the divorce complaint, already filed, and walked it to the sheriff's office for service of process. Under these circumstances, they agreed to put it in their day's workload, but there was no guarantee they'd have them served by the end of the day.

"Not good enough," Suzanne snapped.

The deputy behind the counter eyed her with patronizing ennui. "That's the best you'll get, ma'am. We don't have guaranteed service for anyone here, I don't care who they are."

"Particularly not when a city councilman's involved, I expect."

Indignation made her voice louder than she'd intended, or else everyone simply stopped talking at the same moment. The words echoed for several seconds before the usual hubbub of the sheriff's office resumed.

"You want to speak to the supervisor, lady, I'll call her."

"Never mind!"

Suzanne snatched the papers from his hand and marched out, Maddie on her heels. Granted, the order was only a piece of paper. It wouldn't deflect a fist—or a bullet. But it was what they had. Furious that the deputy couldn't see the inherent menace in the situation, she scoured her mind for other options.

One came to mind. Nick Sansone wanted to play white knight, didn't he? So he could do his part in the rescue of Maddie Morgan.

She pulled Maddie into a nearby coffee shop and sat her at a table. Tapping her cell phone's screen, she found the number for the detective division. As she dialed, her foot tapped, fueled by nervous energy. She found herself observing the crowd and waiting for trouble to surface. The officer who answered put her straight through.

"Lieutenant Sansone."

His voice sent ripples through her. She forced herself to focus on her mission. "Nick, it's Suzanne Taylor. I've got a small problem you might be able to help me with."

He listened while she explained and arranged to meet her in half an hour outside the doctor's office without further question. Maddie protested, arguing that she could take a cab, but Suzanne wouldn't allow it.

"We're in for the whole pound, Maddie. As long as we've got a city officer willing to go with us, you should take the chance."

Maddie left her doctor's office with an envelope of documentation, including more pictures, a prescription for pain and a warning that if her face wasn't better in twenty-four hours that she should go to the hospital for X-rays.

As promised, Nick was waiting for them outside the doctor's office. He greeted Maddie with a warm smile and gentle handshake. "Don't worry, Mrs. Morgan, we'll make sure you're safe, all right?"

He helped her into Suzanne's car, then took the envelope containing the legal papers from Suzanne, giving them a quick glance, since he'd need to explain the import of the paperwork to Greg Morgan. He nodded his approval. "What next? You're the boss."

"Why don't you follow me over there, and you can serve him then? She'll need some things for herself and the kids."

"Fine. Let's go."

Liking the fact he hadn't questioned her expertise, but had just done what she asked, she slipped into the driver's seat of her car, then watched him get into his own, a smile pressing through to surface on her lips.

"He seems really nice," Maddie said.

"He might be." Suzanne grinned and headed for Interstate 376.

****

When they arrived a short time later at the

expensive Shadyside Morgan home, they found the door standing open. Nothing was amiss in the beautifully-landscaped front yard and no one came out at the sound of their car doors closing.

Nick's eyes took on a troubled look. "You two stay here," he ordered. He tucked the envelope under his arm before he removed his pistol from its holster. He disappeared inside the large brick house.

"Oh, my God," Maddie gasped. "What's he going to do?"

Suzanne shushed her, pulling her behind the parked car, now a barrier between them and the house. "If someone's broken in, they might still be inside," she whispered. "Nick will find them. Don't worry."

Expecting to hear shots any moment, Suzanne was relieved when Nick poked his head out the door and beckoned them to come in. "Don't touch anything," he warned as they came to the front step.

"Don't—what happened?" Suzanne asked. Then she saw.

The house looked as if a poltergeist had been through every drawer, every closet. Maddie's clothes were scattered around the living room, slashed to pieces. Furniture was overturned. Some of the children's toys were burned in the middle of their bedroom floor.

But that wasn't the worst of it. Scrawled across the front of the kitchen refrigerator, in what looked like blood, were the words, "You're dead, bitch."

Maddie had managed well until then. Her knees seemed to fold up, and she fell in the middle of the floor and cried as if her heart was broken.

Suzanne took some pictures while Nick called for back-up. Whatever he said to the dispatcher must have shaken up someone, because officers were on scene in fifteen minutes. Suzanne had never seen such a fast response. Granted, her clients in this neighborhood usually got good service, unlike some other sections of the city. But this was phenomenal.

Officers were photographing the scene when Greg Morgan came strolling through the still-open door, dressed in a Versace suit and tie. “What's this all about?” he asked, wide-eyed. “Honey, are you all right?”

Suzanne stepped in front of Maddie, but the woman moved like she’d been hit with a jolt of electricity, fleeing to the bathroom. The click of a lock sounded in the stunned silence that followed.

Morgan eyed Suzanne. “Who the hell are you, and what are you doing in my house?”

Suzanne opened her mouth to speak, but Nick’s voice from the hallway commanded everyone’s attention. “Are you Gregory Morgan?” he asked, coming into the living room, badge in hand.

The councilman’s eyes narrowed. “Are you blind, man? You work for me!”

Before Nick could respond, Suzanne’s sheer dislike for the man shoved words out of her mouth. She wanted to shock and hurt him, even if she couldn’t punch his face into pulp the way he’d done Maddie’s.”I'm Suzanne Taylor. I represent your wife in the divorce action she filed this morning.”

Morgan's jaw twitched slightly, but that was the only indication he understood. He surveyed the destruction with solemnity. “I can’t believe Maddie would go to this length,” he said. “Unbelievable.”

“Maddie?” Suzanne asked, after a silent moment of astonishment at the man’s gall.

“She isn't always stable, you know. She's been on psychotropic medication. Sometimes she doesn't know what she's doing.” He looked at the officers and smiled. “I love the woman but you have no idea what a handful she can be.”

Suzanne saw the officers' expressions start to change, no doubt wondering if they were backing the wrong horse. Morgan went on, “If it wasn't Maddie, then I hope you find whoever did this. Is anything missing?” He walked to the entertainment center, checking the components.

One of the officers shot an irritated look at Nick. “Mr. Morgan, where have you been the last several hours?”

Morgan spun around, outrage flushing his face red. “Me? You think I'd destroy my own home?” He puffed like a barnyard cock, ready to fight. “I've been in a meeting with my managers all day. You can call my office if you don't believe me.”

The officer noted his answer and closed up his notebook.

Morgan walked to the kitchen door and gasped. “Good God. She's more disturbed than I thought,” he said.

Nick had apparently heard enough, because he walked across the room to hand Greg Morgan the envelope with the papers. “In this package is a complaint for divorce and also a protection from abuse order, signed by the judge this morning—”

“What a crock,” Morgan muttered, tossing the papers on a nearby desk without looking at them.

“Sir, this means you are restrained from further abusing and threatening your wife. You are required by order of court to leave this residence, pending a hearing next week.”

“The woman is mentally ill. Don’t you understand that?” Morgan protested to the police officers, who now wouldn't meet his eyes. Pleased her work had rattled him, Suzanne couldn't stop a cocky smile, and Morgan caught it.

“I'm going to sue you for libel, lady. You'll never practice law again,” he said. As he spoke, she saw the eyes Maddie had described from the prior evening. She imagined her hair beginning to smoke. The outrage kicked her chutzpah into high gear.

"Bring it on, pal," she said. "I'm ready for you."

The officers took Morgan to the bedroom, supervising as he packed a small bag of clothes and personal items. Nick gave Suzanne an odd look she wasn't quite sure how to interpret. Despite what she knew about Greg Morgan, at that moment, she wasn't afraid. To the contrary, her adrenaline was pumping and she was ready for a fight. Hyper aware of Maddie cringing behind the bathroom door, and the seething negative energy that was Gregory Morgan, her gaze returned to the crimson scrawl on the refrigerator.

How dare he? He wasn't divine. He had no right to control his woman's life, to terrorize and threaten her. Whatever he had coming, he deserved. She hoped she'd be the one to give it to him.

Morgan came out of the bedroom with a bulging gym bag. Two officers followed him, one warning if he returned to the house, he would be arrested. At the lieutenant's pointed nod, he added that the police would keep watch on the house to make sure he didn't come back. Before he stepped out of his home, Morgan turned to Suzanne, once again the glad-handing politician with a jolly smile. "Tell her I love her, will you?" he said. "Take her to the doctor. She doesn't take good care of herself. Once she's back on her medicine, she'll beg me to come home."

Suzanne stared at him. Morgan's smile widened, and he walked out with the officers, cracking jokes.

After the door closed behind Morgan and the officers, her knees trembled, and she leaned on a nearby chair for support. She hadn't realized how much effort went into withstanding Mr. Morgan's charismatic personality.

"Suzanne?" Nick was at her side before she noticed he'd moved, a hand on her elbow, steadying her. "It's all right," he said.

His recognition of her moment of weakness

straightened her spine. “I’m fine. I’m not a victim here. She is. How could Maddie survive sixteen years with that monster?”

“I don’t even begin to understand. But you’ve helped her take the first steps toward freedom.”

“We both have,” Suzanne said, reluctantly acknowledging it had been a joint effort. “Thank you for sending her to me. It was the right thing to do.”

“I thought so,” he said. “No one better to deal with it.” His eyes were warm. Was he seeking a *quid pro quo*? “I did a favor for you, now you owe me”? She hoped not. Men thought like that sometimes.

Women did, too, she scolded herself. She tried not to. She didn’t want to be indebted to any man, least of all one she actually liked and respected.

He didn’t say anything else, and she didn’t want to give him an opening. They fidgeted in awkward silence for several minutes until the bathroom door opened, and Maddie came out, arms hugged close around herself.

“They’re gone,” Suzanne said.

“But look at this place,” Maddie said, tears still streaming down her face.

Then the children came home from school.

Chapter Eight

Nick didn't know what to think as he surveyed the Morgan house. It seemed to him like they'd entered a world cut from nightmare. As a child, if he had come home to find that kind of destruction, he might have been hysterical. Maddie Morgan's quiet voice reminded him of his mother, but his father had never raised a hand to any of them. The kind of chaos these children must live in, hardly a blink as they stood, silent and pale, on the threshold just long enough to soak it in.

Then the boy tossed his book bag into the middle of the pile and bailed upstairs. The girl gave her mother a hug before she began to help clean up.

"Do you want me to stay and help you, Maddie?" Suzanne asked.

Maddie shook her head. "I'd like some privacy, actually. We'll take care of it."

Nick took one more look around. "Photos. You should take photos before you clean it up." His gaze went to the refrigerator. "Especially that."

Maddie didn't look. She clearly knew what he was referring to. "I'll do it. Thank you for coming."

She walked them to the door, just like any good hostess. Suzanne made Maddie promise to call her if she had any trouble, then Nick walked her to her car.

He scribbled his cell number on the back of his business card and handed it to her. "Now I want you to promise *me* that you'll call if you have any trouble. On Maddie's behalf, or your own."

Suzanne watched the house thoughtfully. "Your people will look after her, won't they? She can call if she's harassed, and someone will be out right away. Right? You and the officer told her someone would patrol to make sure."

An edge in Suzanne's voice stung him. A shot of guilt zinged through him as he admitted, to himself at least, that he might have been overly optimistic about police response. "Come on, Suzanne, you know that was for Morgan's benefit, warning him not to come back. I can't promise that a car will park here all night." Nick shifted his weight from one leg to the other, uncomfortable to be put on the spot. As much as he believed his gut Morgan was the guilty party. Shadyside wasn't his division. He probably shouldn't have spoken for the department. He'd just wanted that smug look to leave Gregory Morgan's face.

In his book, career politicians and evangelical preachers shared a status with low-class used car salesmen, phony through and through. Easy enough to handle them. Smile to their face, and as soon as possible, wash the hand that just shook their slimy one. Something about Morgan had never rung true, but Nick knew the man had cachet with the higher ups. He'd probably hear about this.

When he didn't answer, Suzanne eyed him, her expression conveying disappointment. "At least the police respond to calls in this neighborhood within a reasonable time," she said tartly. "Otherwise, I guess they can be as useless as the rest of the system." She closed her car door, almost before he could step out of the way. He watched her pull out of the driveway, compelled to give her a half-hearted wave, but she didn't look back.

What the hell did she want? He'd known she could handle the legal end, and it seemed like she had it all in order. He had dropped everything to help serve the papers when she called. He couldn't exactly post an officer on this woman's front yard, even if her husband was a crazy bastard.

Annoyed, he stalked to his car, his neck muscles pulling tight. He gunned the engine, backing out onto the street faster than he should have, narrowly missing a pair of empty garbage cans on the lawn across the street. *Calm down, Nick. You can't afford a new bumper.*

He headed back to the station, discontent percolating in the back of his mind.

But the picture that kept returning to his mind was Suzanne's face, at the height of her game, *mano a mano* with Greg Morgan, challenging him with the depths of her soul. She wasn't in the least afraid of a man who was clearly dangerous. The flash of her eye, the straight line of her back, the stance like the proverbial mother lion protecting a helpless cub all revealed something fiery in her soul, someone he admired and wanted to know intimately.

What could he do to get her attention?

****

Two days passed before Nick got his head far enough above water at work to call her. He'd been right that departmental feathers would be ruffled by his appearance in Shadyside, but he'd staved off the worst of it with a personal call to Phillip Johnson, his counterpart. He'd explained what happened, and Phil shrugged it off. Cops did what they had to at any given moment. They all understood that.

He'd arrived home late before he'd decided to call her. Eight o'clock on a weeknight? She had teenagers. Plenty early enough.

His fingers stuttered clumsily on the face of his cell phone as he tried to dial the number he'd saved when she'd called him. The third time, he got it right, silently cursing the fact she made him so nervous.

How many casual dates had he arranged without so much as a second thought?

But something about Suzanne Taylor set his insides twisting.

He turned off the lights in his small living room and opened the sliding glass doors to the wooden deck that ran the length of his half of the side-by-side duplex. He'd owned the building on the outskirts of McKees Rocks for nine years. The tenant in the other half, an older woman who taught junior high school, paid rent that covered the mortgage. The arrangement worked for him.

He leaned on the rail on the deck's edge and looked up at the stars, spotting the constellation Orion in the southwest. As he watched, a spot of light streaked across the sky. He made his wish, like his mother had always taught him to do.

The phone rang several times, leaving him scrambling for something to say should the call go to voicemail. His words seemed to duck into the nooks and crannies of his brain, impossible to find, daring to play hide and seek with his tongue. He was actually grateful when she picked up.

"Suzanne Taylor," she said, all business.

"Suzanne, it's Nick Sansone. Do you, ah, have a minute?"

A hesitation. "Has something happened to Maddie?"

"What?" Not what he had expected. "No. No, that's not why I'm calling."

"Oh. What is it, then?"

"I..ah." He cleared a throat strangled by nerves. *Come on, Sansone. Just tell her what you want.* "I wondered if we could get together this weekend."

Another hesitation, longer this time, then her reply, laced with wry amusement. "Really, Lieutenant, haven't you gotten tired of my company over the last week?"

He considered the correct response. Something serious? A zinger? She didn't seem the kind who wanted hearts and flowers. What answer would get him past the doorstep? "It's either this or hope they play tackle at the next Bar-Badge charity football game." Nick held his breath, waiting to see if he'd chosen the right course. To his relief, she laughed.

"It's kind of you, but I've got serious plans this weekend. Me and a garden rake."

A light breeze riffled through the hair on the back of his neck. "Hey, I love garden rakes," he said, packing enthusiasm into his tone.

"Really."

"Really! I have one. Here. Somewhere." Must be one in the garage. He wasn't sure what all was out there, between what he'd bought and what his father had dropped off from time to time once he had his own house. But a rake, that was pretty standard. People had shovels, hoes, rakes. Sure, he had one.

"Do you know how to use it?"

The biting note both stung him and made him smile. "I'm pretty sure which end to hold. Look, you tell me where and when and I'll be there, fully armed."

"I'm serious about the gardening. The yard's full of leaves and I've got to tuck everything in for winter. I'm tempted to call your bluff, just to make you sorry."

"I dare you."

A soft chuckle came across the phone. "You're on, Lieutenant. Nine a.m., I'll make the coffee, and you'd better be holding your equipment."

He chuckled at the double entendre. "I'll be there. With my Housebuilders belt on."

She gave him her address, and general directions. Worried he might say something to jinx the miracle he'd somehow managed to pull off, he told her goodbye and clicked the button.

When you wish upon a star…

He laughed at himself. "Yeah, pal, look what you've done. Congratulations, you get to spend half a day at manual labor."

But with a companion like that, it wouldn't be so bad. Not bad at all.

****

Since she'd offered coffee, he drove his big silver Chevy pickup truck across town to Moio's in Monroeville for fresh Roman cannolis, a specialty ladylock shell stuffed with fresh vanilla custard and a cherry in the middle. By the time he found a place to park, got in the crowded shop and back out, he'd wasted over an hour. He knew he was trying too hard, but something in his gut insisted he had to set the bar fairly high to impress this woman.

Her house was north of the city in Indiana Township, on a road best categorized as rural. A long stone driveway led up to a white two-story with a side porch and a yard. A huge yard. His heart sank as he saw it. He'd really gotten himself in deep this time.

Grabbing the string-tied box with the cannolis and his rake, as promised, Nick strolled up to the door. She opened it before he could knock.

A lazy smile settled on his lips, taking much more effort than he allowed her to see. "You needed cheap labor, ma'am?"

"Glad you wore your play clothes," she said with a smile. Her hair was up in a ponytail, and she wore jeans that fit just right, with a green T-shirt bearing a Sierra Club logo. She gestured to the box. "Is that for me?"

"For us. You did say you would make coffee."

"So I did. Come on in."

She stepped aside, holding the door open. He entered a shadowed hallway. The family room was off to his right, evidenced by the large-screen television that hung on the wall and video games scattered around the floor. Big windows let light into that room, although the angle of the sun wasn't right for it to reach into the foyer. Neutral-toned furniture posed around a large burgundy Persian style rug and an oak coffee table stacked with magazines.

"Coffee's this way. Come into the kitchen."

She led the way down the short hallway to the kitchen, which was a sunburst of shades of yellow, from the walls to the curtains, to the rack of bright plates that sat above the white-faced cabinets. The closer he got, the better the coffee smelled.

"This is a great place," he said. "It's old, isn't it?"

She smiled and took a pair of thick yellow mugs from the cabinet. "About eighty years, according to the title search."

Nick examined the window casements, then the design of the ceiling. "The window construction postdates the rest of the moldings. You remodeled it?"

"About five years ago, when I bought it." She shook her head. "You're a construction expert, too?"

Nick grinned. "There are a great many things you don't know about me, Suzanne Taylor." He snapped the string on the box and opened it. "I thought we could splurge a bit. I expect you're going to work that many calories out of me before we're done." He took the opportunity to peer out the wide-silled kitchen window, set with half a dozen small terra cotta pots planted with herbs. "Oh, yes. Plenty to be done here."

"I warned you." Her smile was unapologetic.

"What about the children? My mother always volunteered me for these jobs."

"My parents agreed to take them to their activities today so I could get this done." She set out small plates to match the mugs and took half a cannoli. “You really drove all the way over to Moio’s? You must have been up at the crack of dawn. On a Saturday, you can’t get out of there in less than half an hour.”

“I’ve got pull,” he said.

“The badge is useful for more than just catching your reflection, is it?”

Her sarcasm burned him again. He could have explained that his uncle was married to the owner’s sister, but he didn’t want to waste the time. She obviously had some issue with the police. This wasn’t the opportunity to challenge her on it. Not if he wanted to keep seeing her.

“I use mine to serve cheese and crackers sometimes.”

The response provoked a laugh, and she moved on. “Would you like a tour? I’m always up for someone to admire my woodwork.”

He gulped some coffee. “Sure.”He wiped his mouth on the back of his hand and followed her back toward the foyer. She took a right past the stairs, and they entered a room full of plants and books. The central piece of furniture was a rolltop desk along the far wall, piled so high with papers they seemed seriously in danger of sliding off.

“This is my office away from office,” she said.

He ducked a dangling spider plant as he looked out the bay window. The flowered pillows on the seat felt very much like home. Sun shone in, lighting up the bright blossoms on the curtains and sofa. “Kind of like a jungle, isn’t it?”

“Isn’t that great?” She reached out to brush dust off a tall potted ficus. “Especially in the winter. I can close the drapes and pretend I’m on a Florida vacation.”

“Lucky you.”

She picked a couple of dead leaves off the plant and tossed them at the wicker wastebasket next to the desk with a sigh, scuffing one sneakered foot on the thick, nubbly carpet. "Time to quit stalling. I've got to confess, I'm not anxious to play master gardener."

He pulled a pair of work gloves out of his jacket pocket. "Sooner we get started, the sooner we're done. But I'm taking coffee out with me."

"Anything that helps," she agreed.

They retreated to the kitchen to fortify themselves. He found his gaze drawn to her, the curves of her body in the clothing she wore, the hint of strong muscle and yielding flesh underneath. Just as well physical labor lay ahead. Work would keep him distracted from other, earthier thoughts.

They went out through the kitchen door. The back porch wrapped around the west side of the house, but was clearly often inhabited, if the glider and the gardener's bench piled high with pots was any evidence. Not very many signs that children lived here, though. No bikes, swing equipment or other apparatus.

"How old are your girls?" he asked.

"Fifteen and thirteen. Delightful ages." Suzanne stacked up half a dozen clay pots, dropping a trowel in the top one as she changed the subject. "Look, this is what I'd like to get done today. The leaves raked, trees trimmed, and a bunch of the more delicate plants dug up and replanted so I can take them inside. I've also got a basket of spring bulbs we need to put in the ground. Have a preference?"

He surveyed the yard thoughtfully. "Why don't I pile up a bunch of those dead branches and get the leaves raked up? Then we can see what remains."

The work went faster than he'd expected. The warm sun made him shed his police department sweatshirt before long, and he finished his part before she got her plants dug up, even taking into account his judicious pruning of the pine trees.

"If you'd dig holes I'll get the bulbs in," she said, a real note of pleading in her voice. "They have to be down about eight inches to avoid the cold."

"I know." Nick reached for the bag, examining the photograph of the bright blooms on the front. "My mother loved tulips, too. We planted them on her grave, my brother and I."

Suzanne bit her lip. "I'm sorry. As much as my mother makes me crazy sometimes, I wouldn't want to be without her."

A silence passed between them, but it wasn't uncomfortable. He picked up a post-digger. "Point me in the direction you want."

He started making the holes, and she followed after him, adding a little pinch of fertilizer and the bulb, then packing the dirt back into the hole. As they finished the plot she wanted planted, she surveyed their accomplishment, her smile satisfied.

"We make a good team, wouldn't you say?" he asked.

She studied him speculatively. "Efficient, anyway."

She wouldn't even begrudge him a compliment. *Infuriating woman.*

Nick set his rake against the painted porch railing and stretched. His back muscles tightened from the unaccustomed repetitive movement. They'd been at it since ten. Now it was mid-afternoon. Twice a week at the gym wasn't a match for hours of manual labor. He was getting old.

"Is there more coffee?" Nick asked. "If we're allowed to have a break, that is. I hate to ruin our efficiency record."

"Sure. I'm sorry." She brushed dirt from her hands. "I get so…so single-minded." Flustered, she gathered up the garden tools and shoved them in a tall cabinet next to the porch. "Come in."

The coffee pot was nearly empty. She dumped

out the remains and ground beans for a fresh pot. The kitchen filled with the aroma as she poured in the water and flipped the switch. Nick picked up the bag of beans, the side facing him transparent. He'd never heard of the brand, Coffee Fresh, but the logo indicated they came from the Windy City. He had seriously underestimated her tastes. "You order coffee all the way from Chicago?"

"It's the best." Her smile returned, a little shy. "A woman named Carrie owns the business. I think women in business need to stick together, you know. Help promote each other."

She rinsed out their mugs at the sink, and Nick waited till she was done, then washed his hands, the gears in his mind turning. Women banding together to beat men, that seemed to be a common theme in Suzanne's thought patterns. For someone so liberal, equality of the sexes would seem to be a given. Something had happened to her, something that had shifted her world view. He dried his hands on the paper towel she gave him and took a seat at the small dinette table. "Tell me, why do you hate men so much?"

Chapter Nine

"Who said I hate men?"

Where had that come from? They were talking about coffee. Suzanne's psyche prepared to defend the perceived attack, but he raised a hand to stop her.

"I don't mean that the way it sounds. Just not the first time you said something very similar. Makes me think you've been hurt along the line."

She spoke up quickly, purposely creating distance, a skill she cultivated for moments just like this. "Everyone's been hurt, Nick. It's part of the human experience. I'm a big girl. I've gotten over it."

He nodded, and watched her, his dark eyes piercing inquisitors.

She picked at the blades of dried grass stuck to her shirt, wanting to turn away, but refusing to give in. She should have known once she'd opened the door to her self-sufficient life that these questions would start. All she'd wanted was a little help with her yard, since the girls were gone. And she hadn't even really asked. He'd volunteered. For yard work. That's all.

But just like their dinner the other night wasn't quite "just" dinner, this wasn't exactly landscaping without strings. She was in fact a big girl, just as she'd said. She should know better.

She fussed with the cups again, and sensed at last his gaze had left her and moved on. A glance over her shoulder revealed he'd noticed the girls' school portraits, framed in bright green, hanging over the refrigerator. He got up to view them more closely.

She'd steered conversation clear of her daughters, so far, in a purposeful way. Over her years of practice she'd seen many examples of what not to do. One of the most obvious was to keep any potential lover and one's children separate until a relationship developed. Otherwise, the children could prematurely attach to someone who didn't stay, causing damage to their ability to form trusting relationships in the future.

But she knew Nick Sansone wouldn't stop with a look at some photographs. His was an inquiring mind. "The one on the left is Hope," she said. "She's fifteen, and an honor student. Riviera's thirteen, and she's in the flag corps at school."

"They're very pretty girls." He winked. "Of course, how could I expect anything else?"

The comment allowed her to roll her eyes, as he'd surely known she would, and mentally take a step back. "Thank you. I think they're beautiful."

She poured them coffee even before the pot had finished brewing, and set cream and sugar on the table with two spoons. He took a bare half spoon of sugar. Anxious to have something for her hands to do, she focused on adding sugar and cream slowly to her own cup, the *ting* of the spoon hitting the inside of her mug soothing in its rhythm.

Long silence caught her attention, pulled her gaze up to meet his. He seemed to be mulling over something he wanted to say. She could guess what it was. Better for her to bring it up on her own terms, then slam the door on this whole line of inquiry.

"Their father's long gone. We haven't seen him since before Riviera was born." Her lips pressed together.

"Incredible." Nick glanced at the pictures again, the smiling faces clear-skinned and shining in the posed portraits. "So you've done this all alone?"

"We all do what we have to," she said. As soon as the words were out, she resented herself for being so cliché. Could she act any more like a martyr?

"No wonder you're bitter." He dug in the cardboard box for one of the remaining cannolis.

What should she say? Hell, yes, she was bitter. But would a confession frighten him off? Such revelations had scared others away. She studied Nick's face, but saw nothing there of hostility or worry. She guessed he was made of stronger cloth.

She should protest that she wasn't. More polite, wasn't it?

Besides, it wasn't any of his business.

But she really did like him. Maybe enough.

If she was really to have some sort of future with this impertinent, handsome man, he'd know better. She bet he knew better right now. "What would be the point?" she said at last. "I've got more positive directions to use that energy."

A slow smile came to his lips, and she felt she'd been...approved. She looked away, trying not to blush, not needing his approbation in any way.

All the same, she was pleased to have it.

"What else is on the agenda, counselor?" Nick made a point of looking at his watch. A glance at the microwave showed her it was nearly three o'clock. A stubborn small voice in her head insisted she could have done all this work by herself. But she would still have been cutting limbs by dark, with blistered hands. Yes, this was a much better outcome.

"Can I buy you dinner?" she asked. "The least I could do after—"

The front door opened, then slammed. The sudden sound startled her into silence. Her fingers gripped the back of the chair nearest her. Who had come into her house? Did Greg Morgan's reach come this far? Nick got to his feet, watching her face, her reaction warning him something might be amiss.

Footsteps bounded down the hallway to the kitchen, and Riviera poked her head around the corner. "Mom, whose truck is—" She stopped as if she'd come across an angry rattlesnake, staring at the man in the kitchen. "Whoa."

Her sister, more reserved, followed, peering over Riviera's shoulder. "Well, now." She eyed her mother with an arch grin. "So this is what you do while we're not here. Invite men over to play."

Embarrassed, Suzanne shoved her hands in her pockets. "I thought you were staying at Nana's for dinner."

"Too much homework," Hope said. "They brought us home early. Gee, I hope we didn't interrupt anything." Her expression said she absolutely hoped she was.

Suzanne coughed, wishing she had one of those candy bars that the ads said would allow her the time to buy a few minutes to think what to say. "Girls, this is Nick Sansone. Nick, these are my daughters, Hope and Riviera."

"Delighted," he said. He brushed off his hands before reaching out to shake theirs. "You'll have to excuse my casual attire. Your mother had me hauling branches and digging holes today. I'm afraid I'm just not used to all this hard labor."

Riviera cheered, eyes sparkling. "You mean we don't have to clean up the yard?" She went to the window to confirm and turned back with a huge smile. "Yippee!" She dropped her bag where she stood. "I've got to pee." She disappeared down the hall.

Hope shook her head and snagged the bag, tucking it out of the way. The expression in her eyes was decidedly calculating.

"Nana didn't want to come in?" Suzanne asked her.

"Not when she saw you had company. She thought it might be a client." She turned to Nick. "Are you a client?"

The only hint of his reaction to her daughter's directness was the slight raise of an eyebrow. "No," he said.

Impatience in the set of her shoulders and her jaw, Hope waited for more of a response, but Nick just grinned at her. She turned to her mother, hands on her hips.

"Nick is a detective for the Pittsburgh police," Suzanne explained. "We met at court."

"He's a cop?" Riviera said, catching the tail end of the conversation as she returned. She ducked over to the old ceramic cookie jar and grabbed a handful of vanilla wafers. "Cool!"

"'Cool,' huh?" Nick said as she took the seat next to his at the table. "What's so cool about it?"

"You're out there, getting bad guys off the streets, and you get to carry a gun, and...and *be* somebody."

"A gun doesn't make you important."

She shrugged. "Tell that to the kids at my school." She shoved a cookie in her mouth.

"Guns at school. Ridiculous." Suzanne sat at the table, too, awkward in this situation she'd been so cautious to prevent over the years. She didn't want a man involved with her girls, at least not until she was sure he would be part of their future. Nick, however, seemed perfectly relaxed. How did he do it?

"It's a problem everywhere," Nick said. "Students feel threatened by someone and just want to even what they perceive to be bad odds."

Hope added, "One of my friends was shot by some boy who heard my friend was out to get him. My friend didn't even know this guy."

"Guns escalate situations into something deadly." Nick turned back to Riviera. "No one should carry without being properly trained on how to and when *not* to use their firearm."

"How long have you been a detective?" she asked.

"Ten years," he said. "And a street officer five years before that."

"Ever catch a murderer?" she asked, captivated.

He shrugged. "Maybe a couple."

"Wow." Her young face glowed with admiration.

"Wow." He half-laughed, eying Suzanne. "It's not as exciting as you think. Investigative work is painstaking and difficult, not like on television, where everything just magically pops up from the lab in fifteen minutes."

"I saw the bumper sticker on your car," Hope said casually. "You're a Dolphins fan?"

He chuckled. "I was a Dan Marino fan," he said. "Ever since he was at Pitt. I miss him."

"That's tantamount to treason, here in Steeler country." The slim girl sat back in her chair, the overhead light creating a burnished crown on her dark hair.

Nick grinned again. "I'm thrilled a girl your age knows the word 'tantamount.'"

"Avoiding the question." Hope looked back at him, unruffled.

"This apple hasn't fallen far from the tree," he said. "You remind me of your mother in the courtroom."

Hope shook her head.

"Besides," Nick went on, "I've got a confession about that. See, football was always a big thing in my family. My father and brother and cousins and everyone would gather round the TV on Sunday afternoons to watch the games together. All of them, everyone are Steelers men. So, this was my way to rebel."

Hope considered that a moment, then smiled. "You're a real radical," she said. She poured herself some coffee and joined them at the table.

"So have you guys been to a game?" he asked.

"No," Hope said, with a practiced pout. "Mom can't seem to find the time to go."

"Well, that won't do," he said. "You live in one of the biggest football towns in America, and you haven't even gone to a game?" He turned to Suzanne. "How can you let that happen, Mom?"

"I—We haven't, I mean..." She felt like she'd stepped off a pier into icy water. Hope and Riviera both watched her with cat-like expressions, finding it amusing for their usually-incisive mother to be tongue-tied.

"I'll keep that in mind then. For down the road." His eyes twinkling with mischief, he finished his coffee.

"Do you have kids?" Riviera asked.

"Riv, calm down," Suzanne said, uncomfortable her daughter was being so forward.

"It's fine, Suzanne. I've got nothing to hide." He nodded reassurance. "I don't have children. I've never been married."

"Pets?"

He shook his head. "I'd like to have a dog, but with my work schedule, I'm not there often enough to be fair to a dog."

"We can't have a dog." Riviera sulked in Suzanne's direction.

"No professional football? No dog? Clearly you are mistreated, my dear Riviera." He smirked at Suzanne.

She felt a slow burn coming on, despite knowing that he was teasing her. Her gaze met his, and her fading amusement must have connected with him, because he stood up.

"I'll let you all get to your work. It's been wonderful meeting you girls."

"Nice to meet you," Hope said, with a mysterious smile.

"You're much nicer than the cops—I mean police officers—on TV," her sister offered.

"I'll second that," Suzanne said, getting to her feet as well. "Don't forget your tools, Nick. Since you did demonstrate your Farmer John skills as promised." She grinned at the matching confused looks on her daughters' faces. "I'll walk you out."

She headed to the back porch, waiting for him to pick up his hoe and rake, then strolled slowly out to his truck.

"They're great," he said. "Bright, independent, charming. Everything I like about their mother."

She shoved aside the wave of squirmy discomfort that insinuated itself on her conscience. "Thank you." She leaned against the front fender as he put his tools into the truck bed. "Thanks for your help today, too."

"It was my pleasure." He rotated a sore shoulder. He had to get back to regular sessions at the gym. For sure. "I think."

"We do make a good team," she said.

His face lit with delight, and he went to add something, then bit it back. She wondered what he might have said. He pulled open the driver's side door and started his engine, then climbed in. "I'll call you," he said.

"Please do." She turned to face him, finding the door a fine barrier between them. Until he buzzed the window down.

"Have I earned a kiss goodbye at least?"

She glanced at the house, sure the girls were watching. Well, now they'd have something to talk about. She leaned forward and kissed him. Her intent was just to catch his lips, but he leaned into it, then reached out a hand to caress her shoulder, keeping her close. A little dizzy wave wiggled through her. She found she wanted to kiss him just as much as he seemed to want to kiss her. Maybe longer. Maybe more than just kissing.

It had been much too long since she'd been with a man.

He slowly let go, then smiled as he studied her face. "You take care." He waved, then drove out the driveway. She stood, watching him go, arms crossed tight, half wishing the children hadn't come home when they did.

When she went back inside, she could tell the girls had been confabbing. The guilty looks in stereo were carefully controlled by the time she picked up her coffee cup.

"So when did this happen?" Hope asked.

"Nothing 'happened,'" Suzanne said. "He came to help with the yard work. And…and we went out."

"You went out? With him?" Riviera demanded, eyes bright with fascination. "When? Friday? Last night? Did he spend the night?"

"No, he did not spend the night," Suzanne said firmly. "We had dinner. Period."

"He seems really nice, for a cop, anyway," her youngest daughter said, finishing the last of her cookies. "Is he coming back?"

Suzanne chose to eye the clock in lieu of an answer. "I bet I know some girls who have things to do right now. Homework?"

Hope got to her feet. "I think I'd better head up."

"I'm taking a shower." Riviera gave a cheesy grin before disappearing around the corner, her footfalls sounding above them a few seconds later.

Suzanne poured another cup of coffee, considering the stack of work waiting in her office. "I need about six more hours in a day."

"No, Mom, you need to relax sometimes and just

have fun," Hope said. The dark-haired teen pulled the refrigerator door open and inspected the contents. "We never have anything to eat."

"Right. Cupboards are always bare. Try some fruit."

Hope made a gagging sound, but she took a navel orange out of the bowl on the counter.

Suzanne considered her daughter's comment. "You don't think I have fun?"

She shrugged and returned to her seat at the table, knees pulled close and feet flat on the seat of the chair. "I know you enjoy your work, and all. But you don't go out or have a boyfriend or anything like that." Hope's dark eyes, so like her father's, approved of Suzanne. "I think it's great. Nick. You. Going out." She peeled back the thick skin, and both of them inhaled deeply as the first oils filled the air with a delicious scent.

"Give me a piece of that." Hope handed her a piece and Suzanne added a small curl to her cup. Orange and coffee might seem an odd combination, but she loved it. Just like dark chocolate and orange. "So you like him?"

"Yeah, I do. He's funny, and polite, and he *loves* football. Do you really think he'd take us to a Steelers game?"

"You can't count on it, Hope." As Hope started to protest, Suzanne shushed her. "Things change, faster than we ever expect sometimes. You never know what might happen. He may decide to move on at any time."

"You mean like Dad." Hope stared down at the table.

The pain inherent in her words grabbed at Suzanne's heartstrings. She would do anything to make sure Hope's heart wasn't broken again, even if that meant denying herself Nick's companionship. If it came to that. She hoped so much it didn't.

Hope fiddled with the last sections of her orange, and Suzanne soaked in guilt for entering the sour note into the conversation. She did her best to turn it around. "On the other hand, he's certainly the best prospect that's come by for a long time," she confessed with a tiny smile.

Hope smiled back, gathering her peels and throwing them in the compost bowl. She rinsed her hands and dried them on the deep green towel hanging on the front of the stove. "It'll be all right, Mom," she said, giving Suzanne a hug and kiss.

"I know it will."

Suzanne followed Hope down the hall, continuing past the stairs to her office. The cheery flowers sprang to life when illuminated, adding to her sense of well-being. Under the roll-top, files awaited, and she finished reviewing the first before Riviera came down, well-scrubbed and smelling of fruity hair conditioner.

"Mom? Can you come look at my computer a minute?"

"What's wrong? It won't boot up?"

"No. Something else." Riviera's brow was furrowed under the thick blue towel in which she'd wrapped her hair. She chewed her lip, shifting her weight from hip to hip as she stood in front of the desk. This behavior wasn't like her normally ebullient child. Something was wrong. Something bad.

"Sure." Suzanne followed her youngest upstairs to her room, decorated in bright stripes of purple paint and color posters of assorted singing stars. The computer monitor displayed what looked like email. "So what's the problem, hon?"

"Look at that email."

Suzanne slid into the soft chair with the purple cushion, squinting a little to read the purple letters against the green background that Riviera chose for her display. "How you see this thing is beyond me..." she muttered. "Is this from a friend of yours?"

As she read the text, she realized she needn't have asked.

Hey gurl where u been hidin? i been lookin for u at ur school. When I find u, ur gonna be sorry for what ur momma done. Luv u! jonboy

Suzanne's left hand climbed from her lap to cover her heart. "What is this?" she asked, horrified. "Who's this 'jonboy?' Do you have any idea?" Anger shot through her like a hot current. Who would dare to threaten her child? Who would *dare*?

Her outraged reaction drove Riviera back almost against the wall. "I don't know, Mom!" Tears started down her cheeks.

"Oh, honey." Suzanne got up and took her crying daughter in her arms. "I'm not mad at you. I promise. I'm mad at whoever did this. That someone thinks it's all right to terrorize little girls."

Riviera mumbled against her shoulder. "I'm not a little girl."

"You always will be to me, sweet." She smoothed her daughter's hair. "Why don't you leave this computer alone and go down and get my laptop, okay? You're not doing anything... inappropriate, are you?"

She looked up, a pout on her lips. "Mom."

"Just asking." Suzanne's stomach swirled with light nausea as she looked at the monitor screen again. She had to preserve this evidence in some way. Just in case.

"But I've got all my messengers on this one, Mom. And I'm right in the middle of my Gaia game."

Suzanne sat down at the computer desk once again, reading the message. She forwarded it to her own email, and also created a new folder on Riviera's computer, where she saved the offending email. "All right. Maybe it won't hurt to let you keep using this one. But if you get another email from this boy I want to know. Immediately."

"All right, Mom." Relieved, the girl waited impatiently for her mother to vacate the chair.

"I mean it." Suzanne stood up and stepped back, crossing her arms. Riviera jumped back into the chair, opening a different browser window. As Suzanne stayed behind her, Riviera looked over her shoulder. "Mom. Privacy?"

"If you're not doing anything you're ashamed of, why can't I watch?"

More firmly. "Mother. Please."

Suzanne sighed. "All right. But be careful."

Riviera practically shooed her out the door. Suzanne stared at the closed door between them for a long moment. How had they survived without the Internet back in her adolescence? The girls seemed to spend day and night in instant contact with hundreds, perhaps thousands of people. Talk about access to pervs...

Debating what exactly to do about the email, she wandered downstairs to her office. Her first instinct had been, of course, that it had been sent to her daughter because of something Greg Morgan had done. He could have ordered any of his minions to track Riv down. What was his son's name? Not John.

The cyber world of teenagers was something open to threats, though, even discounting Greg Morgan. It could have been a child of any of her clients. It could have been some enemy of Riviera's. It could have been any old mean girl from her school, playing a practical, if tasteless, joke.

Even if Riviera had correctly reported the email to her mother, she didn't seem to be too alarmed by it. Maybe a lot of the kids spoofed each other like this. While the words constituted an overt threat, it would be extremely hard to identify who'd sent them. And maybe a waste of everyone's time.

If Nick had been there, she likely would have asked him. She'd been pleased by their day together. She and Nick *had* been a good working team, and she liked the way he'd interacted with the girls. For the most part, he'd been comfortable as an old sweatshirt. She'd never thought she could feel like that in a man's company again.

Nick might be different. They hadn't known each other for long, but he appealed to her on a level deeper than consciousness. Somehow he reached her, connecting with her, not butting up against her but flowing around her, like water.

Whatever he was doing, it was working.

The realization scared her just a little. She wasn't ready for a relationship. At least she didn't think she was. No need to rush things, not at all. Nick Sansone was a nice man who knew how to use a garden rake. And had good taste in food. And knew just how to appeal to her daughters.

She could handle this herself. She wouldn't bother him with it. It could have been Morgan, or it could have been someone else. It could have been someone just trying to prank one of the girls. No sense in jumping the gun and making Nick feel he was indispensable.

He wasn't indispensable at all. No man was. Suzanne could take care of herself and her daughters. She'd just hold that information till the time was right. A dozen computer experts were available in the city. If she needed to track down who'd sent this threat to her home, she could hire any one of them.

If the culprit turned out to be Morgan, he'd find he had a mama grizzly on his back. And it would be the end of him.

Chapter Ten

Nick sensed Suzanne's interest in him, rising below the surface of that carefully-maintained reserve she affected. Since her attraction complemented his, he knew he couldn't possibly leave the progress of any potential relationship to fate. Fate had a way of dropping disasters when least expected. Better to take matters into his own hands.

Over the next few weeks, he made several attempts to see her again. She turned down dinner, lunch, an afternoon walk along Mount Washington, even the offer of a morning cappuccino from her favorite chain coffee shop. Maybe he'd done something to offend her during that discussion with her children. He replayed the scene in his mind over and over, but couldn't see where he might have erred. The girls were pretty damned spunky, and they seemed to like him. What had he done?

He'd waited too long to get that first "yes" out of her to give up now. He just had to be more clever. Something show-stopping—an offer she couldn't refuse.

The perfect plan came to him, and he executed it immediately.

Fighting noisy mid-afternoon Friday traffic on Carson Street hadn't been part of his calculations. Over the last decade, East Carson had become the trendy place for Pittsburghers to hang out, and particularly drink. It was rumored to have the longest stretch of pub crawl in the United States. Unfortunately, the narrow street hadn't added any additional parking to accommodate its popularity. He cruised the length of the street several times, east and west, before he could slip his truck into a spot scarcely vacated by the car before him, almost close enough to tap bumpers.

With a deep breath, he tucked his keys into his brown leather jacket pocket, then picked up the cellophane-wrapped bouquet of daisies he'd bought at a florist downtown. A cool wind insinuated itself along the back of his collar. He shivered and pulled his jacket closer.

The daisies were pretty, but the real kicker was the envelope tucked inside.

Would she even bother to open it?

He thought she would. She seemed very thorough. She'd at least open it before discarding it. Then they'd see what happened.

A tug on the heavy glass door at the bottom of the steps let him in, and he took the stairs two at a time. Aspiration lifted him upward, a giddy smile on his lips. He managed to wrestle it away before he stepped inside her office.

The waiting room was like a hundred others he'd seen, perhaps made upscale by the plush brown print upholstering the chairs. A heavy-set woman sat at a computer, typing, only glancing up after she'd finished. Her pale pink suit fit awkwardly, pulling at the underarms. Her gaze went first to the bunch of flowers, then to his face.

He smiled, an expert at diplomacy with gatekeepers. His hand slid into his jacket pocket and came out with his badge, which he flipped open for her to see. "Detective Nick Sansone to see Ms. Taylor."

The woman's lips flirted with a smile as she

indicated the flowers. "Business or pleasure?

He chuckled. "Which will get her attention faster?"

With a conspiratorial grin, she lifted the telephone receiver and punched three numbers. "Suzanne, a police detective to see you. Something urgent."

Perfect. He winked his approval.

The inner door flew open, and Suzanne came through it, breathless. "Is it—Oh. It's you."

"Very observant," Nick said, enjoying the flow of expressions across Suzanne's face. Alarm was usurped by surprise, which gave way to suspicion, and finally rolled over into a restrained pleasure.

"Lieutenant." She glanced at her assistant, then back to him. "Won't you come in?"

"Thank you."

He grinned at the assistant to solidify his personal connection, then followed Suzanne into the office. He didn't think he'd ever seen so many books in one place before, outside a library. Two walls were lined with them from floor to ceiling. The flowers in his hand felt awkward now, and he held them out to her.

"For you," he said.

Her fingers tightened into a loose fist for a moment, then she reached out to take them. "Thank you." She leaned the open end of the bunch toward her face, inhaling the slightly musty scent of the white flowers. "You came all the way out here to bring me these?"

"Clearly waiting for you to drop in on me hasn't been fruitful." He crossed to the window behind her, checking out the view toward the river. He'd make her turn around, keep her off balance. Old police trick. "This is very nice."

"You can see what I'm dealing with," she said, waving at her desk. "I'm buried this week."

“All work and no play makes Suzanne a beautiful—but dull—girl,” he said, turning to look over his shoulder, adding a scolding look.

Her jaw tightened. She didn’t seem to have much patience with practiced flattery. “What brings you to the South Side?”

“Just that. I wanted to brighten your day.” He turned completely to face her, then looked at his watch. “But I can’t stay. I hope the day improves.”

“But—” Her brow furrowed with confusion.

“I’m sure glad my desk doesn’t look like that.” He grinned at her, then stepped out into the reception area, giving the assistant a little salute before he left the office. An outright laugh fretted behind closed lips until he cleared the building, releasing it into the fresh air.

How long would it take her?

He walked slowly down the crowded sidewalk to his truck, waiting for his cell to ring.

And waited.

He climbed into the truck and opened the window to catch some of the season’s fading sunlight. And waited.

Maybe he hadn’t turned it on. He pulled the cell from his pocket and eyed the display. Nothing. Not even a text.

Maybe she’d just tossed the flowers after all.

He stared at the phone, crestfallen.

Startled by a knock on his passenger-side window, his fingers contracted on the phone till it chirped. He buzzed down the window, as Suzanne smirked at his discomfort.

“I figured you’d be here. Lying in wait. Like a pirate.”

Heat rose in his cheeks. “Right. I’m here.”

She waved the envelope in the window, a twinkle in her eyes. “These are for me? Tickets to the Benedum Center tomorrow night? Moody Blues?”

"Well, there are two tickets."

"So I can take a date. Very thoughtful of you."

The amusement in her eyes tickled him. She was having fun. At his expense, of course, but he'd brought her happiness. Good. "Thanks. We exist to serve." He grinned at her.

"The sad thing is, the Moody Blues are very old school at this point. Hardly anyone listens to them anymore. Who would I find to go with me?"

Oh, yes, she was enjoying the hell out of this. "I happen to have a clear schedule tomorrow night," he said.

"Really? What a coincidence!" She bit her lip to hide the smile.

"So…?"

"So?" she asked.

He eyed her for several moments, keeping his face carefully straight.

She broke the pretense first. "I'd be delighted to go with you, Lieutenant. Thank you very much. Shall I meet you there?"

"I'll pick you up, counselor." That was the man's role, after all. He'd fully expected to drive up to get her.

"Tell you what, why don't you meet me here? Less mileage. Also, less guilt about leaving work early."

"If you'll leave work early, I'll buy you dinner, too."

"A special occasion indeed. As long as we're not eating at the Donut Connection."

He rolled his eyes. "Very funny, very funny indeed. You be ready at six-thirty. I'll be here."

Wagging a warning finger in her direction, he started the car. She stepped back and waved as he pulled away from the curb. Someone skinnied into the parking place as quickly as he'd taken it on arrival, and he nearly missed her blowing him a kiss in his rearview mirror.

Distracted, he almost ran into the Honda in front of him, squealing his brakes to a stop as horns blared. He didn't dare look to see if she was still watching. She'd find it much too amusing for his ego.

Sweet Mother of Mary, what that woman will make me do...

****

Nick stopped by the precinct after he left Suzanne's office, meaning to check his messages. The sight of Greg Morgan coming out of the chief's office stopped him in his tracks.

The bulky councilman didn't bother to notice him as he headed for the back exit. But Nick came under the laser-sharp eyes of Butch Reickert.

"Chief?"

Reickert leaned against his door frame in his shirt sleeves, his stance anything but casual. He looked ready to chew up his desk and spit it out. "Something you need to talk about, Nick?"

Nick glanced in the direction of the departed Morgan, then back at Reickert, guessing Morgan had filed a complaint about the incident at his Shadyside home. "Can't say I do, chief. It was a good call."

"I know you're too good a cop to let personal involvements leak over into your work. Especially anything that would reflect on the department." The chief held his gaze for several long seconds, then nodded. "Your word's good enough for me." He straightened, rotating his shoulders. He turned to retreat into his office, then stopped. "Be careful, Nick. Be careful."

He went into his office and closed the door.

Careful? Nick scoffed. Morgan deserved the warning, not him. If he continued with the attitude he'd shown Nick and Suzanne, he'd trip himself up, political connections or not. Suzanne was doing the right thing, helping that woman out of a situation she was clearly not equipped to deal with. Perhaps he had let his personal attraction for Suzanne persuade him to cross jurisdictional lines, but it had been justified. He'd do it again if she asked.

A small voice in his head nagged him. If the chief felt disturbed enough to warn him, then there must be something worth warning him about.

Greg Morgan had his hands in a lot of different enterprises around the county. If rumors were true, he wielded more power than just from his council seat, and some of that on the nether side of the law. He could sure cause trouble for Nick, and for Suzanne, too, if he chose to.

Let's hope he's smarter than that.

The squad room was empty. Nick continued through to his office, shrugging off his jacket to hang on the back of his door. He eyed his desk, not as empty as he'd implied to Suzanne, particularly the in-basket. A glance over the case names on the top several files convinced him he didn't want to begin combing through the whole stack now. He'd be there all night.

Instead, he looked over the stack of pink message slips the office clerk had left on his desk. After the third or fourth one, the blue ink blurred before his eyes. Instead he saw the wicked gleam in Suzanne's eye as she teased him about the tickets. He couldn't shake the appealing image.

Come on, Sansone. Concentrate. A cop can't afford to be distracted.

He cleared his throat and sorted through the messages. Nothing that needed to be returned immediately. Leave them for tomorrow.

Tomorrow. When he and Suzanne would sit back and listen to the orchestra backing up one of the bands that shadowed his youth.

He flipped off the light and sat there in the dark

a few minutes, imagining what might happen, enjoying a quiet that was suddenly splintered by the slam of a door in the squad room outside his office. The squad lights came on, and Nick pulled back a little, grateful the blinds had finally been installed. Talk about distracted—when had that happened? Must have been that afternoon while he was out.

"What a load of crap! Transferred to vice for two weeks? You kiddin' me?"

Nick heard Jojo Washington and decided to leave his office light off. Maybe Jojo had forgotten something, and he was going to head out again soon. The last thing he wanted was a confrontation with Jojo. Nick could wait.

A softer, female voice answered Jojo, but Nick couldn't make out the words.

"Tell you what, all this bullshit I put up with, if I don't make sergeant this round, gonna be some hell to pay, that's for sure." Jojo slammed something heavy down on his desk. "No one gonna put me down when I worked this hard!"

"Come, on, Jojo." The woman continued in a foreign tongue, something with a smooth French sound. Clara Malron. Great.

Nick got slowly to his feet, staying low so he'd remain hidden, and moved closer to the door. Might as well find out what the Three Amigos were up to.

"Emilio's right. We got to take things into our hands, Clar. Nothing gonna happen otherwise. Just gotta keep our eyes open. Something will come along."

"Sure it will, sure it will, *doux doux*. Come on, let's bus'off, hmm?"

Nick positioned himself where he could see Clara's face. Her eyes animated and cheeks flushed, she watched Jojo intently. Nick considered again the possibility that the two had a relationship other than professional. He'd seen Jojo with other women, never the same one twice. If Clara had her heart set there, she was doomed for him to break it. Poor kid.

"I'll find a way to kick his ass good, that's what I'm tellin' you."

"Jojo, hush now." She gave an anxious look back toward the chief's office. "You'll get what you deserve."

Another slam. "You bet I will."

Clara got to her feet and walked out of Nick's line of sight, and a few seconds later, their voices dwindled, and the entry door slammed. He stood up, more irritated than worried.

So Jojo thought he'd kick Nick's ass, did he?

Nick wrestled with several reactions and finally laughed. Wasn't the first time some junior officer had given him crap, probably wouldn't be the last. At least for the next two weeks, Jojo and Emilio Vasquez would put in their time with the vice prostitute sweep.

Fourteen days to give him time to figure out what to do next. He grabbed his coat and headed home before anything else could go wrong.

Chapter Eleven

Her hair wasn't right.

She stood in front of the mirror in the frou-frou restroom that served the office and the rest of the tenants on the floor. She hadn't decorated it. The ruffled pink curtains and wallpaper practically bleeding fuchsia butterflies were not to her taste at all.

She took her hair down again. Pinned it back up.

How is it her clients always managed to begin the dating life without difficulty or reservation whatsoever? For Suzanne, it was a major trauma.

She held her hair left, right, her eye critical. The Moody Blues were a sixties band. The Age of Aquarius. Hippies. Free love.

Hair down.

She took her hair out of its band, brushed it, then fluffed it with her fingers.

She'd chosen a feminine silk blouse, black with turquoise medallions, and black dress slacks instead of jeans, since they were going to the Benedum. If the concert had been at Star Lake, they'd have lawn seats and a blanket, and more casual would have been appropriate.

Suzanne thought about Nick, and a blanket, listening to music under the stars...going from zero to sixty pretty fast along that imaginative track. A long time since she'd made love with a man.

She shook her head to clear her mind. *Focus.* Shoes.

The overnight bag she'd brought to the office held a pair of black pumps with a mid-height, chunky heel. She slipped them on, then looked in the mirror again.

Satisfied with her clothing, she dabbed on a hint of makeup, nothing garish, and added small dangle earrings, blue gemstones wrapped in silver, and a spritz of Opium, her favorite perfume. A deep breath gave her a moment to examine her appearance. A little less than professional, a little more than Sunday church. It would do.

She picked up the overnight bag and returned to her office with fifteen minutes left to wait.

Should she be ready when he showed up? Should she be immersed reading papers, so he could see how hard she worked? She paced, trying to decide.

She really liked him. He had a way that connected with her. So many professional men she'd met exhibited personas rigid and ambitious, anxious to get ahead in the world. Pretentious, single-minded individuals immediately triggered Suzanne's defenses.

Nick was different. It was refreshing to meet someone willing to show her a gentler side, someone not trying to control her, but just taking life as it came. It was *fun.*

Realistically, she knew this wasn't a trait that elevated someone through the police department ranks to lieutenant. Inside the man, then, a more aggressive drive must exist. But he was smart enough to know that wouldn't work with her.

That, she liked, too.

Before she could make the decision, it was made for her. Nick appeared five minutes early, announcing his presence by a smooth whistle from the door. "You clean up real pretty, counselor."

"You don't look much like a cop today, either."

The whole package enticed her, the polished shoes, the sharp-creased khakis, the gold-and ruby class ring on his right hand. The top two buttons of his navy print shirt were undone, revealing curly dark hair, thick and especially appealing.

He saw her looking and added a smile. "I wanted to be classy enough to be seen with a member of the bar."

"You may have succeeded," she said. "We'll wait for the reviews to come in before making a final ruling."

"Cautious, always cautious," he chided, but there was a good nature to his words. "Are you ready?"

"Ready as I'm going to be. Let's go."

****

As the concert concluded, Suzanne sat back, the final notes of "Nights in White Satin" still swirling in her head. She looked up at the huge crystal chandelier, one of a number of hanging lights in the Baroque-style setting in shades of brick and terra cotta, all trimmed in gilt highlights and shiny brass rails. The ceiling full of muted octagonal lights gave the interior of the Benedum a gentle warm glow that echoed with the feeling inside Suzanne herself.

The evening had been perfect, so far, tapas and wine at Ibiza, then the music she'd always loved in the darkened theatre. Edge, Hayward, and crew played a fabulous gig, including a medley from *Days of Future Passed.*

Nick and Suzanne waited for the majority of the crowd to leave, Suzanne comfortable in the first-tier level seats, which she knew had set the detective back a few dollars. She'd had several glasses of wine, contributing to the greatest sense of relaxation she could remember in months. Nick had seen to her every need, almost before she'd realized what she needed.

She turned to him with a smile. "Thank you, Nick."

"You're welcome." Something of the excited puppy was in his eyes, delighted he'd pleased her. "What next?"

"Next?" She sat up straight. "It's probably eleven o'clock. Isn't it past your bedtime?"

"Saturday tomorrow. No work for me." A calculating curl of his lips.

"Right."

What to do? Her house was empty. Hope and Riviera were staying with their grandparents, since it wasn't a school night. They hadn't left just because of the date. She hadn't told them. No sense getting their hopes up. Truth be told, she'd been glad they had plans. She'd wanted options, and no reason to have to hurry home.

"What did you have in mind, Lieutenant?" There. Toss the ball into his court.

He stood up, offered her a hand. She took it, and he raised her to her feet.

"First, this." He slipped an arm around her waist, pulling her close to kiss her. She closed her eyes, released the objections that automatically came to her mind and let herself go. He'd worn that aftershave she'd noticed in the courthouse elevator, and as he pressed her against his chest, the scent filled her nose and made her knees weak. Her hands, at first on his shoulders, perhaps ready to push away, soon surrendered with her will, slipping around his neck instead. Their lips met, parted, met again, softly tasting each other, teasing, too. He kissed her a little more intently, seeking something, some answer only her lips could provide, or perhaps only her soul. Heat rose between them consuming all sound and motion, until she lost track of her surroundings.

He let her go slowly. She opened her eyes, finding his so close, so liquid, so overcome with emotion. Hers, she knew, must have looked the same.

"Good beginning," she whispered.

He didn't move. "I know where we can finish that thought."

Her breath caught. Did she dare?

"Will you come home with me, Suzanne?"

Words stuck in her throat, and she couldn't force them out. She wanted to say no. She wanted to say yes. A stray thought crossed her mind that the rush of desire in her body was willing to let him take her right there, and she squelched that as soon as she caught it. But that one made up her mind. She nodded and let him take her hand.

They walked, hand in hand, along Seventh Avenue to the parking garage at Theater Square. Night sounds of traffic and happy concert-goers floated around them. Suzanne couldn't speak, afraid she'd jinx what seemed to be the best chance for the right one she'd had for many years. While she would have been concerned to walk in this area by herself on a weeknight, the presence of a city police lieutenant considerably allayed her fears.

Nick exchanged greetings with the security guard on the first floor of the garage, then they continued up to the second parking deck. As they approached Nick's pick-up truck's passenger-side door, a man in a black hooded sweatshirt and jeans walked up to Suzanne and jabbed a large manila envelope in her direction. She took it without thinking.

"What's that?" Nick asked, his brow clouding up.

"For the lady," the man mumbled. His shoulders hunched, he kept his face turned away from the parking lot lights overhead. Not as tall as Nick, he slouched away, disappearing around the corner toward the exit as Nick reached for the envelope.

"Do you know that guy?" Nick asked.

"Hard to tell." Feeling a little sick, Suzanne pulled the envelope away from Nick's outstretched hand. Her independent streak wasn't ready to give in just yet. So far, this was her problem. "All thugs in black look alike in the dark, hmm?"

"I'll go after him."

"Nick, don't. We don't even know what it is." She started to open the envelope, but he just growled at her.

"Come on, get in the truck." Nick stood straight now, like a guard dog at alert, his eyes surveying the garage. "You can examine it inside."

She didn't argue when he opened the door, but climbed in obediently. Her mind returned to Riviera's email, and the threat therein. What was in the envelope? Another threat? A letter? Something worse?

Nick closed the door behind her, moving swiftly around the truck to climb in the driver's side. He gunned the engine, taking off in the direction the man had gone. The man in black was not to be found. Nick exchanged a few brusque sentences with the parking attendant, but got no answers. His foot slammed on the gas pedal and peeled out of the lot.

Her shoulder slammed into the passenger window as he took a hard left onto Sixth. Her stifled gasp brought a quick look of contrition and an apology, but he didn't slow down.

"Suzanne, I'm sorry. I just didn't want the chance that someone was looking to take a shot—"

"Take a shot? What the hell are you talking about? It's an envelope, for heaven's sake."

He reached forward with his right hand to snap on the interior map light. "No return address," he said, his voice tight.

She eyed the envelope, turned it over. No markings of any kind, not even dirty fingerprints.

"We could take it to the station," he suggested.

"It's probably nothing."

Even as the words left her lips, she chastised herself. She didn't think it was nothing. She just didn't want her evening with Nick Sansone to turn into a crime event. It wasn't fair.

Annoyed, she opened the clasp even as Nick protested, grabbing for the dashboard as the truck swerved. "Look, damn it, you drive and I'll look at this, all right?"

His breath came in short but heavy spurts, and his right hand hung in the air between the steering wheel and Suzanne, as if he waited to yank the envelope from her hands. "All right," he conceded. He turned his attention to the road with a glance in the rear-view mirror. "You said the girls are at your parents.' Right?"

"Mm-hmm." She tilted the envelope, peering inside. No white powder. Too flat for a scorpion or other creature. Just a couple sheets of paper. She reached in and slid the papers out. When she saw what was on them, she nearly dropped them as though they were white-hot.

"Everything all right?" he asked, his tone indicating he knew it wasn't.

She adjusted her grip on the papers, trembling fingers a little more solid against the sheets of plain office paper as she studied a dozen color pictures of Hope and Riviera at school, in various rooms and groups of young people.

She didn't know how long she stared at the prints, steeped in shades of horror. Her heart raced, as if his foot on the gas pedal sent her flying forward into the unknown. The clock said only ten minutes had passed, but she felt like it was nightmare-laced hours before Nick pulled the truck to a stop. She dragged her attention up, to look out the window, to discover they were in some office building parking lot in Greentree. "What are you doing?" she asked softly.

"May I?" he asked, but he didn't wait for her answer. He took the pictures from her hand, shuffling through the pages at a brisk pace. His jawline tightened to stone.

"So. Someone is taking pictures of your children. This says they know where your children are. And they bring the pictures to you after a concert at the Benedum, which means they know where *you* are." He eyed her. "Stalking is a crime in this state. But I don't have to explain that to you, I'm sure."

"No, you don't." Suzanne tried to focus her thoughts, which had followed the same chain of logic. Who had the resources and tenacity to pursue her like this?

One obvious answer.

Nick growled. "Well, we've both got fingerprints on them now." He slipped them back in the envelope. "I can turn them over to the lab techs tomorrow. Unless you already know who sent them."

She shook her head. "I don't know. Not for sure."

"You're thinking it's Councilman Morgan."

A shrug was her only response. If she was wrong, she'd cause both Maddie and herself much more trouble than it was worth. He spoke for her.

"I'm thinking that's who it is. Unless it's standard behavior for crazies to hire people to track you down."

"To tell you the truth, Nick, I deal with a lot of people who are unstable. I mean, for heaven's sake, it's the worst time in their life. They're losing their partner, their house, their kids. How are they supposed to react? I try to give people the benefit of the doubt."

"That's crap." The edge in his voice could have

sliced through the asphalt they parked on. “No one has a right to terrorize you or your girls.” He studied her in the light reflected from the overhead parking lot lamps. “But this is part of a bigger picture, isn’t it? This isn’t some random crazy.”

She closed her eyes, the relaxation she’d experienced earlier in the evening quickly dissipating. “Yes.”

He took another long look into the rear-view mirror, then suddenly bailed out of the truck. He marched around, muttering, words she couldn’t hear, but his tone was clearly angry. She understood. She felt the same taut wire coiled inside herself, ready to spring loose. But she had other priorities.

She reached in her pocket for her cell and dialed her mother’s number. Long seconds passed while she waited for an answer, during which she watched Nick’s frustrated walkabout. Finally her mother answered. “Hello?”

“Mom? This is Suzanne. Is everything all right?”

A hesitation. “Of course everything’s all right, dear. The girls had some friends over to watch a movie, but everyone’s getting ready for bed now. What’s the matter?”

Suzanne counted to ten. The last thing she needed was to get her mother riled up at this time of night. She put a smile on her face, hoping it would come through in her voice as well. “Nothing’s the matter. Someone tried to call my phone but it cut off before I could see the number.” Okay, it was a lie, but it was for a good reason. “I just didn’t know if it was one of you.”

“No, dear. Your father’s taken his milk and cookies up already, so it wasn’t him. The girls are washing up.” A pointed moment of silence. “The dogs will let us know if anyone shows up who’s not supposed to be here.”

Suzanne bit her lip. It figured her mother would have guessed Suzanne wasn't being completely honest. "What? Of course they would. I'm not going to worry about any of you at all."

"That's fine, dear. You have a good time."

Did she know about Nick? Had Suzanne let something slip to the girls? She hadn't thought so. Of course, they were a combination of beauty and brains, the both of them. Hmm. "All right, Mom. Thanks. You call if the girls need anything, all right?"

"Of course I will. Good night."

As she hung up, Nick marched back over to the vehicle, and gunned the engine. "All right then." He sped off into the night. Several times, she tried to open a conversation, but couldn't think of something that wasn't a subject so glaringly distracting, it was an obvious non sequitur. He probably wanted to discuss the pictures, root out the culprit. It was, of course, what he did every day. Suzanne, though, wasn't sure she wanted a face on her potential tormentor. As long as it was a nebulous "someone," she could avoid open confrontation.

And she wanted to avoid it, for now. Someone this focused could be very dangerous, especially if pushed. If she simply let it ride, maybe…just maybe, the moment would pass.

She frowned as she recognized some of the landmarks entering McKees Rocks. "Where are we going?"

"Somewhere I know you'll be safe."

A nervous chuckle escaped her. Irony always seemed a good weapon in inexplicable circumstances. "Maybe I should assume you planted that guy so I'd feel like I had to come home with you."

His sharp look pricked her conscience.

"Nick, I'm…teasing. I know this isn't you." She

fidgeted in her seat. "Look, it's scary, all right? But I don't want to take it too seriously. If I do, I give him power."

He jumped on the word like a pouncing cat. "'Him?'"

"Him. Her. Whoever."

Nick pulled into the driveway of a good-sized duplex and parked. The front light was on, revealing a bare minimum of landscaping. Apparently he didn't use his garden equipment much at home. She had no real objection to being there. In fact, she did feel safer. She'd noticed him watching to see whether someone followed them. If she'd gone home, she would have been terrified. *Whether I would have admitted it to myself or not.*

She didn't wait for him this time, but opened her own door. He met her on her side of the truck, then locked the door with the push of a button, his eyes scanning the street above and below the duplex. She felt a bit like a celebrity or politician, with an official bodyguard guaranteeing her safety.

It felt good.

He walked her to the door, staying on the street side, not touching her, but very close. Inside, he hung his keys on a hook next to the door, then lit a small lamp on a thin polished table under the hook, before he reset the house alarm.

"We won't be disturbed," he said in answer to her raised eyebrow. "Now come here." He hooked her waist with one hand and drew her close, wrapping his arms around her. She hadn't realized just how much she'd wanted him to do that—how much she needed comfort. This had frightened her more than she wanted to acknowledge. She let her arms slide around him, too, laying her head on his broad chest. His heart beat, strong and quick, filled her ears. He was worked up about what had happened. In contrast, the longer she stayed in his arms, the more she calmed down.

Finally, she pulled back just enough to look up into his eyes, which were warm, welcoming. He leaned down, seemingly in slow motion, and brushed his lips against hers, several times, very lightly, as if testing her.

In a single breath, she returned to that feeling that had encompassed her at the theater, when he'd kissed her. The envelope faded from her thoughts as the roar of passion took over, parting her lips as she responded to him. He reacted in a rush of heat, holding her tight, pressing his lips against hers—impossibly soft lips for a man, but full and firm and exactly what she needed right at that moment.

He slowly backed her up against the closed door. Its unyielding surface against her spine reminded her of herself, so often, unwilling to even open herself to a man again. But her focus moved from her back to what waited in front of her. He let go, not touching her, the tiny distance between them drenched in heat and longing. She felt each inch of her almost reaching out for his, wanting the warmth of his skin next to her again.

The magic she'd sensed when he'd kissed her at the concert returned to replace the fear caused by the man with the envelope, and she mentally grabbed for it, needing a real dose of magic. Aware of his hands, now one on either side, flat against the door, maintaining that space between them, but containing her, she should have felt trapped, but instinct spoke, telling her nothing threatened her here. She slipped a hand around his waist to draw him closer, but he held back, going slow, letting his mouth speak for him.

She went with his intuition then, as their lips first brushed softly against each other, then became more insistent. His tongue tasted her lips in a gentle circle, a cautious explorer in unfamiliar territory. A moan of pleasure escaped from her, and her tongue met his, inviting him to continue.

His hands moved to her shoulders, his fingers exploring as he leaned closer to kiss her more deeply.

She let one hand slide up his back, fingernails trailing along those broad muscles she'd admired so often. He moved under her hand, a growl coming from his throat. She pulled him close, wanting to feel the length of the man along her own body. He allowed it this time, and she reveled in his strength and heat, let him press toward the fantasy world of lovemaking, where she could set the real world aside, the burdens and responsibilities, and just be in that moment, just for herself.

His kisses, relentless in their demands for her desire, felt like hot brands as they moved from lips to cheek, to throat. Distracted by his lips, her fingers fumbled at the buttons of his shirt. Persisting, she pulled the shirt open and found her fingertips buried in the thick hair she'd noticed earlier. She let them frolic there briefly before sliding them around to the muscled back once again, drawing Nick to her.

Only after she'd removed his shirt did he move to do the same to her. She guessed he remained partly on alert, despite his precautions. Regardless, he let her set the pace...whatever part of her brain was still thinking logically noted this. The rest was overcome in the rush of long-suppressed ardor. Like Pandora's box, when this hidden cache of libido was released, Suzanne knew she wouldn't be able to control it.

Once their flushed bodies touched one another, naked flesh against naked flesh, there was no doubt where they would end up. Nick's hands set her afire, caressing erect nipples, smoothing along the curve of her hip with an almost possessive feel. Her fingertips traveled his contours, finding him mostly well-toned muscle, taut with wanting her, ending with the most obvious evidence of his desire, the erection that pulsed against her thigh.

"Are you sure?" he whispered in her ear, his breath a hot burst of stimulation.

Her thoughts were awhirl, anticipating their union. "Yes, hurry," she said.

She caught the smile on his face as he turned off the light and took her to the bedroom, pulling the covers aside in one smooth movement. He crawled onto the white sheets before reaching for her hand.

"Come here, *bella donna*," he said, persuading her with a squeeze of his fingers.

She slid next to him, the cool sheets doing nothing to slack her carnal appetite. Arms and legs tangled, seeming to fit together so perfectly. They learned each other from every angle, their salty taste, their scents. She reveled in the molding of his strong sinews; he whispered his praises of her soft skin.

Finally, poised above her, he looked down, lust in his eyes. She moved her hips in rhythm with his urgent thrusts, the building explosion in her loins held off as long as she could, savoring the feelings, delaying that final satisfaction until they burst together with cries of pleasure.

In the cloud of sated warmth that followed, Suzanne's fingers traced Nick's strong chin with something close to reverence. No man had ever made her feel this way. She tried to put off her thinking mind, the one that wondered where the police lieutenant had learned his skills as a lover, the one that allowed worries to trickle back in.

This moment. Only this moment.

She laid back and closed her eyes, half-aware of Nick covering her with the blankets and snuggling close to her as she let afterglow take her away into blissful sleep.

Chapter Twelve

In the morning, Nick watched Suzanne as she slept, her brow unfurrowed by worries. He considered the weight she must carry on her shoulders each day, responsible not only for her own two daughters, but the lives of so many others. Some of them unhinged, apparently. Yet she carried on—and could still sleep like an innocent child.

His leg started to cramp, and he stretched cautiously. It was enough to disturb her. She rolled over, the light from the window over the bed revealing a small blue butterfly on her left shoulder blade. He reached a finger to gently trace its wings. She stirred at his touch.

"Sorry," he said. "I didn't mean to wake you. I just—"

She smiled, a rush of pink coming into her cheeks. "Yeah, yeah, who knew there were lawyers with tattoos, huh?" She covered her tousled head with the sheet.

"You'd be surprised." Nick had, in fact, been surprised when he'd belonged to the upscale fitness club that catered to Suzanne's colleagues. While keeping himself toned, he'd noticed a number of interesting bits of ink normally concealed in court by those Armani suits. Who knew?

"A permanent reminder of a temporary feeling," he said with a chuckle.

"What?" She peeked out over the edge of the

sheet.

"Something Jimmy Buffett said." He turned to his back, showing her the bright-colored parrot on his right shoulder. "Confessions of a Parrothead."

That made her laugh. "Secrets all over the place." She pushed herself upright, blinked at the light coming in the window. "What time is it?"

He looked at the bedside table. "Ten."

"What?" She nearly jumped out of bed, and he got his first chance to view that lovely body in daylight. Just seeing it reminded him of the night before, and his body reacted, stimulated by those memories. He'd not be coming out from under the sheets, not just yet.

"You have someplace to be, counselor?"

"Um. No. Just..." She bit her lip. "Just getting my bearings, I guess. Which way to the bathroom again?"

He pointed her the way, grateful as it gave him a chance for a more sedate recovery after she stepped out. He grabbed his blue terry bathrobe and tied the belt around his waist before he went to make a pot of coffee, one of his favorite brews, the beans roasted dark as night. Suzanne would probably like it.

While it brewed, he retrieved another bathrobe, this one in maroon velour. He listened at the bathroom door a moment, heard the water running in the shower, and just opened the door a crack to hang the robe on a hook inside. He thought a moment about joining her in the steamy tub. As much as another romp appealed to him, he'd worked too hard to win her trust to jeopardize it by rushing her into something. He decided against it, and closed the door instead. Besides, he needed to make sure they were safe.

His service revolver had been in reach all night, and he'd slept lightly, half-listening for anything amiss. Nothing. He stepped out onto the front step to retrieve the morning paper, taking a long look around. No suspicious signs of a foreign presence appeared, no footprints, no marks on the truck, as far as he could see, no tire tracks in the driveway. His effort not to be followed as he left the city apparently succeeded.

He locked the door again, retreating to the kitchen to check on the progress of the coffee. Now that he saw the living room in daylight, he noticed that mad rush to the bedroom had created quite the piles of detritus. A bit chagrined, he snatched up his own clothes and took them to the hamper in the bedroom.

The fact that someone had tracked Suzanne to the Benedum alarmed him more than he'd let her know. If someone had come to her office, or her home, that would have been at least expected. Clearly whoever had sent her the pictures meant to give her a message that she could be in danger anywhere.

It was just the sort of thing Greg Morgan would do.

Nick's decision to recommend Suzanne to Maddie had been for all the right reasons: to put Maddie into the hands of experienced counsel who'd take care of her through the circus that was the system. He'd never have done it, if he'd known it would set Greg on Suzanne's tail. Though he knew Maddie through some social contacts at his mother's church and community center, Nick had run afoul of Greg Morgan on a couple of occasions, when Nick was interested in pursuing his duty, and Morgan was trying to get away with something. Nick had never been important enough for Greg to remember his name. Until now.

First, Morgan coming to talk to Reichert about Nick, now this? Oh yes, something was up.

His mind turned to more practical considerations. Even though he'd hoped he and Suzanne would spend the night together, he hadn't really planned for it. "Breakfast," he muttered to himself, tearing his thoughts away from the woman in his shower. He wasn't sure what he had in the refrigerator. He sure hoped there was something.

He leaned on the door as he studied the contents of his refrigerator. Half a pizza in a plain white box. Some Italian takeout from the week before. Four bottles left from a six-pack of dark beer. Half a carton of orange juice. A loaf of sourdough bread. Mustard, horseradish. On the bottom shelf he found some chopped ham and a carton of eggs, which seemed promising till he looked inside. Three eggs? Really?

Nick sighed.

He stared a little longer, as if he could magically change what lay on the shelves in front of him by sheer force of will. The shower quit running. A few minutes later, the bathroom door whispered open, and he caught a glimpse of a maroon robe coming up behind him. She moved quietly, but he restrained himself from a startled reaction. *Never sneak up on a cop, honey.*

"I'm starving," she said, her voice soft like syrup.

"That's a shame," he said. "We could get dressed and—"

"Oh, no," she said. "Let's not." She pushed past him, taking the juice out of the refrigerator, along with the ham, bread, eggs and mustard. "This'll work."

He watched, amused, as she slathered mustard on four slices of bread, then scrambled the eggs in the microwave, layering them on the bread with the ham. A minute under the broiler, and they had breakfast fit for—well, for a single man, and a woman used to making do.

"A woman of many talents, I see," he said.

"You have no idea." She chuckled. "Least you could do is pour the coffee."

"Well, if it's the least I could do..." Nick laughed and took a second cup from the cupboard, and filled it to a half-inch from the top. He thought he remembered she took cream. If he had cream. Frowning, he looked in the refrigerator again. Nope. He had the powdered stuff in the closet, though, so he got that out. His Boy Scout leader would be horrified at his failure to be prepared. He might even lose a badge or two.

Suzanne didn't seem dismayed in the least at the false cream, though. She seemed like a different person, not self-conscious, not closed up, not pushing him away. Something between them had changed overnight, but he didn't think it was simply the act of making love. After what had happened with the pictures, she'd decided to trust him.

Finishing the impromptu breakfast, he licked his fingers and sighed. She seemed distracted now, picking at the pages of the *Post*-Gazette. What he really wanted to talk about was her safety. A small voice in his head nagged him for making the events seem so dramatic. Her "life" hadn't been in any particular danger. *But it could have been.* He didn't need to lecture her—surely she had that speech memorized and delineated, as often as she must give it to her own clients. But to let her know she could count on him if she needed help. Not just for a single night, but for as long as she needed it.

"So what are you going to do about those pictures?" he asked.

She froze a moment, then closed the newspaper. "I suppose I'll hang on to them. Until I have more."

"Last night you said there was a bigger picture."

"Actually, you're the one who said it." Her head cocked at a sassy angle as she studied him. "But this isn't the first incident about the girls."

"Will you tell me what's going on, Suzanne? I'm not trying to get into your business. I just want to help."

She pulled the robe closer around her. "Someone sent Riv a threatening email the other night. The day we worked on the garden, actually."

Nick's lips twitched into a frown. "No one she knew?"

Suzanne shook her head. "I would have written it off as just kids screwing around, except for the comment that this person would come after Riviera for something her mother had done."

"So you didn't think it was kids."

Suzanne shrugged. "I don't know who it was. It could have been some high school kids trying to prank her." She looked away. "It could have been more."

"Did you report this?"

"I didn't want to overreact."

His blood pressure hit the escalator. "You—overreact? When your child is threatened? Are you kidding me? There's no such thing as overreaction."

She pulled back from him physically, and a veil of distance came into her eyes.

Nick realized too late he'd stepped across an invisible line. "I know, I don't have children. So my opinion may not be relevant. I'm just—"

"And you don't have my life," she said tartly. "Believe it or not, I've managed to take care of myself and my children all these years before I met you." She stood up.

"Suzanne! Please." He stood up, too, feeling helpless, knowing he could make her stay and listen to him if he so chose. But he wanted her to want to stay. "I have resources."

"In the city. I'm in State Police territory. Believe me, I've advised clients over the last fifteen years to report incidents like this. You know what they get? They get 'Oh gee, I'm sorry I can't help you unless you can prove who sent that.' Not very useful." She eyed him for a long moment, then relented. "Look, Nick, I saved the email. I'll save these photos. If it's really…him…I can go after him when we're done. I'll take action when it's safe. For everyone."

"You mean for Madeleine Morgan."

She nodded. "I mean for Madeleine Morgan."

He tried to understand. He did. At least they agreed on that. Maddie Morgan needed to be protected. But did it have to be at the expense of Suzanne and her daughter?

"To timing," he said, raising his cup.

"To timing." She clinked her cup against his, then drained it. "I should be getting home."

Disappointed, he finished his coffee, too. "Sure? We could take in a movie or catch the new artist at the Mattress Factory."

"I appreciate the offer. Maybe another time." She stood up, tightening the thick cloth belt. "Thanks for breakfast."

His hand reached up to cup her cheek, her skin soft under his worn fingers. Just as he wondered whether he could persuade her to stay, she pulled away and escaped to the bedroom. The door closed with the distinct sound of the lock being turned. So much for that. He ran some water onto the dishes in the sink and waited for her to come out.

When the door opened, he was surprised to see she'd appropriated one of his Jimmy Buffett t-shirts instead of the fancy shirt she'd worn the night before, wearing it over her dress slacks. She blushed when their eyes met.

"I hope you don't mind," she said. "I just—I thought it would be more comfortable than what I wore last night."

He found her curves no less appealing in his

shirt. *Something light, Nick. Don't upset her.* "I was hoping you'd found the night worthy of a souvenir."

Suzanne's face warmed into a smile, though she stayed across the room from him. "Well, it certainly was that." Her hands smoothed the shirt down across her stomach, a little longer than was necessary. "Look at it this way. As long as I have the shirt, we'll have an excuse to get together sometime."

"That sounds like a deal." He mumbled something about getting dressed. "Have some more coffee if you want," he said. In the bedroom, he grabbed a pair of jeans off the back of a chair, pulling them on in a hurry, nearly falling over as he hopped on one foot. A police gym t-shirt went next, and a Dolphins sweatshirt on top. Nothing fancy. He wasn't a fancy kind of guy.

Which made it all the more strange that he'd fallen so hard for a lawyer.

"Not that you're going to have to buy a tuxedo any time soon, Nicky boy," he scolded himself. "Got to win her first."

He ran fingers through his close-cut hair and shoved size-ten feet into some worn off-brand sneakers. Checking his reflection in the mirror, he thought he'd pass for a lazy Saturday. *Especially if he was spending the rest of it alone.* He forced a cheery smile onto his lips and headed back into the living room. "Ready?" he asked.

Suzanne stood before the wall of framed citations Nick had received in the course of his career. Nick wasn't vain about the awards. The fact he knew his mother had used her pin money to have each of the six commendations matted and framed out of her own sense of pride in her son's accomplishments made them more valuable to him. He hadn't the heart to take them down. In truth, he hardly ever noticed them since he'd made lieutenant.

He spent too many hours on the job to rest on any laurels, even well-framed ones.

"You're some hotshot, hmm?" she asked, without turning around. "No wonder you got promoted."

His turn to blush. "Thanks. I just do my job."

She looked over her shoulder at him. "Thank you. For doing your job, I mean. It has to be rough. We count on the police to put themselves at risk every day. Like what you did at Maddie's."

"Me? You're the one I thought was going to elicit some imminent violence!" He hesitated on the way to the door. "You apparently hit your mark. If Greg Morgan had come unglued there, you could have been smack in the line of fire."

She chewed her lip. "I suppose that's so. The bastard burned me, the way he just expected all you men to take his side." As he bristled, she raised a hand to halt him. "Not that *you* did. But you saw those other guys."

"I did," he admitted. "Maddie seems to me to be a good wife and mother. She and the children shouldn't have to live in that kind of household. I'm glad we can help her."

"Me, too," she said, relaxing into a faint smile. "Don't worry. He won't get to us. We'll kick his ass. Give him a little of his own medicine." She gathered her purse and other belongings from the floor where she must have dropped them the night before, and waited awkwardly near the door. He could tell she was ready to escape.

"Come on, we better get you back before you turn into a pumpkin or something." He held the door open for her, then they headed out to his car amidst a cool late autumn wind ripe with the scents of fallen leaves and wood smoke.

They didn't speak much on the way back to the lot off Carson Street where she'd left her car. He struggled with warm words he wanted to say but was afraid to speak, since she seemed so touchy. Wanting to make sure she was comfortable, not wanting to scare her off after he'd worked so hard to get to that "yes", he held back what he might have said to some more casual partner. He found that he needed to devote plenty of attention to Saturday morning traffic around the Strip, popular this time of year for the final farmer's markets before the cold set in. When they pulled up to the lot, he made her wait while he checked her car locks for signs of tampering, or any wires that didn't belong. Nothing.

Apparently Morgan had made his point.

After a few moments of awkward silence, Suzanne walked up to him and gave him a quick peck on the cheek. "Thanks again, Lieutenant. For everything." She got into her car, and she was gone.

He turned the truck around in a nearby driveway, feeling suddenly bereft. The need for company settled into his bones. He could stop by the office—always plenty to do there. But the thought of encountering the Three Amigos changed his mind. Instead, he set his course for the small apartment where his father lived alone. Two guys together, that was the ticket.

They could talk football, family and finally, women. Stubborn, mystifying, maddening women. Maybe Joe Sansone would guide Nick's heart in the right direction to make sure this one didn't get away.

Chapter Thirteen

Suzanne was already on the interstate when she quit burning over Nick's comments. She'd thought about retreating to her office but Nick might have followed her to continue his lecture. She'd held her tongue, tried to be polite, even appreciative of his motives. But the last thing she'd wanted was more conversation with him.

How dare he criticize how she raised her children?

She'd taken care of them on her own for thirteen years. She didn't need advice from some self-important police lieutenant with a knight-in-shining-armor complex. Maybe it was irrational, but in the morning light, particularly when he wanted to get back into the discussion of the pictures, the emails, all with a critical note in his voice, her back just came up. It was her natural tendency, and she knew it, ready to toss the baby, the bathwater, the basin, all of it, just to save her pride. Wasn't the first time it had happened. Each time she thought it would be the last. But it wasn't.

She'd managed to be polite, even once the criticism started. They'd had a wonderful night. She sighed. A really wonderful night. Remembered sensations of their lovemaking tingled her skin and brought a rush of blood to her face.

God, I'm an idiot.

She was human. And a woman. A woman who

had physical needs. Needs she'd denied herself for a long time, worried about just this happening. A man feeling like he had the right to control her life.

Calm down.

He'd checked her trunk thoroughly, seeming sincerely worried about her. He probably was. She was glad for that. All the same, since the moment she'd allowed him to "rescue" her from the goon in the parking lot, when he'd sped away with her in his car, muttering about stalkers and danger, she'd been under his control.

Once she'd closed the door and was alone, she started to feel more like herself again. Driving out of the lot, she didn't look back. Nick Sansone was the best man she'd met in a long time, but he wasn't right for her. She should have gone with her gut and left this one alone from the beginning. Cops were trouble. That's all there was to it.

Trouble wasn't on her agenda. What was on her schedule for the day was the drive north of the city to her parents' house in Perrysville, to pick up the girls.

She never expected the ambush that awaited her there.

Perrysville was a nice small town, enough local services and shops to provide her retired parents with their daily needs, and an easy drive to the city if there was more they needed. Paul and Maureen Young lived just outside town. A hundred years earlier, the old white house had once been the home that ruled all the lands within view, but financially-pressed owners had sold off bits of property until all that was left was the house itself on a half-acre of land, set amid a stand of maple trees, now in a blaze of fall colors. The yard was big enough for her mother to grow flowers and some tomatoes and beans in the summer, while her dad could putter in the two-car garage out back and easily maintain the grass with his small riding mower.

Their Airedale, Maggie, came running to meet Suzanne's car as she pulled into the long driveway. Suzanne carefully avoided the enthusiastic dog and pulled into her usual parking spot next to the daylily bed. The old stems had been clipped and a pile of wood mulch sat next to the bed, ready to tuck them in for winter.

She greeted the dog, who'd finally learned not to jump on visitors—it had only taken thirteen months—and kept her at arms' length as she walked up to the porch that lined the north side of the house. This wasn't her shirt. She didn't want to be responsible for any claw holes in it. Besides, she was more of a cat person. "Mom? Call off your guard dog!"

"Suzie, I didn't hear you come up." Wrapped in the old green wool sweater she'd brought back from a trip to Scotland a dozen years before, her mother came out the screen door. The sweater smelled like mothballs and wet dog and almond hand lotion, but her mother refused to set it aside for the new ones Suzanne had bought her in the interim. She clapped her hands. "Maggie, come here, girl!"

The brown dog scampered up on the porch, tail wagging.

Suzanne hugged her mother, noticing a few more graying threads in her auburn hair. As her mother's mouth opened to speak, no doubt ready to jump on the subject of the odd phone call the night before, Suzanne chose the topic of conversation instead. "You look great, Mom. Did the girls give you any trouble?"

"Honey, when do they ever? Those girls are just angels."

"Angels? Of course." Suzanne laughed. The girls knew how to play their cards, that was true. Their doting grandparents were patsies in the hand.

Which suited Suzanne just fine. Her parents got the chance to meddle in the girls' lives instead of her own. The frequent visits between grandparents and granddaughters also gave the girls the opportunity to be more rambunctious, a little more needy and be coddled just that much more.

"They'll be back soon. They were just down the road at the neighbor's house helping her put up some apples." Her mother petted the dog once more, then held the door open for Suzanne to enter the kitchen. The homey blue gingham curtains were familiar, replicas of ones that had graced the kitchen of Suzanne's childhood home, some ten miles south in Mount Lebanon. The kitchen smelled of baking cookies. Off to the left, sounds of some sports event drifted in from the living room, where her father was absorbed in front of his large-screened television.

Suzanne poured herself a glass of fresh lemonade from the refrigerator and sat on one of the polished oak chairs at the kitchen table, feeling like a little girl again.

Wouldn't it be nice to be able to just be a kid and let someone else make all the big decisions? Not to have to worry about bills or bullies or relationships? Adult choices are hard.

Like choices about love. Suzanne's thoughts strayed to the improvised breakfast with Nick, the little-boy rumple to his hair, the warmth of his smile...the depth of his frown at his disappointment with the bold way she decided to handle Greg Morgan. The memory annoyed her. She'd let her outraged ego run free after what she'd seen at Maddie's house, instead of her sense of propriety. Perhaps it would have been better to be more diplomatic. What she'd wanted to do was slap Greg Morgan silly. She'd just done it verbally instead.

But that police officer had no right to pass judgment on her.

She hated being so torn. No wonder she usually kept her distance from interested men. If only Nick wasn't so damned appealing...

Her mother bustled about with a clean rag in hand, wiping up messes that Suzanne couldn't even see. "Now I've just put a macaroni casserole in the oven for lunch, honey, so tell me you'll stay."

"Mom, I've got so much work to—"

"No," she said, raising a finger. "You have to eat, and work can wait. Besides, the girls tell me you have a young man." A smile inched onto her mouth. She sat in the chair opposite Suzanne, eyes sparkling. "Tell me about him."

Suzanne felt the furrow between her eyebrows dig deep. First off, she'd hardly describe Nick as a "young" man, and second, he was hardly "her" man, and third... She eyed her mother. "Mom," Suzanne said, her tone calculated to discourage further inquiry.

Her mother's face radiated innocence. "I know. You're a big girl now and you know how to take care of yourself. And it's none of my business." Suzanne nodded. "That being understood, when are we going to meet this detective of yours?"

"He's not 'my' detective, Mom. He's..." How would she describe what had gone on between the two of them? Her mother wanted to hear that there was something promising in these beginning steps of their relationship, but Suzanne's current mood would prevent any further meetings...no matter how well they'd melded between the sheets. They surely hadn't approached the meet-the-parents stage, by any definition. "Nick Sansone isn't the kind of man that I could make any sort of commitment to, all right?"

Her mother chewed her lip, but it was her father who commented from the doorway behind her. "Well, no wonder. He's a Dolphin fan."

Suzanne rolled her eyes and turned to face her father, who was also dressed in long-owned, comfortable clothes, black slacks and a blue plaid flannel shirt, always worn over a clean white t-shirt. A former steelworker, he was decidedly unconcerned with his wardrobe. But that clean white undershirt was mandatory. “Dad. It’s a *game.* You can’t judge a man’s character on what team he likes in a sporting event.”

“Bite your tongue, girl. The Steelers reign supreme here.” He pronounced the word “Stillers,” like most Pittsburgh natives. “Your man is clearly delusional.” He crossed to give her a brief hug on his way to the coffeepot.

“He’s not ‘my’ man!” On the other hand, she thought, “delusional” might just define that attitude.

“Don’t get yourself worked up, honey,” her mother said, more gently. “He’ll get over the Miami thing. Bring him to dinner some night, and your father will set him straight.”

Recalling Nick’s explanation for his fandom, Suzanne found it hard to believe that any outsider would change his mind. More to the point, she considered appropriate retribution for a couple of young ladies who couldn’t keep a secret from their grandparents. She’d be ready to inflict it once she got them home.

“The girls think he’s wonderful,” her mother said, her broad farm-wife face lit up with satisfaction. “Maybe by Thanksgiving you’ll feel comfortable bringing him to dinner. We’d look forward to it.”

Her father joined in, his gruff voice usually a comfort to Suzanne, but this time it rubbed her like sandpaper. “’Bout time you found someone new. Woman isn’t meant to carry the load alone. Need a man, that’s what I always say. Thirteen years is a long time to waste, in my book.” He raised his coffee cup in emphasis and wandered back to his overstuffed chair in the living room.

A slow burn filled Suzanne. "I've hardly wasted my life, Dad. Women don't *need* a man," she said. "I've managed just fine without one."

Her mother beamed. "Of course you have, dear. You always have been just amazing in every way. But, a man can be a wonderful thing to have, whether you need him or not." She stood up and started cleaning again, with that expression that meant she was happy as a clam. "Do ask him for Thanksgiving, hmm?"

"Mmm," Suzanne replied without the slightest intention of meaning "yes." She held the chilled glass against her lips, letting it block any further comment. This perpetual discussion never had a resolution. Each time, she tried to shut it down before it degenerated into hurtful comments. She hated the feeling of inadequacy the talk sparked in her, and she hated being mad at her parents for their interference in her personal life. Most times, she succeeded. Not always.

This time she was spared further effort by the arrival of her daughters, who came through the back door in a burst of chatter and chilly air.

"Mom!" Riviera said, shoving a quart jar into her hand. "We made applesauce!"

"Great," Suzanne said. She examined the jar, the contents flecked with dark brown specks of cinnamon. It was still warm. She glanced up at Hope, eyebrow cocked, her jaw tight, trying to decide how to put her daughters' wagging tongues to rest.

Hope's intent gaze switched from her mother, to her grandmother, to her mother again. "You told!" she said to her grandmother.

"Yes, I did, just to let your mother know how much we care about her. Now go get your things packed, and we'll have lunch in just a few minutes."

She herded them across the room and down the hall toward the guest room.

Suzanne put down the jar and sighed. Good intentions did tend to take people on some pretty long roads. A deep breath restored a bit of calm and half a smile to her face. No sense in getting riled over speculation about a certain police lieutenant.

Who knew?

If she was lucky, she wouldn't see Nick Sansone again, at least in other than a professional capacity. Thanksgiving was six weeks off. Their lives could change completely, or even end between now and then. If whoever thought it a fine idea to stalk Suzanne and her family kept up his antics, a lot of lives might change. The only way to find out for sure was to take things a day at a time.

Her mother bustled back into the kitchen, already reaching for plates to set the table before she got to the cupboard. "Now who's ready for some macaroni and cheese casserole?"

Chapter Fourteen

Joe Sansone seemed glad enough to see Nick, though he was a little surprised when he opened the door of his apartment. Nick felt exposed there on the welcome mat, several of his father's neighbors peeking out to see who had a visitor. Pop dressed as he did every day, in his pressed navy blue pants, blue undershirt and a wool sweater. Today his sweater was red, and his hair still trimmed according to police regulation.

"Everything okay, Nicky?" he asked, brown eyes deeply crinkled at the corners under bushy gray eyebrows.

"Sure, Pop. Can't I come to see my old man?"

"On a Saturday morning? Without calling?" The old man looked across the hall and gestured Nick inside. "Don't give Mrs. Dailey an eyeful."

"Mrs. Dailey's spying on you?" Before his father firmly closed the door, Nick checked out the thick-bodied older woman wrapped in a pink bathrobe over her purple polyester slacks.

His dad grunted and turned away, going for the remote control to the television, which he'd left on the arm of the chair. He put on some news channel and turned up the volume. "She's probably listening right now."

Nick chuckled. "I think she's harmless, Pop."

"You don't know that woman," he said. "She's got her mind set on marriage." He waved his hand in the direction of his kitchenette. “Coffee’s on. Get yourself a cup. Get me one while you’re at it.” His father finally grinned and retreated to his recliner, the brown vinyl one he’d bought to celebrate his retirement five years before.

Nick poured them both a cup of the steaming brew and came to take the easy chair next to his father. “Pitt’s playing this afternoon.”

“Mm-hmm. That’s not what you came to tell me.” His father’s bright eyes studied his son, making Nick feel like he’d brought home a bad report card.

“I was just out, Pop. Thought I’d come by to see if you needed anything.”

“Trouble at work? Being part of Command’s a bitch sometimes.”

“No, nothing at work.” Nick thought for a moment about his issue with the Three Amigos, but he thought he had that pretty well under control. Once the two troublemakers were on the vice patrol, he’d have some time to defuse their discontent.

“So what then? Oh wait, I know. It’s the woman.” His father smiled with an air of mystery.

“Woman? What woman?” Now who was spying on who?

“The one you took to dinner at Mama Rosa’s.”

Concetta was a tattletale. Nick rolled his eyes. He should have known word would get back to his dad. “I don’t suppose taking the Fifth would help me at this point.”

He chuckled. “It’d just prove you had something to hide, Nicky.”

“Nothing to hide, Pop. Just… nothing to tell. Dinner doesn’t exactly—”

“Don’t even try it, boy. Your old man’s been watching your face a lot of years. I know when you’re full of it. Just lay it out straight. She’s more than just dinner. I can see it.”

Nick sighed. He didn’t even want to get into the

problem of the stalker. He just wanted some reassurance that his own pursuit of Suzanne Taylor was well-founded. "Yeah, yeah. All right. She's something special. She's a lawyer."

His father's eyes sparkled over the rim of his coffee cup. "Oh, I see. Moving into the country club set, are you now?"

"Very funny." His tone made it clear he didn't find it amusing at all. "She's dedicated to her work. She helps a lot of women, victims of abuse."

"Plenty of that in this town. Used to hate those calls."

"We all do. She's really good at it." Nick shifted in his chair, his mind flashing back to courtroom moments when he'd first seen Suzanne, then to the more private scenes from his house. *Best tuck those away.*

"Did you mean that she's a workaholic?"

"What?" Had he said that? He replayed the words he'd used.

"Usually 'dedicated to her work' means a woman who doesn't have time for a home and family, Nicky."

"Not at all. She's a single mother, actually. Two daughters, teenagers." He felt a smile hiding behind his lips. The girls were distinctly different, but both reflected their mother's personality.

"Mmm," his father said.

"'Mmm'? What does that mean?" Nick found it hard to keep irritation from his voice. Why was it that he thought talking to his father would help him clarify what he wanted to do? He hadn't really expected a full-scale interrogation...maybe a little pep talk. That was all. Nick rubbed his forehead.

"That means..." Joe chewed his lip a moment, then shrugged. "That means you're a big boy now, Nicky. You know what you want."

"I want what you and Mom had."

His father nodded. "Me and your mom fell in love when we were both just out of school, when we were young and had our whole lives in front of us. No ties, no kids, no jobs. We could grow together that way. I can't imagine what it would be like to take two grown people who've already got all their priorities set and try to fit their lives together." He emptied his cup and set it on a coaster on the table next to him. "But things are different these days."

"Sure are." Nick shared a sheepish grin with his old man, and pushed himself up and off the chair.

"And they don't make 'em like your mother anymore." Joe chuckled and changed the channel to the pregame sports show on KDKA.

"Probably not, Pop." Nick took his cup to the sink, then came back to man-hug his father. "You need anything, something from the store?"

"I'm fine. Went to the grocer earlier today. Harry's coming tomorrow. Thought we'd take a run out to Fort Pitt before winter sets in, make sure they've got everything socked away. They don't want our old bodies volunteering out there in the snow and ice. Think we might break or something." The older man's jaw set at a stubborn angle.

"They're just looking out for you."

"Damn lawyers."

Nick couldn't help a twitch, but his father just kept looking at the television. "Oh, I don't mean your girlfriend, Nicky. She's a woman. Can't be much of an ambulance chaser, you know? High heels and all." He chuckled, mostly to himself.

"Very funny. Very funny. Maybe you should head out onto the nightclub circuit, now that you have all this free time, Pop," Nick growled and headed for the door.

"You take care, Nicky."

His dad was still laughing as Nick closed the door behind him. Mrs. Dailey's door swung open as the Sansone door latch clicked, her frizzy-haired head poking around the frame.

Angela's years of training in manners kicked in, even as Nick cringed. "Hi, Mrs. Dailey," he said.

"Hello, Nick. Everything all right with your father?" Pale blue eyes blinked behind thick-lensed glasses. The smell of cooked cabbage came from her open doorway.

"Everything's fine. Just checking in." He nodded and started down the hall.

"Because if he needs anything, he can always call me. We're neighbors, right? He needs a cup of sugar, whatever, he can always ask me."

He stopped and looked over his shoulder at her, wondering if she'd get the hint. "Right, Mrs. Dailey."

"It's no trouble at all, Nick. Your father's a nice man."

Realizing he'd be trapped all day if he let himself engage, he gave the woman his best charming smile. "He sure is. I've got an appointment, so I'll see you later. You take care now."

Feeling only a little guilty that he'd cut her off, he walked away, his brisk steps not giving her time to change gears. The crazy old bat probably didn't have anyone to talk to, and anyone who came along brightened her day. No wonder Joe practically barred his door.

Nick took the stairs down, avoiding the slow-moving seniors at the elevator. He'd clarified one thing during his talk with his father. He wanted a firm commitment from the woman he loved, the same kind his parents had shared. He was ready to make one.

Suzanne was capable of these commitments—he saw them with her clients, and with her daughters. The real question was, could she make that kind of commitment to Nick? Especially considering the way they'd left things that morning, when he'd stuck his nose where he had no business? Would she come around to that commitment after all?

He hoped so. He'd misstepped that morning, that was obvious. He'd have to approach it again. Take it like a suspect's interrogation, whittling away at her composure, her reserve, until he broke through the wall to find out what she was hiding. Make her see that cooperation, working together had its benefits. For both of them. How many interrogations had he done over the years? Hundreds. Could one sweet redhead stand up against him? He couldn't see it.

Should be a piece of cake.

Chapter Fifteen

Cases from work began to eat up a huge part of Suzanne's time, not the least of which was the case she'd filed for Maddie Morgan.

Gregory Morgan hired a big corporate gun from downtown to handle the matter, probably someone who dealt with the family business. This worked in Suzanne's favor, since her counterpart, Frank Rosenblatt, wasn't particularly experienced in family law.

Though delayed several weeks by Rosenblatt's legal maneuvering, the hearing for a permanent restraining order proceeded without the battle Suzanne had expected. On reflection, she realized it was just another part of the man's game. Greg conceded the entry of the order, without admission of the acts alleged in the complaint. The law permitted him to do this. Such a choice would prohibit a finding of abuse on the record—a step many defendants chose to keep their records clean. Respectful, humble, he'd stood before the judge in the large county courtroom, soberly dressed in a well-tailored gray suit, as the attorneys negotiated and dictated the order the judge would sign.

The gallery was half-full, likely because so many protection orders had been on the docket for the day, but perhaps some were there because the city councilman was one of them. This wasn't a criminal matter, so nothing would be permanent. As long as

Greg abided by the order's terms, it would quietly evaporate in a year after its term expired. That didn't mean, of course, that the *Post-Gazette* and others wouldn't find it a juicy tidbit.

After the Morgan case was handled, the judge took a recess. As he left the bench, Suzanne saw smug satisfaction cross Morgan's face, and the look he gave Maddie, the one that said "You'll be back!"

The only minor blessing was that Maddie hadn't seen the look. Through the whole hearing, she'd stared into her lap, where her hands twisted and pinched each other, white with tension. Even in a $500 suit and shoes at least half that, the woman hadn't had the courage to do more than whisper an answer to anything the judge asked her.

Suzanne stood as the courtroom cleared, doing the best she could to remain a physical barrier between the Morgans, despite her own distaste for the man. Frank Rosenblatt packed his papers into his briefcase without saying anything further to his client, ignoring Greg's penetrating stare at the other table. Those eyes, so full of passion—be it obsession or hatred—had the power to frighten Suzanne. She didn't want Maddie to have to deal with them.

"Call me Tuesday," Frank murmured to his client, then after a nod to Suzanne, he left the courtroom. As soon as he'd cleared the door, Greg walked right up to Suzanne, perhaps a foot from her. Well within arms' reach. It was all she could do not to shove him away.

"Don't think you've won here, counselor. Our dance has scarcely begun. I'm going to take that bitch down. But that's not all. You chose the wrong side in this case. I'll destroy you, and yours. All of you."

Even before she faced him, Suzanne could feel his presence, a red-hot ball of anger. Since she didn't have Maddie's expensive wardrobe to act as a shield, she'd have to wing it. She turned slowly and looked Greg Morgan in the eye.

"I've heard that speech before…where was it? Oh, yeah. *The Wizard of Oz.* 'You and your little dog, too.' As I recall, that character didn't survive till the happy ending."

His hand, closed into a fist, came open as she finished speaking, and for a moment she thought he was going to hit her right there in court. She didn't flinch, though, not wanting to give him the satisfaction of knowing he could get to her. She glanced inside the bar for the broad-shouldered bailiff, but he was occupied, flirting with the court clerk. By the time she looked back at Morgan, he'd stepped back from her with a wide smile.

"Someone's not going to get out alive here. That much is true."

He started to whistle then, and turned away, walking out of the courtroom as if he had no care in the world. Frozen, she watched till the door closed behind him. A little whimper behind her caught her attention, along with the shout of someone in the gallery. Maddie had fainted.

The bailiff abandoned his post at the clerk's desk and hurried over, faster than she'd expected for a man of his bulk. "Clear the courtroom. Now!" he bellowed. A couple of sheriff's deputies who'd attended the protection hearings came forward to move the onlookers away from the fallen woman. Suzanne helped the bailiff lay Maddie on the bench behind the table as the room fell silent. The bailiff left to summon help, and Suzanne pulled a chair over to sit next to her client. The clock over the door ticked several minutes by until Maddie opened her eyes, seeming a little surprised to find herself looking up at the ceiling.

"What—did he hit you? Did he hit me?" Mystified, Maddie's hand went to her cheek as if checking for bruises. She pushed to a sitting position and glanced around, clearly expecting to see her husband nearby, but the wooden benches outside the bar were empty.

"No. He's gone. Everyone's fine. I think. Are you all right? The bailiff went to find a paramedic."

"Oh! No, I'm fine, please don't..." Flustered, Maddie got to her feet, too fast, apparently, because she fell back to the seat, her knees not holding her upright. "I don't need anyone checking me."

"Maddie, please calm down. I think maybe you should get looked at. Have you been to the doctor lately? You've lost weight, and you're shaking like a leaf."

"They're just going to want to put me on pills. I don't want to be on pills. Greg gave me pills all the time, and they made me...they made me so crazy." She grabbed Suzanne's arm. "No pills. Promise me, Suzanne, no pills." Her eyes, dark and liquid with fear, beseeched Suzanne to listen.

"All right, honey. No pills." She glanced up as the courtroom door opened and the bailiff came in, followed by two uniformed paramedics. "Just let them check you, all right? Then we'll go down the hall and talk."

Maddie reluctantly agreed. She tolerated the touch of the men as they took her blood pressure and listened to her heart, her gaze locked on some nameless point in her personal horizon. Her answers were monosyllabic. When they'd finished, one packed the equipment back into their case while the other asked if she wanted to go to the hospital. She declined.

"No more we can do here," he said to the bailiff.

"Miz Taylor, judge wants his courtroom back," the bailiff said. "Plenty of people waiting for the second half of the docket."

She nodded. "Of course. Thank you all for your

kind attention." The paramedics stood up. "Maddie, can you make it down the hall to the conference room?"

Maddie tensed when she looked at the door. "Greg will be out there, won't he?"

"I don't think so. It's been nearly forty-five minutes."

"Why don't I let you out the back hall, Miz Taylor? There's a direct hall to the conference room from there." The bailiff smiled with the warmth and sweetness of a Sistine cherub.

Suzanne glanced at his nametag. Since he'd moved to a more personal level, she should, too. "Thank you, Mr. Ramirez."

"*De nada.*" The bailiff dismissed the paramedics, then offered Maddie Morgan his arm, half supporting her as they walked out the door that was usually reserved for jurors He led them down the back hall to the conference room. He made sure Maddie was seated and had a fresh pitcher of cold water within reach before he went back to his duties. Suzanne heaved a sigh of relief as she took a seat at the solid walnut table.

"We can stay here as long as we need to, so don't worry," she said.

Maddie nodded silently, her bitten-down nails scratching at the wax on the outside of her paper cup.

Suzanne looked over the new order, wondering whether Morgan hadn't already violated it with his comment about how someone "wouldn't get out alive." Frank Rosenblatt would probably be able to convince the court that Greg hadn't meant Maddie, so he didn't violate the order. He could threaten Suzanne without crossing that line. Was it enough for Suzanne to press charges on her own? Probably not. The vague reference could be just someone spouting off under pressure. Just like the email and the pictures.

How would I explain to someone that look in his eyes, that hatred, that heat, that burning malevolence? It was something that had to be experienced.

The recollection made her shudder.

"He does that to people," Maddie said in a voice like the breath of death.

Embarrassed that her thoughts were so easily read, Suzanne bit her lip and raised her shoulders in a small shrug. "I shouldn't let him get to me. That's what he wants."

Maddie agreed with a nod. "But you know what? Now I can picture him pedaling away on a rickety old bicycle with a basket on the back, just like an old witch." She actually smiled. "I think that vision's going to help."

Suzanne laughed, half-embarrassed. "It was the first thing that came to me. I probably shouldn't have said it. But I'm glad it helps." She poured herself some water. "So, how's your new place?"

"You were right about the gated community. The men at the entry have a copy of the protection order, and they know not to let Greg in, even if he's dropping off the children." She sighed. "He just doesn't give up, though. He sent me flowers at work. Roses. Lilies. Huge baskets of flowers."

"That's in violation of the order."

"I know. He sent them to the nursery school where I'm working as a teacher's aide. The other teachers find it charming—they tell me they wish their husbands were so thoughtful!"

"You should have told me. I could have reported him." Suzanne growled, frustrated. The gesture wasn't charming at all, but another sign of control, announcing to his wife, "I know where you are and what you're doing." Seemed to be a common theme with this man.

"And what would the judge have said? 'You want me to punish the guy because he loves his wife enough to send flowers? That's not a crime.'"

"But it is!" Suzanne's face flushed with a rush of angry blood. She couldn't protect a client who wouldn't act to protect herself. "He could go to jail."

"I don't want him to go to jail, Suzanne. My son's already rebelling. He wants to be with his dad. My daughter's temperamental, too. They don't like the changes." As Suzanne started to interrupt, Maddie raised a hand to cut her off. "I know, I know. You said it would happen. Look, I just want Greg to leave me alone. That's all I want. The less trouble I cause him, the less likely he'll persist."

Maddie's expression was earnest. Suzanne knew she wouldn't change her mind. She'd have to find out for herself. A man as determined as Greg Morgan had no intention of giving up so easily. Suzanne knew. Maddie would learn.

Maddie took a deep breath and stood up. "So you'll go ahead with the divorce?"

"Of course. We can start discovery, find his assets. Now that we've got the permanent order, he'll hopefully be less likely to act out." Suzanne gathered her belongings. "Do you need a ride home?"

"I've got a car. I borrowed it from a friend, so Greg can't take it from me." Maddie's smile faintly lit her face. "I'll be fine, Suzanne. I'll just hold onto that mental picture of the witch on the bicycle. With the music in the background." She hesitated for a moment, cocked her head, then laughed. "Oh, yes, definitely with the music." Maddie came around the end of the table to embrace Suzanne. "Thank you for everything you do."

"You're welcome." Suzanne held back most of what she wanted to say. She couldn't live Maddie's life for her. "Call me next week, all right?"

"I sure will." Maddie left the room. Suzanne

stood in the silent vacuum created by her departure, wondering about Greg Morgan. Should she take steps to protect herself?

She could call the police.

She could call Nick.

She took out her cell, held it in her palm for a moment as she considered it, then slipped it back into her pocket. *Hell, no.*

Suzanne had no intention of letting that man tell her how to run her life today or any day.

This one, she could handle on her own. Greg Morgan was just a sad little king who believed he was in charge of something. He'd find out he was wrong.

Chapter Sixteen

Nick found his schedule over the next few weeks constituted a barrier to time with Suzanne. His days were easier due to his problem children spending time with the vice squad, but end of year also meant budget crunch and late nights choosing what hours, personnel, and programs he could do without.

He had made a few efforts to contact her, but they'd all been rebuffed by an ever-present voicemail system. His personal schedule didn't allow him the kind of time he'd like to have to pursue her more aggressively. How could he get this relationship back on track?

His answer came in an opportunity from the police department itself. After a thirty-year career, Division chief Raymond Sandoval would celebrate his well-deserved retirement with a banquet. Most of the brass around the county would attend, along with political officials, family and friends. It was the kind of event that most business people chose to get their faces out in the social circle. There would also be so many people that Suzanne wouldn't have to feel she was on the spot with him. A perfect occasion to see Suzanne, and to be seen with her.

All the same, he didn't bother to call first before he drove to her office over a lunch hour to ask her to accompany him. She shouldn't have a chance to say no before he could use his best bad-boy grin to persuade her. When he arrived, the secretary grinned and waved him in. He stuck his head inside Suzanne's office door. "Do you have a moment?"

Her eyes widened and she got slowly to her feet, her face unwelcoming. "What are you doing here?"

"I have a favor to ask." He stepped in and closed the door.

She came out from behind the desk, a vision in a soft knit sweater in shades of brown and rust and a slim pair of brown slacks. "I'm not sure I can help you with the city budget, or your personnel issues."

He held up a hand to cut her off. "I've got plenty of aspirin and antacids for that."

"I don't envy you at all. So you're not here to borrow a calculator. What can I do for you?" She sat down on one of her love seats and gestured for Nick to do the same.

He cleared his throat as he shrugged off his leather jacket and sat down. Small sofas didn't make sense to him. A good sofa was at least six feet long and let a man put his feet up. This was...abominably short. He sat forward, on the edge of the seat. Humor seemed the best approach. "I wondered if you're a fan of rubber chicken."

Her eyebrow went up.

"Ray Sandoval's retiring, and I need to make an appearance at the shindig. Banquet. Whatever."

She continued to study him, intent, like a scientist seeing some new sort of cell through a microscope.

"It's probably not really rubber chicken. They booked the Renaissance. Menu there's pretty good."

"A whole evening with a room full of cops and liquor. Now there's a recipe for fun." Her green eyes warmed slightly from cut emerald. He had a chance then. He felt his shoulders relax, and even smiled.

"Isn't it? Look, I hate these things, but I've got to show up. I thought maybe since we hadn't had much time together, at least we'd get free dinner and a couple of drinks and then we could slip out and find something more interesting to do."

"More interesting?" Speculation in her eyes. And a flash of heat, quickly concealed. *Oh, yes. That would be interesting indeed.* "Who did you say might attend?"

"There's an open invitation to anyone in the police ranks, but usually it's the higher-ups, couple of county officials, someone to make a proclamation, you know, Ray Sandoval Day, or whatever."

"And when is it?" She went to her desk, pulling a thick datebook from her left-side drawer.

"About a week from now. November 20th. The Saturday before Thanksgiving." When he said "Thanksgiving," she bit her lip and closed the book with a snap. "Something wrong?"

"Wrong? No." She returned to her seat near him. "Looks like the Saturday is clear. I'm sure it would fulfill some civic duty or other for me to attend."

He ignored the lack of warmth in her tone. If fate saw a way, perhaps that heat he'd glimpsed could be encouraged into a small fire. "Then it's a date. Good. One worry off the plate."

"I'm sure we both have plenty of those."

"Still fighting with Councilman Morgan?" He debated mentioning Greg Morgan's visits to the precinct, but decided she had enough to worry about on that score. He'd protect her from further harassment. If he could.

"That's between me and my client, don't you think?"

Whatever he'd done, she clearly hadn't forgiven him yet. "Of course. I was just..." He straightened his shoulders. "Maybe when the budget's done, I can take you and the girls to a Steelers game."

"Maybe." Her tone was less than enthusiastic.

He studied her for clues. Was she unhappy about attending a sports event, or worried about protecting her girls? *How much safer could they be than with a thoroughly-trained police detective who carries a gun?* "If you don't think I'm a threat," he prodded.

Her eyes widened but she didn't offer a response.

"Any more emails? Pictures?" It still burned him that she hadn't let him follow up on the packet she'd received. It's not like he could make her do it. He had to let this one go until she was ready. With any luck, Morgan would back off. Not much percentage for him in escalating this fight, as a public figure, was there? The councilman seemed to have plenty in his private life he didn't need brought into the light.

"Nothing."

Her voice was firm, but she didn't look him in the eye. Damn it, the woman was stubborn! He hadn't done anything wrong. Why wouldn't she let him in?

He took a deep breath, then blew it out slowly. "All right. If you need help with that, you know who to call."

She nodded.

A moment of silence stretched out between them, then they both came to their feet, not looking at each other. "Guess we should get back to work," Suzanne said.

She stood close enough that he could smell her perfume, something spicy and layered. Memories of the night they spent together flooding in. He reached for her without thinking, pulling her close to him, her head against his chest. He half expected her to shove him away, but she didn't. She didn't put her arms around him, either. It was enough for him. His lips curved into a smile, and he closed his eyes, wanting the moment to last an eternity, but a few beats later, Suzanne's secretary knocked discreetly on the door frame.

"Sorry, boss, but your one o'clock is here."

"Thank you, Donna," Suzanne stepped away from the tall detective, her eyes a little softer, and a smile twitching at her lips. "I'll see you next week."

"You bet." Feeling a little like he was on top of the world, Nick grabbed his coat and headed for the door. He didn't look back, but he did give Donna a little salute.

The encounter kept his attitude sunny the entire afternoon, even through the hot glares of Clara Malron, the only one of the three sergeants not on temp duty with Vice. The chain of command being what it was, though, there wasn't much besides glaring that she could do. Nick could set his mind in more positive directions.

****

Suzanne usually didn't like those kinds of events, the grip-and-grin retirement gift presentations, the false line-up of speakers who dragged out something nice to say about the man or woman who was stepping down. It often seemed to her like the slimier the retiree was, the more flowery the accolades.

She'd met Sandoval a couple of times over the years she'd practiced in Pittsburgh, and didn't have much respect for him. At the scene of a domestic disturbance, if he found a bruise on the woman's cheek, while the man ranted that the woman had attacked him first, Sandoval would tell the woman if she wanted to press charges, he'd have to take them both in, and the kids would go to foster care. Not a solution in Suzanne's book. *Way to support victims of domestic violence, guys.*

He wasn't the only one who used this method to avoid dealing with conflict, of course, which was one reason Suzanne didn't have much use for the police generally. She didn't have any more to do with them than she had to.

Which made her attraction to Nick that much more confusing.

So why bother going with him?

She'd thought about Nick's words, his perceived criticism regarding her girls and the emails, and finally realized he hadn't been intruding on her prerogative at all. His attitude had less to do with his opinion of her parenting and more to do with that narrow-eyed paranoid cop outlook that every one of them seemed to have. He had spoken out because he really cared. That should be a good thing.

It *was* a good thing.

His invitation was certainly an effort to make up for what he'd done, and she made a conscious decision to accept it in that spirit. Secretly she was glad he'd come to see her. She missed him. Not just the physical, though she found herself remembering the touch of his strong hands when she was achingly alone in her big bed at night. More than that, she missed the challenge of his conversation, the rapport they seemed to have. He was educated without being overbearing like some of her colleagues, with a strong sense of right and wrong, and a generous helping of care and concern. He wasn't a "typical" cop, and he wasn't a "typical" man in her view. He deserved another chance.

Her hope was that he could read her as well as she believed he could, and that he'd realize the children were off-limits. For now.

In the meantime, Suzanne and Nick could continue to explore the feelings they held for each other.

Besides, despite most people's idea of the so-called glamorous life of a big-city attorney, in reality, it had been a year, at least, since she'd attended a fancy party like this. She wasn't fussy about frills in her everyday appearance, but she liked getting all dressed up as much as any other girl. She'd had the slinky black dress for several years—that standard cocktail-party standby, but a few pieces of thick gold jewelry from a shop on the South Side, and a sweet updo of her hair made it seem new again. It might not be Maddie Morgan's expensive suit, but it felt a little like armor.

Preparing to face a room full of police and government officials, she felt that she needed that boost, a bit of distance. Even though she worked in the system, she disagreed with plenty that went on there. The police and the sometimes heartless people who worked for the county, all of whom were "'just doing their jobs," often cost her clients, in time and money.

Nick showed up at her office in full dress uniform, sharp and official, gold trim emphasizing the cuffs and hat. She felt compelled to salute, which provoked a grin.

"No need to be formal, Miz Taylor. No one here but us chickens." He entered the office, crossed to her side and gave her a gentle kiss on the cheek. "You look spectacular."

Now that was pure validation. "This old thing?" she said, fully sinking into the ironic tone of her voice. "But seriously…thanks."

She meant it for the compliment, and for even more, for being persistent, for understanding her quirks. His warm smile seemed to encompass acceptance of all those underpinnings. She picked up the small black sequined purse she used for evenings out, very different from the big bag she usually carried half her life in. Just enough for a small card case, her phone, a lipstick, her keys and a few other items.

"Shall we?"

"Into the lion's den?" he asked, showing her he understood very well her feelings about his brotherhood.

A sheepish smile came to her lips. "Something like that."

"I'll protect you, miss. To serve and protect. That's the motto, right?"

"So they say." She took his proffered arm, and they walked down the stairs, into the cool night air.

During the brief ride from Carson Street to the Marriott, Suzanne studied an uncharacteristically silent Nick, wondering what had him so preoccupied. Perhaps she'd shaken his confidence, and he didn't know what subjects might be safe. Maybe it was something at work beyond the vagaries of the annual budget. Just as well she'd kept him out of her problems with Greg Morgan. The stalking, at least, had stopped, after he'd come into the open with his threats. Maybe now that he'd crowed his little bantam announcement, he'd feel self-justified and knock off his juvenile games.

Once he'd parked the truck in the Marriott's designated lot, Nick became more attentive. Whatever he wrestled with, he apparently intended to set it aside for the next few hours so they could share the time together. "Have you ever met Ray Sandoval?" he asked. "He's an interesting guy. Served in the Marines during Vietnam, then came home to Pittsburgh and changed uniforms..." Nick launched into a lengthy accounting of the man, more than Suzanne had ever wanted to know about the retiring Captain, his teacher wife, and his son at Annapolis. Inside, she recognized the county manager, a few other county officials of middle-range authority, a number of State Police uniforms, and an assortment of officers from around Allegheny County, even a few from up in Indiana Township. Nick didn't stop to make introductions but swept her in, straight to the bar, where he ordered a scotch for himself and a glass of white wine per Suzanne's request.

The room was large and festively decorated with looping bands of silver ribbon stuck on nearly every flat surface. Each of the forty-plus tables had a fat centerpiece with silver flowers, plastic fruit and ribbon, multiple place settings and sparkling glassware. A raised dais and table in the front was clearly reserved for the guest of honor and the other brass. Sipping her wine, she hoped Nick was permitted to sit out of the way somewhere, where they'd be "just part of the crowd," and could spend the evening relatively undisturbed.

Nick waved down an older man in uniform, and Suzanne was pleasantly surprised to find a familiar face. Suzanne hadn't seen detective Ferguson for years. His family had lived next to hers when she was an adolescent. He and Suzanne's father had been great fishing buddies, and he'd always had a teasing word for Paul's red-haired daughter. He'd aged so since then—but of course she had, too. As Nick formally presented her to his former partner, Hank Ferguson, the balding man's eyes narrowed, then he broke out in a smile.

"Suzie Young?" he said. "No need for all the foofarah here, Nick. We're old friends. Where did you stumble over this troublemaker?"

She shook his hand warmly. "Mr. Ferguson, how are you?"

"I'm well, honey. Still haven't bought a bullet, so we count our blessings, right?" Hank tapped on the shoulder of a white-haired woman behind him, wearing a well-worn blue formal. "Dottie, look who's here! It's Suzie Young."

When she turned, she looked closely at Suzanne, her round cheeks reminiscent of Mrs. Santa Claus, then her mouth dropped open."Is that Maureen's skinny little girl? Well, you have grown up." She reached out for Suzanne, crushing her fondly against an ample bosom.

Grown up. Right, that was it. Ooof. Gradually she managed to disentangle herself. "It's good to see you both. How is Jordan?"

"He's just fine. He's working out in California, doing something with computers. I don't know what, exactly. He's tried to explain it to me a couple of times, but I'm just not good with this tech stuff, you know." Hank turned to Nick. "Suzie was such a tomboy. She and my son Jordan used to tear up the neighborhood good! Sweet heavens." He laughed. "So how's your mom and dad? What are you up to these days? Still here in town, I see."

"I'm an attorney. My office is—"

"Wait a minute! This...She's the lawyer you've been seeing?" Hank's eyes opened wider as he stared at Nick.

"Really!" Dottie's interest perked upward into full-blown curiosity. "How long have you two been dating?"

Suzanne felt her private life slipping from her control and took a long sip of wine. "He talks about me, then?" she asked with a sidewise glance at the lieutenant.

"Oh, not like that," Nick said, a little too quickly.

"Mmm." *Not like that?* Then like what? She let the vista of uniforms and ladies in cocktail dresses around the room distract her from her thoughts, taking in the buzz of conversation around them, wondering if it was time to be seated soon, before all the old stories started coming out. "Mr. Ferguson, my mom and dad are fine. They live up in Perrysville now, almost in the country. Dad will be so pleased I saw you."

Nick smiled, a mysterious gleam in his eye. "So now I know where to gather a little background intelligence on this woman."

"What might be more important is for me to warn Suzanne what she's in for," Hank said. "I was this man's partner for seven years, my dear. I learned things no one else knows about him."

"Now that sounds like a worthwhile investigation," Suzanne said, amused as Nick's face registered serious consternation at the prospect of his own secrets seeing the light.

"Ah, the evil that men do follows them everywhere they go. Women, too," Nick added with a small smirk. "Let me introduce Suzanne to the chief before all the speeches start." Nick cleared his throat. "Save us some seats at your table, will you?"

"Of course. We'll be over in the south quadrant." Hank gestured in the direction of a quiet corner behind them, which Suzanne approved. He and his wife smiled as Nick and Suzanne moved toward the front of the room, Nick's gaze searching the crowd before them.

"I had no idea you and Hank were old friends," Nick said. "That's an interesting coincidence."

"I haven't seen them in years, probably since I went to law school. Mom and Dad sold the house shortly after that." She turned to look over her shoulder. "They look good, though. He must be close to retirement, hmm? He and Dad were nearly the same age, I thought."

Nick nodded. "I'm sure he'll step down within the year. He hasn't been well lately." He hesitated in his search, then crossed through the crowd more purposefully, bringing Suzanne along behind him.

Suzanne recognized Butch Reickert, the department chief, from television appearances rather than personal encounters. He wasn't particularly tall, but his barrel chest made him seem larger than those around him as he joked in his gravelly voice. His white hair was combed back from his face in a thick mane, like that of a lion lording it over his pride. He smiled as wide as any politician when Nick introduced Suzanne.

"Pleased to meet you in person," Reickert said. "I think I've received memorandums from you through the court, scolding us for the way we choose to enforce domestic violence orders."

Suzanne took the sparkle in his eye as one of good humor. This wasn't the time to engage in the battle. She let her firm handshake demonstrate her strong commitment to continue the discussion. "All of us can benefit from constructive criticism from day to day."

"Regardless of what you think, we take these things seriously."

"I should hope so. Better to protect a victim than investigate a homicide, wouldn't you say?"

"Yes, ma'am. Yes, ma'am, I would." Reichert let go of her hand to reach out to someone just behind her shoulder. "Councilman Morgan. How kind of you to come tonight. I'm sure the Captain will be honored."

Suzanne stiffened as Reichert spoke. Nick took her elbow and pulled her gently aside as Greg Morgan strutted past, resplendent in a crisp black tuxedo and bow tie, shaking Reichert's hand as if he were on the campaign trail.

"I'm pleased to be invited, Chief. The police officers in our county do fine work. Fine work indeed. Even the misguided ones." Morgan let go of Reichert's hand, and pivoted just enough to include Nick and Suzanne in his purposefully-beneficent gaze. He studied those at the front table, then looked Suzanne up and down with an insolent eye. "Counselor. How very nice to see you again."

"Mr. Morgan," she said, a chill settling on her words so crisp that she was surprised they didn't snap.

"We'd better find our seats," Nick said, his voice pitched just so he remained polite. The tight grip of his fingers on her arm showed his agitation. "Chief."

He nodded, then turned away from the two men, imposing his body between them and Suzanne. Relieved to be out of Morgan's proximity, she didn't miss the irony of Nick doing exactly what she had done for Maddie in the courtroom.

Had Suzanne now become the "victim"? If so, she didn't like it one bit.

Nick found the Fergusons at a table far from the front of the room. "Good," he said. "With any luck, we won't even be able to hear the speeches." He winked at Suzanne, then got them each another drink from the bar, a gesture Suzanne felt was not only appropriate but appealing after the unexpected encounter with Greg Morgan. Hank insisted on sitting next to Suzanne, "to catch up on old times," and they settled in as the salads were served.

The subject settled on her girls, and Hank and Dottie insisted on hearing all about them, right down to the proud-mama photos Suzanne had on her cell phone. While she bragged, Suzanne couldn't help but notice that Nick was distracted once again, but not by Morgan. His gaze was several tables over, scrutinizing a trio of young ethnically-diverse officers. The officers, two men and a woman, watched him with the same intensity.

"I just can't believe you're a mother," Dottie said, admiring Riviera's cheerleader photo. "Jordan hasn't even settled down yet."

Suzanne refrained from commenting that she didn't think Jordan was likely to settle down with any woman. While she'd indeed been a tomboy in those young years, Jordan had been her confidant and good friend with whom she'd shared an interest in several of the other boys in their class. If his mother hadn't figured it out yet across the miles, it certainly wasn't Suzanne's job to tell her.

While she listened, Suzanne saw Hank had picked up the silent, but definitely hostile, exchange between Nick and the others. His expression was one of concern. Suzanne glanced among them, trying to divine what might be happening, but when neither commented openly, she returned to the greens in front of her.

Hank reached across Suzanne to pull on Nick's sleeve. The gesture refocused Nick into the party atmosphere, and dinner proceeded without paying much attention to the droning accolades to the retiree. Suzanne tried to ascertain where Greg Morgan had finally landed, just so she was prepared to avoid him, and found him at one end of the dais. *Insufferable man.* Reinforcing his importance only gave him permission to continue his highhanded ways.

After dinner, a musical trio began to play big-band music, and several of the older couples got up to dance. Although she'd originally planned to try to sneak out after dinner, Suzanne found that what she really wanted was a slow dance in Nick's arms. His efforts to engage her during dinner had reminded her of everything she found charming about him. Her curiosity was also piqued by his visual exchanges with his subordinates. Maybe she could pry some details out of him.

"Care to hit the floor, Lieutenant?" she asked, laying her hand over his.

His eyes widened a little, but he wasted no time getting to his feet. As they stepped onto the dance floor, the band segued into "Someone to Watch Over Me." The irony didn't escape her.

"Did I tell you yet that you look beautiful?" he said, holding her close enough to spark memories of the night she'd spent at his house. Every place his fingertips touched her generated a spark of excitement.

"At least half a dozen times," she said, feeling heat in her cheeks.

"Ah. Well, I won't bore you by telling you again." He winked and continued guiding her around the floor, his movements skillful and practiced. She loved to dance, especially with a man who knew what he was doing. Another plus.

She looked up at him, carefully pitching her voice so it held no note of challenge, only concern. "Maybe you want to tell me what's up with you and those guys over at the table on the west end of the room."

He grunted and glanced away. "Nothing that should matter to us," he said.

Suzanne knew enough about people to tell when she was being put off. Should she push harder? He would tell her if she forced him to. But she didn't want to spoil the gentle détente they'd reached over the course of the evening. Instead, she laid her head on his shoulder, and let the music chase the questions from her mind.

Hank claimed the next dance, as Nick partnered with Dottie Ferguson. They switched back and continued through several numbers, letting the music remove them from their troubles. Suzanne enjoyed the subtle movement and the warm, gentle buzz of the alcohol taking effect. The pleasant moment was interrupted when a tall dark-skinned officer stopped in front of them.

"Mind if I cut in?" he asked. Suzanne recognized the man as one of the officers Nick had been watching earlier.

"Yes, I mind," Nick said. His hand closed on Suzanne's, and he started to walk away.

"Hey, man, chill. I'm trying to follow the social protocol in the uppity world." Disrespect practically dripped from his voice, and his eyes held an open challenge.

Suzanne's curiosity, handed an unexpected chance to discover the source of the young man's hostile attitude, drove her to take a risk. “Nick, it’s all right. One dance with this gentleman will just about be my limit for the night. Then we can go.”

Nick’s expression hardened to stone, but the officer just grinned. “That’s cool,” he said. “Thanks, Lieutenant.”

Hank came up behind Nick, saying a low-voiced word or two in his ear. Nick’s hands were clenched. Whatever was between Nick and this man must be serious. She studied the officer as he swirled her away from Nick and Hank. He smiled down at her but something unpleasant in his eyes didn’t match the friendly gesture.

“So, you’re the Lieutenant’s main squeeze,” he said.

“Squeeze? I don’t know about that.” The man had foregone the conventional stance and was instead holding her much closer than strangers normally danced. Determined not to cause a scene, she simply acquiesced. “You work with him?”

“You bet I do. I’m one of his peons. Sergeant Washington,” he said, winking at the other officers at his table as they passed. “Far down the food chain.”

“I gather you’re not pleased with that status.”

“You’re smart, girl. That’s what all the education will get you,” Washington said with a hint of insolence. “Think you know it all, right? Miss Lawyer? You know it all?”

“Just making conversation, Sergeant,” she said, realizing she’d likely made a mistake, and wishing the dance would end. At some point she passed Greg Morgan, who was talking to several men she didn’t know. As Washington guided her onward, Morgan’s hot gaze fastened on her, making her even more uncomfortable. They continued around the floor, passing Nick twice more, Washington holding her extra close each time. Finally the music ended and

Suzanne purposefully detached herself from him.

"You ever get tired of old Saint Nick, you come on round and see me, Miss Lawyer," Washington said just loud enough for her to hear. "I'd take good care of you. Mmmhmm, I sure would."

She didn't dignify his words with an answer, but walked back to the spot where Nick fumed. "Let's get out of here," she said.

Nick's earnest gaze searched her face. "Did he say anything? Did he threaten you?"

"He's just a kid with a crappy attitude. What did you do to tick him off, anyway?"

"Some people just live angry," he said.

They walked back to the table, Hank and Dottie both insisting on a hug from Suzanne for old times' sake before she could leave. As Nick helped her on with her coat, Suzanne spotted Greg Morgan making the rounds, smiling, shaking hands. When he reached the table with Nick's three malcontents, the glad-handing seemed to last a long time, accompanied by quite a bit of intent conversation. Birds of a feather, now, weren't they?

Intrigued by that meeting, Suzanne walked out with Nick, noting his brooding silence. Halfway to the truck, she slipped her hand in his. "Want to talk about it?"

He grunted and shook his head. "Not your problem," he muttered.

She squeezed his warm fingers. "All right. If you do, I'll listen." He didn't reply and she concentrated on keeping up with his long strides. *Guess we each have our off-limits areas…I can respect that.*

He came to her side of the truck first, unlocking the door with the fob button. When he pulled the door open, a blast of foul-smelling white smoke billowed out like a vent from hell.

"Get back!" he yelled, yanking her arm before she could even move. She found herself by the rear end of the truck while he cursed up a storm of obscenities worthy of a third-tour Marine. Eyes burning, she choked on the air around them, turning away to try to clear her lungs.

The smoke continued for fifteen or twenty seconds, then stopped. He stalked around to the driver's door, opening it. The free flow of air cleared the putrid smoke from the cab pretty quickly, and Suzanne inched closer to see what had happened. The smell remained overpowering, and she covered her mouth and nose with her hand. "What was that?"

Nick rummaged through the detritus on the floor, poking the mess with a pencil, coming up with tattered paper and a can punctured with holes. "Homemade smoke bomb."

She glanced left, then right. "Someone sabotaged your truck while you were inside? Right here in a public lot?"

He tucked the pencil tip under a heavy-duty wire that led to the passenger door. "Here's the trigger. I guess they expected me to be a gentleman and open your door first."

"I'll call the police," she said, only realizing afterward how ironic that statement was. "They're handy, after all."

"No." His denial was fast and sharp. "I'm not giving them the satisfaction."

"But—"

"I'll call you a cab." He fumbled for his cell.

"No. I don't need a cab. I'll..." She sniffed the air. "It's not so bad. I bet it'll air out in a minute. If you're not going to have the CSI-types look for evidence—" She paused, expecting him to cut her off again.

"I know who it is," he growled.

That raised her eyebrow. But she didn't ask. "Why don't you just drop me back at the lot and I'll get my car?"

Surveying the mess, he rubbed his forehead as though he encouraged his brain not to explode. He backed out of the doorway and gingerly opened the hood, studying the parts inside.

Alarmed, she joined him, though she wouldn't know what gadgets or wires belonged under a hood and which didn't. It made her feel useful just to be there. "You don't think they got in here, do you?"

He hmmed and grunted. "Don't see anything out of line. Let me clean out the cab." He returned to the front seat and gathered all the bits into a plastic bag he'd had stuffed under the seat. A rag he had under there as well served to wipe the residue from the seats and dash. "There, counselor, I think we're safe. I'd suggest you wait over there until I start it, just in case."

A homemade stink bomb was one thing; the potential of getting blown up starting the vehicle was a whole other animal. The thought sent a chill through her. "Nick, honestly, you should report this to someone before you get hurt."

He looked at her, his dark eyes intent and glittering in the reflection of the garage lights. "Before which one of us gets hurt? I think I know who did this. It's the kind of juvenile prank officers rig for each other. But I suppose when we look at the clues, how Morgan knew where to find you that night at the Benedum, and when someone knew I'd be opening my passenger door first, ostensibly to let you in, there are other possibilities." He looked over his shoulder at the entrance to the stairwell. "Best advice I have is to get the hell out of here before we come face to face with whoever it is."

Several protests came to her, but she silenced them at the look of deadly seriousness on his face. "All right. I'll…I'll wait over here." She pointed behind a large SUV. He nodded and she took herself there, all her muscles clenched and tense, peering out around its hind end. When Nick put the key in, her breath caught and she thought for just a moment what she'd feel if she lost him. It pained her.

A moment later, he turned the key, with no fireworks or other consequences. She watched him visibly relax, his eyes closed. Deferring to his expertise, or just his gut, she waited till he beckoned her to the truck. As bravely as she'd spoken before, she found that, climbing in, she half expected something to go off. She seated herself carefully. *I can always take the dress to the cleaners if I have to. The important thing is to get out of here.*

That was clear in Nick's expression, in his body language, in the way he gripped the steering wheel as if he could choke it. He watched straight ahead as he went through the exit booth, showing his badge to the attendant. He drove along Fort Duquesne Boulevard, staring out the windshield, with no seeming destination.

"Where are we going?" she asked quietly.

He gave an odd little laugh. "I suppose that depends which one of us they're after. "

You're not paranoid if they're really out to get you, isn't that what the poster says? She sighed, picking at a loose piece of trim on her clutch. "You said you thought you knew who it was."

He glanced in the rear view mirror, then flipped on his turn signal for a left. "Yeah. Yeah. It's some guys at work who are unhappy with their lives. Think it's my fault." He pulled smoothly into traffic on Commonwealth Place. "I don't think there's an issue, really. They knew where the truck would be, and I think they just took advantage, that's all."

Indignation filled her like a rush of hot liquid. "That's it? Big joke? Let's prank the boss?"

As she sputtered, he surprised her by laughing.

"That's the juvenile boy's club for you, counselor. As you've pointed out on multiple occasions, we're not the most sophisticated of professions."

Stung at first that he'd laugh at her, she finally realized he was laughing with her instead. She still found it hard to relax, recalling the intent discussion between Morgan and the officers Nick had been on edge about. "So it looks like I'm the one who has to watch your back tonight."

"Appears that way." He took another left.

"I can do that best at my place. Surely the kiddies won't follow you all the way out there?"

"Your girls?" he asked.

"My mother took them outlet shopping in West Virginia this weekend." He was at least being sensitive to the issue, and she made sure to appreciate it. At the same time, she was already imagining what might happen between them given some quiet and privacy. The quiver that ran down her spine wasn't due to fear at all.

"A very practical suggestion. Let's pick up your car, so you won't have to get it in the morning." He drove a little further, took a right, and they hit the Liberty Bridge.

Slowed down by Friday night Carson Street traffic, Suzanne wrested her thoughts away from impending moments between the sheets, anticipation already grabbing hold of her libido. "Trouble," she muttered.

"What?"

"Trouble. Dating a cop…"

"Cop? Dating a lawyer's plenty of trouble on its own, thanks. Especially one with brass balls."

The expression made her blink, though it wasn't the first time someone had applied it to her. "Why can't a woman be independent? Surely you can't think that every woman should be a doormat like poor Maddie Morgan!"

"Of course not," he said, adding, "And don't call me Shirley."

"I—" Oh, he'd tagged her that time, with a well-worn line. She rolled her eyes and leaned back on the seat. Frustrating, confounding, baffling man. *And don't call me Shirley.* The ridiculousness of the line, the nonchalant delivery, got to her at last and she started to laugh. By the time they got to her parking lot, they were both laughing, letting the tension of the evening release itself in a very natural way.

"Cute. You're very cute." She wagged a finger at him.

He winked. "Don't you forget it."

He got out to check her car again, as she waited nearby, her eyes searching the cars passing by on Carson Street a block away. *Now who was paranoid, hmm?*

When he was satisfied she'd be safe, he held the door, waiting just a few moments too long until she came close. But she was ready for him. She slid into his arms, his earlier transgressions forgiven, set aside in light of the events of the evening. When their lips met, invisible sparks of passion zipped through her, spiraling down through her body, where they collected, waiting for the opportunity to burst like firecrackers that would come once they were alone.

When he spoke, his voice trembled. "I'll be right behind you all the way, Suz. I won't let anything happen to you."

She just smiled. "I know you won't."

Before he could tempt her to delay further, she got into her car and closed the door. Twenty minutes away from heaven. She could hardly wait.

Chapter Seventeen

The week before Thanksgiving began with Sandoval's dinner and two days Nick spent at Suzanne's house making her feel like a queen. From there, everything went downhill.

Holidays always seemed to set off families in crisis, and the Morgans were no exception. The first call she received Monday morning was from Maddie Morgan. The woman's voice was near hysterical.

"Suzanne, please, you've got to do something! He's gone!"

"Who's gone?"

"Joshua. He didn't come home from school on Friday."

"Friday? That was three days ago." Suzanne tapped her pencil on her desk. What the hell was Maddie thinking? She'd waited three days to let anyone know. "Did you call the police?"

"Of course I called the police." Maddie blew her nose. "He's with his father. They didn't want to get involved."

Suzanne's muscles tightened, rejecting that news. "We'll get him back. There's no custody order other than the Protection from Abuse order. That says you have custody. Greg's in violation. He'll go to jail." She began scribbling notes to herself.

Maddie whispered, "No," so softly Suzanne could barely hear her.

"No what?"

"Greg can't go to jail. He'd blame me." Sobs came through the phone line.

Suzanne stabbed the pencil into her desk blotter, breaking the tip. When would Maddie get it through her head that she wasn't responsible for Greg's happiness? "So if you don't want me to enforce the order, what would you like me to do?"

Silence greeted her question, delivered with a little more harshness than she'd intended. Suzanne immediately regretted her shortness.

"Maddie, I'm sorry. Let's think about our options, shall we?" She took a deep breath, counted to five. A calm approach was needed. "You want Joshua home, right?"

"I…yes. No. I don't know. He was…awful. He cursed at me, broke things. I want him home, but he doesn't want to be here anymore. I can't make him stay."

"The court order can."

"He says he didn't agree to the terms of the order, so he doesn't have to follow it."

Suzanne raised an eyebrow. Technically, the little snot was correct. He wasn't a party. But an order was an order. "I can get him home, even via sheriff, if I have to. But if he's determined not to stay, you're just going to make yourself crazy trying to get him to live there."

More sniffling, then a determined honk. "I know. He misses his room, and the boys in the neighborhood. His dad promised him a sports car."

What insanity was this? "He's not old enough to drive."

"I know that. But a shiny red sports car waiting for him in the garage....Greg will hold that over his head till he *is* old enough to drive. I'll be lucky to even see him again." Maddie sounded absolutely defeated.

"What about Katie? What's she say about all

this?"

"Oh, I'm not worried about her. She's determined to stay here. She doesn't even want to talk to her brother."

"Well, that's something." Suzanne sighed, swiveling her chair so she could see out the window. Snowflakes twirled past, floating gently down over the city. They weren't big yet, maybe the size of dimes, but they were forecast for squalls that night. *Better head out early*. "You could push for a custody hearing, but that could open you up to an order saying Joshua should live with his father. You're probably better off to have that PFA as a custody default. That way, if there's any trouble or anything happens, you can always have it enforced."

"That's it? Either I take him in on a violation and he goes to jail, or there's nothing I can do?"

"Any contempt of a PFA carries at least a $300 fine. But jail's a possibility. Especially with his crappy attitude." Even if Morgan cleaned up and talked pretty to the judges, Suzanne bet she could make him lash out. The anger in him shone like a red hot light just behind his fiery eyes, just under his expensive clothes. Just the right spark and he'd go off in front of the judge. He'd reduce his own case to rubble and lose it all. All it would take was the right catalyst.

Maddie didn't speak for several long seconds, then she said, "All right. We'll let him stay there for now."

Might as well look at it from a hopeful angle. "Maybe he'll realize that it's not as great as he thinks it's going to be."

"Maybe." Maddie thanked her and hung up.

Suzanne slammed the phone down, feeling useless. What an ass Morgan was! Taking Maddie's child from her was just another stab at control. If she wanted her son back, she'd have to go home and drop her restraining order. Then he'd have her back under his thumb again. Only this time, he'd probably squash her like a beetle.

Several other clients with troublesome cases checked in that week, fires brewing across the board. Holidays meant chaos in the world of the family law attorney. Suzanne was glad her Thanksgiving would be peaceful, spent with family, sharing turkey and stuffing by the big fireplace.

Except for one thing.

Nick.

She hadn't taken a man home for a holiday dinner since she was married to the girls' father. Not that there had been many men, but she had never been this serious with one. The last time she'd allowed herself to consider permanence with someone so fast was John Taylor. She certainly didn't think Nick and John were comparable in any way. But still...

She held her cell phone in her lap all the way to Perrysville, just waiting—maybe daring—it to ring.

Nick eyed her from the driver's seat. "You know, your office is closed. People don't have the right to nag you twenty-four hours a day."

Suzanne bit her tongue and listened to the girls' chatter from the back seat about school and friends. She'd already taken one call from Maddie that morning while she was getting the last touches on the sweet potato casserole she was bringing to her parents' dinner. Maybe it was her day off, but her old case, the one where her client had been murdered, jabbed at her conscience. She didn't hand out her personal cell number to just anyone, only to those she thought might have a legitimate emergency. If someone needed her, she should be available.

And she certainly didn't intend to debate that point with Nick Sansone.

Change the subject, that's what she needed to do. "So, what game is on?" she asked.

"Detroit and Atlanta," Nick replied. "Should be a good game."

Riviera pouted. "Steelers would have been better. Grandpa will be ticked."

"I suppose then we'll have to concentrate on interaction between people, instead of staring at the tube," Suzanne said, a taste of tart on her tongue.

"No way," Hope said. "Football is an American right, like carrying a gun."

"Don't blame your mother, girls. She just doesn't understand." Nick and the girls continued to compare rosters and quarterbacks and scoring per game for the season. Suzanne didn't care, it was true. On the other hand there were plenty of Monday mornings, she'd been lost in motions court while the other attorneys' primary topic of discussion was the Steelers' game of the week. She always felt shut out from those conversations as the "old boys' club" had time to bond even further. At least her daughters wouldn't end up in the same position.

"The Bengals blew their best chance for a trophy, for sure," Hope protested. "Traded off the best quarterback they'd had in years!"

Suzanne gave up trying to follow the conversation and went on to mentally check-off the landmarks as they neared her parents' home. Her mother had been coy when Suzanne called to tell her Nick had agreed to come to dinner.

"So, we get to meet the great detective," Maureen had said. "It's about time. The girls seem to think you might be thinking about marriage."

That made Suzanne gasp. "What? No way."

Maureen, of course, heard what she wanted to hear. "Good. They need a father."

And Suzanne heard the unspoken corollary that

accompanied that—'you need a husband.' "Mother!"

"Can I help it if I want to see you happy?"

Suzanne's woolgathering was interrupted by the girls shouting, "Turn here! Turn here!" She got a ragged glimpse of Perryville's charming main street with the double-globed streetlights as Nick's tires squealed, barely staying in their lane as he took the corner much too quickly. A couple of miles out of town, the roof of her parents' house came into view over the top of a hill. The butterflies in her stomach did the lambada as they pulled into the driveway. Nick came around to open her door, but the girls didn't wait, leaping out to romp with their grandmother's Airedale in the six-inch layer of snow.

"It's not a big deal, just turkey and pie," Nick said low in her ear as they walked together up to the house.

"I know. It's just that I haven't brought anyone here like this since John. It seems so—official."

"Really?" He smiled broadly. "I suppose I should be more honored then. Maybe I should have worn a tux." He squeezed her elbow and winked broadly. *Idiot.* Despite his teasing, or maybe because of it, she felt much more comfortable.

They climbed the porch steps and Suzanne launched into the mechanics of proper introductions, letting the formal protocol trump her nerves. "Mom, Dad, this is Nick Sansone. Nick, these are my parents, Maureen and Paul Young."

"A pleasure to meet you both," Nick said. He shook their hands like they were visiting heads of state.

"Come inside, come inside," her mother said. She patted each of them on the shoulder as they came past her into the kitchen. The girls raced upstairs with their overnight bags since they were staying the weekend. Nick offered to be the porter, but Maureen shushed him with a quick wink of a sparkling brown eye.

"No, no, you're a guest here, Nick! Let Paul show you his masterpiece."

Nick and Paul detoured into the living room, their voices covered by the drone from the television. Suzanne frowned. "Masterpiece? What masterpiece?"

"You know men, honey. That entertainment center your father built is always a talking point when they get together."

"Entertainment center. Right." Suzanne rolled her eyes and continued into the kitchen, which smelled of sage and garlic, a trace of cinnamon lingering as well. Pumpkin and mince pies sat on racks on the spotless counter. The wooden cabinets around the walls were polished to a shine, and the area around was orderly and clean, even in the midst of dinner preparation. Such a neatnik, her mother—clearly genes that hadn't been passed to Suzanne, whose organizing skills were strung out on life support.

The scent brought back memories of other holidays, when her mother's table had buoyed up Suzanne, made her feel whole again when her life was out of control. As independent as Suzanne liked to be, something about being back in her mother's kitchen allowed her to let some of her worries go. Even if it was just for the hours she remained there.

"He's nice looking, your lieutenant," Maureen said, a twinkle in her eye as she poured them both a cup of coffee and set out the cream. "So tall."

"Yes, he certainly is." Suzanne read her mother's face, seeing only approval. "Just what the fortune teller ordered." *Tall, dark and handsome, wasn't that the usual lingo?*

"You went to a fortune teller?" Maureen gasped.

"No, Mom. I didn't go to a fortune teller." Suzanne laughed. "I'm teasing you. I told you Nick was a nice guy. He's very thoughtful. Believe me, he wants to look out for us in every sense of the words. It's his job, you know."

"Of course. Is work going well?"

Maureen gave Suzanne her cup and a spoon, then sat at the oak table, still bare but with the cloth and dishes to go on it piled at one end. The girls' footsteps sounded overhead, then Suzanne heard them come downstairs to join the men in the living room.

"I'm staying busy." A nice, safe answer. Her mother didn't need to hear about any dangers inherent in Suzanne's work. She had enough to worry about, managing her husband's blood pressure and the farm, too.

"I worry about you, Suzie. I know you're one of these new liberated women who can take care of yourself and handle everything." Her dark eyes searched Suzanne's face, emotion intensifying as she continued. "Last year, when I almost lost your father, I learned that we all need to love and be loved. Facing the prospect of being alone scares me to death. You're human, too. Your children love you, but not in the way each adult person needs, love, support, understanding? No man is an island—and no woman, either."

Silence hung for a few seconds in the kitchen, then Suzanne's phone buzzed in her pocket. She took it out to look at it. A text message from Maddie. "Excuse me a minute, Mom."

She selected the message. *He's taken Katie!*

Irritation prickling through her skin, Suzanne apologized with her eyes and stepped into the pantry for some privacy, dialing Maddie's number. When she answered, Suzanne said, "When did he take her?"

"She must have slipped out this morning. I thought she was studying in her room, but she's gone." Maddie's voice cracked with the effort of holding back tears.

"Did you call the police?"

"Not yet. I called you first. I don't believe he's doing this! He knows the children are the only thing I care about." The sobs tore loose, and Suzanne heard a loud clunk, as if the phone had been dropped, then anxious voices.

"Maddie?" A growl of frustration escaped her. If Greg had broken into the house, someone should call the police. *Do something.* "Maddie?"

A moment later a scrabbling noise on the other end of the phone and then a relieved Maddie. "She's here. She's back. Joshua took her for a walk, but she told him she wasn't going to Greg's." The hint of a smile in her voice. "I'm so sorry for disturbing your holiday. I promise I won't call again."

"Don't be silly. If you call, I'll be there for you, Maddie. That's what I'm here for."

Maddie said goodbye and Suzanne held the blank phone in her hand a moment, glad the pantry door was closed. Maybe she could stall off her mother's persistent nagging a little longer. Or at least formulate a coherent response.

She only wants to see you happy. By her definition, that is. A happily married woman, at home, caring for her man.

Suzanne shuddered. *No, thank you.* She enjoyed her independence and intended to keep it.

The door opened suddenly, startling her. She nearly dropped the phone as she took a step back, ramming her shoulder into a thick shelf of canned goods. "Ouch!"

Nick studied her curiously. His broad shoulders blocked the kitchen from her view. "What are you doing in here? Did your mom put you in time-out or something?"

"I had a phone call."

"Suz, I thought—"

"And I thought you weren't going to interfere with my work. I don't tell you how to handle perps, do I?" The edge in her voice was intentional. *He'd better take the hint.*

He held up his hands in surrender. "Sorry. I was just making sure you weren't living the life of a football widow." He stepped out of the doorway, turning to give her mother a friendly smile. "Anything I can do?"

"No, dear. Suzie and I can handle it. Here, let me get you some fresh coffee." Her mother poured him a cup, and poured a second one, too. Suzanne thought at first it might be for her, but her mother handed it to Nick. "Give this to Paul, would you?"

"Of course. Thank you." He carefully held the full, steaming cups in front of him and headed for the living room, pausing a moment to wink at Suzanne.

Slick, Mom. Very slick. Suzanne bit her lip, feeling a little sheepish and definitely torn between her responsibilities. Her mother looked at the old black and white clock on the wall by the stove. "Dinner is in about half an hour. Let's set the table."

The two women laid out the white linen tablecloth that had belonged to Maureen's mother, the one used only for special occasions. Even with infrequent use, the cloth had acquired certain stains that would only have come out with bleach too harsh for its aged threads. Suzanne recognized the mark left when a too-eager Riviera had decided to serve everyone blueberry cobbler one Easter Sunday when she was much younger. Coffee and tea alike had left traces over the years, and somewhere she remembered a blood stain left from some rare roast beef. A quick scan didn't reveal it. Perhaps time had removed it from view, just as time tended to cover over memories, letting them fade away.

She laid out the Fiestaware plates, alternating

their assorted shades of green around the table, then the salad bowls and cups and saucers, while Maureen placed real silverware at each setting. Suzanne remembered the wooden box that had been carefully carried to America by one of her great-great aunts, inside enough silverware to set a table for sixteen. Every year the utensils must be rubbed with the anti-tarnish cream before they were used; now the forks and knives gleamed with the polishing Maureen had surely given them the day before. *A special occasion indeed.*

That task complete, her mother surveyed the kitchen, tapping her finger to her lips. "The salad is tossed, and the service bowls set out." She opened the refrigerator and closed it. "I'll have your father come mash the potatoes in a few minutes." She turned to Suzanne and smiled as a roar went up from the other room. "I think I've got everything else under control. Why don't you see what trouble they're getting into?"

In the living room, she found Nick ensconced in a recliner chair, focused as closely as her father on the football game. They waved their fists at the television almost in unison as a play ended and the girls broke into excited discussion.

"He didn't make it."

"It was too a first down!"

Paul pointed to the screen. "They're bringing out the chains."

Suzanne snorted. "Chains? Are they dragging someone to the dungeon? I didn't think they could do that for a penalty."

All four turned to her with a deadpan look of disbelief. Hope finally said, "Mom. Don't be an idiot. They're measuring."

"Oh. Okay." Suzanne shrugged a bit, chastised. She leaned on the back of Nick's chair, watching her family as much as the broad screen in front of her.

After a few moments, she felt the touch of Nick's hand on hers, on the far side of the chair from where her father sat. She glanced at him and found a warm smile sitting on his lips. She let herself return it. *Everything will be all right.*

Even once they all sat at the table for the meal, Nick mesmerized the group, handling the conversation with deft expertise. He discussed politics and farming with her father, then home repair and the preparation of perfect gravy with her mother. He went on to tease Riviera about her new boyfriend, and Suzanne wondered how he'd gotten ahead of her on that.

"Your boyfriend?" she asked her daughter. "When did that happen?"

Riviera turned three shades of red. "He's not my boyfriend. I mean, he's a boy, and he's a friend, so…I mean. Ugh." She rolled her eyes. "It's nothing."

"Right," Hope said. Her eyes twinkled with a sarcastic glint. "Nothing at all."

Riviera elbowed her sister. "Shut up."

"Where did you meet this boy who's a friend?" Suzanne's mother asked, taking over the interrogation. Suzanne knew from years of experience that it was impossible to escape her mother's determination. Maureen was much more stubborn than her sweet face would lead one to believe.

Apparently Riviera knew, too. "He goes ice skating on Saturdays down at the rink. He was just showing me some moves, that's all. Then we started talking online. He's really nice." She stared down at her empty plate. "Isn't it time for pie, yet?"

Suzanne's mother laughed. "It must be. You girls clear the plates and bring in the pies, will you? The whipped cream is in the refrigerator."

The girls did as they were asked, even bringing the adults the coffee pot, which they passed around, emptying it into their four cups. When the pie had been served and eaten, Nick offered to help with the dishes.

Suzanne's mother shook her head. "Suzie and I have a routine, Nick. You and Paul go relax, and we'll have this cleaned up in no time."

"Are you sure? I take orders pretty well, or at least Suzanne thinks so." He winked at her again, and she knew he referred to the day she'd done her fall cleanup. But it did him no good.

"No, no, you go on, dear. Have Paul show you his workshop."

The men left the kitchen, quickly followed by the girls, retreating to the living room to catch the end of the game. Suzanne cleared the table, pausing before the window over the sink to admire the view. As dusk set in, the moon appeared, hanging just over the horizon, reflecting off the snow in a silent and peaceful landscape.

Her mother wiped and stacked the dishes for Suzanne to dry, methodically moving from soapy water to rinse, a ritual that was the product of fifty years' practice. The two worked in silence, washing and wiping, until the kitchen was restored to its normal sparkling appearance. "The girls seem happy," her mother remarked. "Like normal sisters. You never had that problem—or the joys of sisters, either. I always regretted that we couldn't have another child. Everyone should have a sibling."

Suzanne dried her hands on the damp dish towel and hugged her mother. "I'm sure I did just fine without, Mom."

"You've done well, honey." Maureen held her close. She whispered, "I like him."

"Good. So do I."

Maureen let go and put the last few plates away. "He's more educated than I thought."

"Well, you never know when a police officer will

need to quote Shakespeare on the beat." *Really? After the entire dinner conversation, that's what her mother noticed?*

Mother and daughter sat at the kitchen table again, and Suzanne felt the presence of ghosts of déjà vu. This table had hosted marathon nights of canasta, neither willing to quit until the other was thoroughly beaten, the planning of Halloween parties in the big, dark wooden barn, shared confidences, The Talk about sex, worrying over her dad's health.... But always a very safe and peaceful place, compared to Suzanne's daily life of telephones, emergencies and court calendars.

Maureen took a sip of her cooling coffee. "So we'll bring the girls home Saturday night?"

"That will give us time to get homework done. Sure, thanks."

The group in the other room broke into cheers. Apparently their team had won. A few moments later, Nick came into the room, one arm around each girl. Hope and Riviera seemed ecstatic. Paul shuffled in behind in his worn slippers. "Nothing good ever came out of Detroit," he muttered.

"What a nice looking family," Maureen said, her eyes fastened on man and girls. Paul came up behind Suzanne and patted her on the shoulder before leaning down to kiss the top of her head.

"Don't let this one get away, okay?" he warned her.

Et tu, Dad? "Right." She looked at Nick, feeling tears sting her eyes. It was a nice looking family. Maybe one of these days...

Nick cleared his throat. "Suzanne, the Weather Channel said something about more snow later. We'd better—"

Saved! "Right. We'd better." She got up quickly, careful not to run the chair over her father's instep. Riviera and Hope gave Suzanne hugs and kisses, and then, to Suzanne's amazement, did the same to Nick before they returned to the television. Odd to see them treat Nick like a father.

His approval rating seems to be unanimous. Why am I the only one who's reluctant?

Chapter Eighteen

Nick entered the month of December delighted with his life. Despite the attempts of Jojo Washington to get under his skin, he'd navigated the retirement dinner without losing his temper. And he'd Met The Parents. They really seemed to like him, too. He couldn't ask for anything more in his life.

What an irritation, then, halfway through that first week of the month, when he got hauled into Reickert's office for a dressing-down.

The summons was scrawled on a pink message slip on his desk when he returned from an investigation of a theft in mid-afternoon. Having his problem children on temporary assignment might make the squad room more pleasant, but it also left him shorthanded. He found himself on the streets more than he'd been in a few months. It felt good to get out, work hands on, instead of juggling paperwork all day like the rest of the bureaucrats.

But when the chief called, you went.

He stuck his head into Reickert's office. "What did you need, Chief?"

The old man didn't get up. "Take a seat, Nick. And close the door."

Well, that wasn't a good sign. What the hell... Nick did as he was told, suspicion making him hyperaware of everything going on around him. It was just the chief, no one from Internal Affairs. So it couldn't be a mistake he'd made on the street. So what then?

Reickert seemed to be fumbling for words. Not one to waste time, Nick leaned forward, hands on his knees. "What's going on?"

The old man cleared his throat. Twice. "Nick, I'm getting some pressure here. You know I'm not one to bow down to city hall, but..." He trailed off, his expression one of helplessness.

Was Reickert in some kind of trouble? Nick had never seen him like this. "You want me to talk to someone, boss?"

"Actually, we'd all be better off if you quit talking to someone." Reickert had the good graces to look embarrassed as Nick guessed the subject of the discussion.

"Seriously? This is about Suzanne Taylor?" Even the thought of Morgan stooping this low raised his blood pressure.

"Now, Nick, I'm sure she's a fine woman, and you have every right to see who you want to see," the chief sputtered. "I'm not telling you what you can and can't do, but—"

"Damned straight you're not." Fury gave way to disbelief, then segued to a sort of morbid curiosity. "What is it Morgan said exactly?"

The chief stiffened as Nick used the councilman's name. "I didn't tell you that's who it was."

"You didn't have to. What did he say? Did he threaten her?" Now that it was confirmed, Nick's thoughts began to spiral off into what-ifs. Surely Reickert wouldn't have bowed to any open threats. He would have reported those immediately, like he should. Nick studied his boss, seeing Reickert slumped in his chair, as if he were ashamed to even be there, more like he wished he could vanish under his heavy oak desk. *By God, he'd better have.*

"He didn't threaten anyone, Nick. Th-That's the thing. He didn't really *say* anything so much as implied it. You know our budget's up for approval before the council, and we're in a bad way with the economic downturn. We need every dime just to keep everyone on that we have now, and we may still lose some of our part-timers." He straightened up a little, at least looked him in the eye. "I can't let my troops down. All I'm asking is for you to cool it off for awhile, at least till after the budget passes at the first of the year."

Incredulous, Nick stared at him. "You're serious. This is all about money. Money?"

"Money's what keeps this place running and keeps the citizens of Pittsburgh safe. You're damned right I'm talking about money. I'm asking you for a personal favor. Just hold off seeing her for another three weeks, till the budget passes. I'm asking you to take one for the team. I'm sure she'll understand."

Stunned, Nick leaned back in his chair, wondering if he'd stepped off his world onto another planet that morning without noticing. "You're going to let that man run the private lives of your officers, because he doesn't want the world to know what kind of consummate asshat he is. That he's an abuser. And an abuser of power." *And a whole lot of other things I better not say under the circumstances...*

Reickert shrugged. "You can do what you want, Nick. I'm not taking any action either way. Like I said, I'm just asking this as a personal favor. Three weeks. Doesn't seem like such a hardship to me, considering all the good it'll do for thousands of people."

No, I guess you wouldn't think it was a hardship. Nick felt sick inside, like he'd eaten broken glass. How would he explain to Suzanne that after the successful dinner with her parents, that quintessential step to the next level of a relationship, that he couldn't see her? He sure as hell couldn't tell her it was because of Morgan. She'd go off on some legal white steed, all dressed in her white knight armor, ready to joust. He eyed Reickert, not trusting himself to respond. He hated politics. He hated bureaucratic garbage. He hated lying. This mess was the bastard offspring of all three. Clearing his throat, disgust filtering into his mindset, he sat straight in the chair. "Is that it?"

Reickert's chin sagged. "Sorry you're caught up in this. Three weeks, Nick. I promise."

Nick growled and shoved himself up from the chair. "We'll see." He stalked out of the chief's office and back to his own. Clara Malron looked up as he came through, her face lighting with interest at his scowl.

How was he going to deal with Suzanne?

He pushed the door closed, gaining some small satisfaction as it hit the frame hard enough to rattle the glass. Plopping into his chair, he leaned back, tension settling right into the muscles of his neck. The last thing he wanted at this point in time, this precarious point, would be to jeopardize what looked like a hopeful development. He'd enjoyed his day with Suzanne's parents, and they'd seemed to accept, no, welcome him with open arms. Suzanne's father Paul had practically added him to the family roster already.

But now I have to avoid her?

What might work? Nothing about a conflict of interest; anything in that line would pique her professional curiosity, and he'd seen her work. *She never gave up on that kind of thing.* Not like he could fake a three-week trip away. Maybe a contagious disease? That could be dangerous, if she was the drive-out-to-drop-off-chicken-soup type. He didn't think she was. Well, at least not just yet. But he couldn't take the risk.

For now, he'd have to stall her with murky, vague complaints about the budget process or something. Not like that was a lie, exactly. This was tied right to the budget.

Nick was more upset that he'd been left in this position by the weakness of his boss. *Shame on Chief Reickert for not having the backbone to stand up to Greg Morgan.* The respect he'd carried for the chief all these years took on a tarnish, and faded a little. The man in charge was supposed to protect his officers, not leave them vulnerable to attack.

He'd go along with this request, just this once, because of the long-term association and deference he had with Reickert. But it wouldn't happen again.

****

Suzanne finished reviewing the last file she'd brought home and rubbed burning eyes. What the hell time was it? Exhausted, she glanced at the clock. Half past midnight. *Well, no wonder.* She carried her empty teacup to the kitchen, setting it in the sink. All the locks around the downstairs were fastened and chained. Flipping off the last light in the hallway, she headed upstairs.

She turned off the hall light, but not before she caught the sudden extinguishment of the light in Riviera's room. A frown edging onto her face, she opened her daughter's door, finding the room dark and her daughter ensconced under her thick pink comforter. "Riv?"

Nothing.

"Riv, I saw the light."

Still nothing.

Annoyed now, she turned on the light. "I'm not playing around. What are you doing up?"

Riviera stirred, then peered out from behind the edge of her bedclothes. "Sorry, Mom. I'll go to bed now."

"What were you doing?" Not homework, Suzanne surmised. Otherwise, she'd have been protesting up on side and down the other. She glanced around the room. The laptop was missing. "Where's the computer?"

Riviera sighed. "Here." She pulled it out from under her blankets.

The admission fired Suzanne's annoyance into full-blown irritation. "You know better. Bedtime was ninety minutes ago. Are you gaming this late?"

"I'm not!"

Another admission. Sometimes it was almost unfair to her kids that she was a lawyer. "Then what?"

"I..." Riviera bit her lip, looking down at the computer. "It's just...I mean... Joss wouldn't let me get off. He needed to talk, Mom. He's having a hard time with his parents, and he didn't have anyone else to talk to."

"Tell you what. If he needs therapy at midnight, he can call the crisis line. Give me the computer. You need your sleep so you can get up for school in the morning."

"But, Mom—"

Irritation was moving up the scale to medium hot. "You want to argue with me? I can keep the computer for a week."

Riviera pouted. "No."

Suzanne took the laptop, feeling it warm in her hands. The kid must have been burning up the modem lines for hours. "Get some sleep, dear. Life as you know it will continue in the morning."

Her daughter didn't reply, but Suzanne heard the under-the-breath muttered reply as she left. A little smile crossed her face. *Complaint department's down the hall.* Although the fact that her daughter had a boyfriend, a normal life, was somewhat reassuring. Everything was so dramatic at that age, seeming to encompass life and death in a split second. The instantaneous nature of the Internet didn't help parents out in the least. As far as she was concerned, her job as a parent was to make the kids toe the line.

If only she could make her clients do the same.

Chapter Nineteen

Nick struggled with those next weeks. He'd even had to turn down an invitation from Suzanne to come to her house for the weekend, explaining—lying—that he was on a stakeout detail. Not being honest with her made him sick to his stomach, and frankly pissed him off, especially when he didn't know if she'd ask again. Winning her trust had been such a huge part of his effort to date her.

And now he was letting it all go, for the money to sustain his department.

The Tuesday before Christmas, he arrived early, and took the stairs two at a time, travel mug in hand, briefcase in the other, ready to start the day on fire. The squad room seemed to be unnaturally quiet, especially for morning, but he greeted his co-workers and continued to his office. Through the open blinds, he noted speculative eyes upon him. The eerie feeling increased as two dark-suited officers from Internal Affairs came off the elevator and headed for his office.

Damn it. What's Vasquez and Washington done now? Couldn't they even handle one vice assignment? So far, he thought the temporary transfers had gone well. In addition to those two, other officers from around the department had filled in shifts when needed. He'd even done a couple himself, though it had been a long time since he worked vice. Still too many young girls, too many kids strung out on drugs. The streets, he found, didn't change much.

He rose to his feet, his hand extended as the two entered his office. They both shook his hand, then one of them closed the door.

"Gentlemen," Nick said, taking a seat behind his desk. One of the IA guys was silver-haired, tall and Caucasian, with lieutenant's bars on his collar. The other was more compact and clearly of Latino derivation. Both faces were vaguely familiar, but he couldn't put a name with either one. Both faces were also grim. "What can I do for you?"

"Lieutenant Jackson," the taller one said by way of introduction as they sat across from him. "We're investigating a report of inappropriate conduct."

Nick nodded. "From vice?" Here it came. What had his bad boys done now?

The other officer looked surprised. "Exactly, Lieutenant Sansone. We've received allegations that last month you sexually assaulted a young woman in your custody before you brought her in to be booked."

"What?" Nick rose to his feet, stunned. He was sure he hadn't heard correctly. "That—would you repeat that?"

"Sit down, Lieutenant," Jackson said, his voice pitched at just the right tone to "handle" him. "We're not done with our investigation. Obviously we'll want to interview you. You may want an attorney present." He cleared his throat, then waited for Nick to return to his seat. "Or you may want to talk to us now."

Nick considered the alternatives, still reeling. He'd never touched any of the young women he'd arrested. Ever. Never. He couldn't imagine that anyone could sustain such an allegation. Or any reason.

"Lieutenant?" Jackson had the decency to look embarrassed.

"I—I'm sorry. I need a moment." Nick stared at his desk as if he could possibly find the answer there. He didn't.

A knock came at the door, then it opened. Butch Reickert stepped in. He pulled the door closed behind him. Nick thought he detected a few more lines on the older man's face, and the expression it currently held was one laced with guilt. Was this more fallout from Morgan's arm-twisting? "Nick, you know the routine. You'll be on suspension pending the investigation. I need your shield and your gun. Shouldn't take too long, right, boys?"

"No, sir, Chief," Jackson's companion murmured.

Nick stood and took off his suit jacket, ready to punch someone and trying hard to control it. Through the window to the squad room, he could see Clara Malron studiously applying herself to the work on her desk for the first time he could remember. *Maybe this wasn't something that originated with Morgan. He had his own issues to deal with. Could this have come from his ongoing dispute with the Three Amigos?* Jaw set tight to keep himself from saying what he knew would only hurt him, he took the department-issued Ruger from its holster, ejected the ammunition, and handed the clip to Reickert, then did the same for his police shield.

Jackson cleared his throat. "We'll need you to make yourself available for questioning, Lieutenant."

"I'll call you," Nick said, his mouth dry.

"The sooner, the—" Jackson continued.

Reickert interrupted, his voice like granite. "He'll call you."

"Of course, chief." Jackson studied Nick, pity in his eyes. "Let's go, Lieutenant. We'll escort you out."

"Chief, come on," Nick said. "You can't believe this crap."

Reickert wouldn't meet his eyes, holding the gun and shield before him like burnt offerings. "Not up to me, Nick. Department policy. You know it and I know it."

Anger boiling up in him, Nick couldn't control the words that came out. "I didn't think being a coward was department policy."

That got his attention. Reickert stood up tall, his voice whipping like an Arctic wind. "Watch yourself, lieutenant."

Lieutenant? Really? Considering the personal sacrifice I made on your behalf, pal? This was a serious crock of crap.

Nick picked up his jacket and his briefcase, leaving his coffee. He'd lost his taste for it. Holding his head high, though every fiber of his being wanted to crawl away and hide, he walked with the IA officers to the elevator, passing longtime co-workers who stared, speechless, as they proceeded. No question what might be going on here. The IA guys always had a certain look to them. Like career executioners.

The men didn't speak to him, though Jackson shoved a business card into his hand. They walked him to the front door, then waited inside as it closed behind him.

He found himself out on the street with nowhere to go.

****

Suzanne was deep into typing a brief when Donna poked her head around the door frame. "Nick Sansone's on the line. He..." Donna pursed her lips a moment, thinking. "He sounds like he's lost his last friend."

Now that was odd.

She'd tried to get in touch with him several times over the last couple of weeks, but he'd been standoffish. First he'd pled preoccupation with last-minute budget negotiations, then he'd been unavailable because of some kind of vice stakeout.

Whatever the reason, she was glad to hear from him. *And about bloody time...*

Suzanne picked up the phone. "Nick?"

He didn't waste a second on small talk. "Can you take a break?" Donna was right; his voice was haunted.

Suzanne wondered which disaster this call might relate to. Possibilities clicked thought her mind like a slideshow. If something had happened to Maddie, he'd have come personally to tell her. Same if he'd gotten a heads-up on something with her children. So, something else then. She'd never heard him sound so unsure of himself. "If you need me to, of course."

"At the coffee shop at the Warhol in fifteen minutes?"

"All right." The Warhol? What an odd meeting place. Even more curious now, wondering what new hell had appeared on the horizon, she scrambled for her jacket and purse, then the door. Donna started to ask, but Suzanne just waved a hand. "I'll let you know when I know, okay?"

She drove as quickly as she could in morning traffic, heading for the museum. Neither of them even liked Warhol's wacky art. At first she'd thought maybe he had a surprise for her. As she drove, her fears reinforced that thought—all indications were, however, that it was a very bad surprise.

As she entered the café, accessible from outside the museum on Sandusky Street, she found Nick sadly out of place among the minimalist glass and chrome tables. The hand that held his coffee cup shook like someone who was freezing.

"Maybe coffee's a bad idea. Hell on the nerves," he said, with a ghost of his usual smile. "You want some?"

Suzanne shook her head and studied him. She'd seen him angry, elated, jovial, disappointed, but she'd have to call *this* Nick frightened. It was something new. She didn't like it.

He began to speak several times, but couldn't seem to transfer his thoughts to spoken words. A jelly-like quiver formed in her belly which grew larger as she waited. Whatever it was, this was big.

"Bastards!" The word tumbled out of his mouth, accompanied by the slamming of his fist on the table. Amid the rattle of glassware, and the shocked stare of the effete young man behind the serving counter, Suzanne wondered if anger was better than fear. She reached for Nick's hand before he could slam it again. Tight with emotion, even the pressure of her hand didn't relax him.

"Nick, come on, tell me what happened." She squeezed his hand, ignoring the looks of the old couple at the other end of the counter. "I'll help if I can. Is it Morgan?"

That was the word he needed to release the dam that trapped his words. He looked into her eyes. "I don't know."

Then he told her, first, about the "request" Reickert had made of him about the budget, then about the happenings of the morning, not letting her interrupt, no matter how hard she tried. Finally she just sat back to absorb it all, almost too disgusted with the whole situation to be incensed.

No wonder he'd sounded so bad.

How could this have happened? While he fiddled with his cup and stared, lost, out the window, her mind filled with rushing images. The precinct. The park. Scenes of dark streets where prostitutes patrolled like starving tigers, waiting to pounce on the unwary. What kept coming to the top was Sandoval's banquet and that intent conversation between Greg Morgan and the three young troublemakers.

Morgan by himself was a dynamo of bad attitude and acts. Adding in the energy of three others with an ax to grind jolted the potential impact and trouble to the next level. Maybe this level.

"Did you see any kind of written statement? Did they tell you who?"

"No, and they wouldn't let me know who, anyway. Protocol. But my record is solid. They've never had a complaint against me. I can't understand why they believe this woman. Even Reickert's someone I just can't count on for help this time." His eyes were fixed on the dark liquid quivering in his cup.

"I can't believe he'd cave to Morgan about the budget. That's garbage." Her foot tapped nervously against the table, drawing the attention of the couple again, and finally even getting under her own skin. She stopped. "But Morgan and your little friends may be working on this together."

When he showed interest in her theory, she shared what she'd witnessed at the banquet. "If what you say is true, Morgan has way too much influence on what's going on in your office already, and if Washington and the others are out to get you, there's no question this situation could have been created, tailor-made."

"Or 'Taylor'-made," Nick growled, his outlook clearly on a downhill slide.

"Now you can take your share of the heat for this, pal." She tried to inject a teasing note into her voice. "Don't forget you're the one who sent Maddie to me in the first place."

His sharp look warned her, his sense of humor had pretty much faded away.

"Okay, okay! Honey, I'm teasing you." She squeezed his hand again. "You can't lose it here. If you're going to get through this, you need to focus."

She thought of the case as if he had come to her as a client in crisis mode. Seeing his heart break was more painful to her than she'd estimated.

"If it's not them, it might be someone else you've busted looking for a payback. Cops make enemies on the street every day."

Nick nodded, slowly coming around. "That's possible. Any of the last three drug busts we've done had enough big-name defendants that someone could have felt too threatened."

"Do you have any guess who the complainant might be?"

"I don't know. Maybe. I've worked with Vice for a couple of weeks, just a few shifts to help them out. I didn't make too many arrests, but there was this young hooker I picked up on Prospect. She came up and hit on me at a stop light. I probably should have just put a good scare in her and sent her on her way, but she looked impressionable, the kind to be scared straight. So I did. The scared part worked—she was shaking like a leaf and terrified about going to jail." He rubbed his forehead. "Someone came and bailed her out before my shift was over, but I never found out who. Didn't think it mattered."

"This is unbelievable." Outside the doors to the cafe, the sun shone in the clear autumn sky and people went about their business as if nothing had just happened that would destroy a city servant's life and a career. What crap! Suzanne preferred a straight-on attack to guerrilla warfare any day. Continuing in attorney problem-solving mode—that hurt less—she asked, "What does this mean in terms of your pay and benefits?"

"Huh?" He looked at her blankly. "Who knows? I haven't got that far. I guess they're still in place. I'm suspended during the investigation. They took my badge and my department firearm." He shrugged, and Suzanne could almost read his mind. He had enough other weapons, some even better than the one the department paid for. But what would really eat at him was the deprivation of the daily challenge of his work and the desire to root out the culprit responsible and even the score.

"Criminal charges?"

"Possible under the Crimes Code, I suppose. It depends on the evidence, if they even have any. What am I saying? They *can't* have any. But I don't know what this girl told them or why." He looked at her in disbelief. "I don't even want to consider that. You shouldn't consider that, either. I didn't break one damned rule!" His breath caught, ragged in his throat. "What am I going to do now?"

She wished she had an answer for him. The shock of being betrayed by one's own colleagues was a formidable one. Knowing a criminal, a stranger, was responsible might have been easier to comprehend, but if it was someone in the department, that was much worse. Not knowing who the bad guys were just wasn't in the police vocabulary.

"Have you talked to a lawyer?" When he raised a eyebrow, she added, "Besides me. You know this isn't my thing at all. You should be talking to Jerry Goldstein, or Roy White. They can tell you what you should say and what to watch out for."

"Suzanne, I don't have anything to hide, because there's nothing to find. I didn't do anything!"

"I know you didn't." The story in his eyes told her it was the truth. Despite what they disagreed on, she believed she knew his character. He wasn't the type to take advantage of a young prostitute. Not at all. The fact he kept saying it meant he needed something from her, something she was wholeheartedly able to give him. "Nick, I *know* you didn't."

Nick's jaw tightened. "That means everything,

Suzanne." His voice trailed off, and Suzanne guessed if she had looked up, she would have caught a glisten of tears in his eye. But she allowed him to clear it away before she met his gaze.

"Regardless of where the complaint comes from, IA works in a certain way, right? Routine. The t's need to be crossed and the paperwork filed, whether accusations were made about you, Washington or even Reickert. So obsessing about the procedure isn't going to get you anywhere."

"You're right. But this just makes me sick. All the years my father....my grandfather... my record is spotless. None of us ever had a shadow of this kind hanging over us. None of us were dirty cops." He shook his head and gave up on the coffee. He shoved the saucer to the other side of the table.

Sounds around them seemed exaggerated—the clink of silverware, the soft voices of the two women in designer shoes. Seeing how wounded he was by this, something that at least partly sat at her door, Suzanne forgave him for his earlier concern over her safety, which at the time she'd chalked up to an overstepping interest in her life, and paranoia. Apparently there was something to be paranoid about. Instead her instinct to help the underdog kicked in, big time.

Nick finally spoke first, after a sigh Suzanne thought would never end. "You better get back to the office. One of us unemployed ought to be enough. I'm sure you're right. It'll all shake out, in a matter of time."

She stood and slipped an arm around him, hugging him. "I'm glad you called. I just wish there was more I could do personally."

"I'm glad you came. I'll call Roy, I think. Just to cover my ass." He took a deep breath. "Even if I did nothing, the fact that evidence of any kind might be out there leaves me vulnerable."

"Exactly. Hey, I've got an idea. Come to dinner. Plan to stay for dessert," she teased, hoping a light response would help push the thunderclouds from the horizon.

"Thanks, Suzanne, but I don't think so." He threw two dollar bills on the table. "I'll call you later. Maybe nine o'clock?"

"All right." His attitude was coming around. Her prodding had set that sharp detective mind onto a new path, one with purpose and determination as he set out to confirm the identity of his persecutor. Once he hooked up with Roy, those sparks would begin to change to spotlights. They walked out together. He made sure she reached her car safely and that it started, as he usually did.

In her rear view mirror, Suzanne watched him taking slow, thoughtful steps toward his car and gesturing vaguely. She imagined him trying to put square pieces in the round holes before him. So many doors would be closed to him while this was going on. She hoped he'd let her help him get through it.

Chapter Twenty

That night at home, Suzanne was distracted by Nick's situation, and she didn't balk when Riviera asked to take her dinner up to her room so she could do homework. She and Hope ate at the table alone, without much conversation. Hope didn't seem to mind. They finished dinner, then Suzanne stacked the dishes in the sink and began the brainless task of washing them. As she wiped and rinsed the plates and silverware, her mind explored the possibilities of who had done this to Nick.

What a horribly vicious way had been chosen to discredit him. From her years of experience with custody cases, Suzanne knew once sexual allegations were made, they stuck like glue, true or false. This would stay on the minds of his fellow officers like no other misconduct, prosecution or not. His career could be finished.

Which meant Nick would be, too.

In the months as she'd come to know him, she'd learned one thing: Being a police officer was his life. Since he'd been a small boy, he'd wanted to carry on the tradition of his other family members and protect and serve the public. If he was not cleared one hundred percent, he would consider it a stab at his personal core. He'd never be the same.

She dumped the water out and dried her hands. The house was quiet. She checked the locks on the doors, then retreated to her office. A shuffle through the folders and files on her desk showed her nothing that demanded immediate attention. *That's just as well. Do you really think you can concentrate?*

Delaying any decision about work, she assumed a position which she had done often in her younger days when she dabbled in yoga—lying on her back, with her feet propped on the back of the love seat. She alternately flexed and pointed her toes to force the blood out of her lower legs, and hopefully, back into her brain.

As she lay there, even the bright flowers on the curtains around her failed to cheer her. She got up and watered the plants lightly from the green pitcher she kept in the office, her attention returning to Nick's problem. The biggest obstacle to sorting out this mystery would be Nick's loss of access to crucial information, now that he was suspended.

So the key would be finding someone with information, someone who trusted her. She hadn't met many at the banquet who seemed the trusting kind. Particularly Washington. But there was always Hank Ferguson. Maybe he could—

The phone rang before she could finish her thought. As she scrambled up, she glanced at the clock. Nine-thirty. Nick. She grabbed the receiver and held it to her ear as though she could hold him close to her as well. Just like any other mother, she wished she could "make it all better." "I'm so glad you called."

"I knew you'd be waiting," Nick replied softly. His voice had lost that taut sound.

She visualized him sitting on the old brown sofa in his living room, or maybe already tucked in bed. "How are you?"

"Better. Not as shocked. Still can't believe it."

"It's ridiculous. How far do you think it will go?"

"Who knows? No sense in worrying, I guess. The investigation will run its course, then everything will blow over."

Hearing him paraphrase her words reassured her. He'd listened. First step on the path to being all right. "Exactly."

Several breaths came and went. Nick cleared his throat. "Of course, the fact that someone tried something this outrageous means they felt pretty secure in their ability to pull it off."

With Morgan's backing, it would be easy enough. Suzanne's sense of right burned thinking about how she'd like to deal with the crooked councilman. "We're not going to think like that. When will you be able to confirm that it was the same girl you picked up? Would Hank check for you? Anyone else?" Suzanne had to assume that Nick's co-workers would be as shocked as Nick himself. Many might be wondering about their own safety, if someone so obviously clean could become a target.

"Hank probably would. I'll have to see when the dust settles. In the meantime, I have plenty of yellow pads. I'll just start putting down everything till I can see a pattern."

"Did you talk to Roy?"

"He was in court this afternoon. I left my home number for him to call me in the morning."

"Hopefully, he'll knock this thing down before any criminal charges. God, I hope it doesn't come to that." Frustration at the injustice of the whole scenario crept up on her, tears suddenly constricting her throat.

"Try not to worry about it," he said in a voice which was forced with its effort to be light. "I'll be fine. Hell, I need a few days off after that budget haul. This is my problem. I'll handle it."

"I worry about you, Nick. If you need me later, no matter when, call me."

"Thanks, love. I appreciate your support. Good night."

The line closed with an abrupt click. She was alone with her whirling mind, many questions, few answers. She looked at the pile on her desk and realized she wouldn't do much good if she began any work there. What then?

She didn't have to decide. A tap came on her door and Hope peeked around the edge. "Mom, can I come in?"

"Sure, honey." Suzanne cleared off the small love seat so she and Hope could sit together. She wondered as she stacked files whether Hope had overheard her conversation with Nick. Hope and Riviera both liked Nick, a lot. She hadn't intended to burden them with this just yet. "What's on your mind?"

"Mom." Hope sat, shoulders hunched, hands holding each other, tight, in her lap. "Mom..."

Troubled her usually ebullient daughter wouldn't even look her in the eye, Suzanne wondered what new hell had descended on them. "Hope, just tell me. If it's bad, just tell me fast. We can handle it."

Hope opened her mouth, but nothing came out. She tried again. Suzanne's heart sank. It was bad, whatever she wanted to say, bad enough that Hope didn't want to tell her. *Damn.*

Finally Hope looked up. Suzanne tried to look as encouraging as possible. "Is it something at school?"

Hope shook her head. "It's Riv."

She couldn't help a glance up at the ceiling, knowing her child sat nearly above her. The reluctance with which Hope proceeded was starting to rattle Suzanne. "What about her?"

Hope took a deep breath. "You know we stick together, Riv and I. We try to take care of each other, so you don't have to worry."

Holy mother, what could she be going on about? She tried to keep her reply free of the dread that threatened to overtake her. "I've suspected that."

"I can't keep this to myself. I'm so worried about her." Hope's voice broke and a tear ran down her cheek.

Suzanne swept the girl into her arms, holding her close. Her daughter clung to her, sobs obscuring any opportunity to speak. Once she'd calmed down, she gradually let go. Suzanne found her own face damp. She got them a tissue box from the desk and sat down again.

"What about Riv?"

"You know that boy she's been seeing?"

A hot fear ribboned through Suzanne's midsection. "Joss?"

Hope nodded. "They had a fight this afternoon."

A fight? Sure, Riv went to her room for dinner, but what's the problem? Is she just sulking because she had an argument with her "first love"? Suzanne frowned. She'd expected something more than this. "So, they had a fight. And?"

"And he beat her, Mom. She's all bruised and—"

Suzanne was out of the chair and through the door before Hope could finish her sentence. She marched up to Riviera's room, her heart racing, her temper dangerously hovering on the out-of-control mark.

Riviera lay curled up on the bed, holding a pillow in her arms. The laptop lay conspicuously not in use on her desk.

"Let me see," Suzanne said.

Riviera didn't even protest, though she shot a look of betrayal at her sister, who waited, anxious, in the doorway. She sat up and set the pillow down, revealing purple bruises on both her forearms. Her cheek near her left eye was swollen and starting to darken, too.

Unable to help herself, Suzanne gasped. "What

the hell is going on here?"

"Don't get all that way, Mom." She picked up the pillow again, cradling it to her chest like a shield against her mother's anger. "It's my fault. I picked the fight."

Hearing the same minimizing and self-blaming phrases come from her own child that she heard so often from her clients, Suzanne lost it. "No! No, it's not justified for a boy to hit you under any circumstances. What's this boy's name? I'm calling his parents right now."

She took the pillow out of her daughter's arms and examined the bruises on her arms. Those were definitely thumbmarks. The boy must have grabbed her with pronounced force to leave these marks—Riviera had been a tomboy from the early days. She didn't bruise easily. Biting back a strong of obscenities that rushed through her mind, she leaned closer to see the marks on her cheek. The eye was probably safe, but she wasn't sure. They were making a trip to the emergency room. Riviera hadn't answered. "What's his name?"

"Mom, please, don't call. We'll work this out. I—I won't see him for awhile till he cools down—"

Suzanne growled, "His *name*. Now." She started rummaging in her daughter's dresser for an outfit to wear to the hospital.

Riviera stared at her, a deer-caught-in-the-headlights look.

"Now!"

"Joss Morgan."

The words hit Suzanne like a punch to the stomach. "Joss?"

"His name's Joshua, but his dad calls him Joss."

No.

It couldn't be true.

Forcing words out of a throat that had suddenly dried up, Suzanne turned to her daughter. "Joshua

Morgan? The councilman's son?"

"Yeah." Tears welling up in her eyes, Riviera fidgeted on the edge of the bed. "I thought you'd be happy that he wasn't the kid of some homeless guy, you know. His dad's Somebody."

"His dad's somebody, all right."

So many emotions rushing through her, she could hardly think of a direction to move. She sublimated her first instinct, to go after Greg Morgan with a sharp instrument. *Maybe later*. How had this happened? She prided herself on her confidentiality, trying very hard not to discuss or involve her family with her cases in any way. She might have mentioned that she was handling cases with a domestic violence focus, but she wouldn't have said who. Or suggested that her daughters stay away from those children. Or even realized that those children could be dangerous.

How had this happened?

Morgan's son had met her daughter and they'd begun a relationship. They didn't go to the same school; they'd met at the skating rink, she'd said.

A dark suspicion came to her, and she rejected it the first time. *No. Not possible that Greg Morgan had sent his son out to do his dirty work. His own son?*

But as she recalled Maddie's desperate calls Thanksgiving week about Joshua's defection back to his father's house, it didn't seem so far-fetched.

"Get dressed," she snapped. "We're going to the emergency room."

Chapter Twenty-One

The next morning, a Friday, Suzanne called the office to tell Donna she wasn't coming in, and she kept Riviera and Hope home from school. They'd been up much too late, dealing with the hospital and the police. The woman doctor confirmed that no permanent damage had been done, commiserated with Suzanne, and had been stern with Riviera about the boundaries of a healthy relationship.

The police officer who came to the ER had been less stern and more skeptical. "How old's this kid?" he asked.

"Almost fifteen."

"And he did this? You're sure?" He held his pencil in midair, not even taking notes anymore.

Suzanne bristled. "If my daughter says he did this, then he did. Would you like my card? It says attorney on it. I wouldn't waste your time with anything I didn't believe was true." *Jerk*, she added silently.

She debated calling Nick, but he certainly had enough on his plate. She could manage pressing charges by herself.

"All right, well, I'll give the Morgans a call, see what they have to say." The officer shrugged and eyed Riviera like she was a hysterical attention seeker, which couldn't have been farther from the way she'd conducted herself. Suzanne was actually proud of Riviera's quiet acceptance of her treatment and the honesty she'd displayed talking to both the doctor and the police officer.

"And then you'll file the assault charges."

He turned his intent stare on Suzanne. "If the evidence bears it out."

"You're looking at the evidence, you idiot!" She regretted the words as soon as they were out. The officer dismissed her and left the curtained area Riviera had been assigned. Chagrined and flustered, she forcibly reined in her irritation and put on a more upbeat face. "Guess calling the officer an idiot was a little much, huh?"

Riviera managed a ghost of her usual smile. "You think?" She slid off the bed and hugged her mother.

Suzanne felt her heart breaking that she'd had any hand in causing this injury to her own daughter. Rocking the girl who was nearly as tall as Suzanne herself, she smoothed her hair and kissed the top of her head. "I'm so sorry, Riv. We'll handle this."

"I know, Mom. You handle everything."

That little expression of confidence did what it could to assuage Suzanne's feelings. Action was what would help her get back on the horse.

Action was what she intended to take, now that it was the next day and she could see her way a little clearer. She called the precinct to follow up, but the officer had gone off shift. She was assured by some minor functionary that her complaint would be taken care of in the ordinary course of events, and that she shouldn't worry.

Which, of course, started her worrying.

She debated the utility of filing a restraining order against Greg and Joshua. If the assault charges went through, one of Joshua's bond conditions would be that he wasn't allowed contact with the victim, so that would do the job for them. That wouldn't keep Greg Morgan's long reach from interfering with Suzanne's life, but it would be a start.

Besides, getting a restraining order against Greg would be harder, since she'd have to prove that Greg was behind the attack. She couldn't imagine that the son would voluntarily admit that his father had put him up to it. The publicity that could be generated by the press finding out she'd filed it could help her case. Or it could backfire against her if he bought that judge, too, and threw out her case because she had no hard evidence it was him. So she was in the same place that Nick was, knowing something in her gut that she had no way to convince others was true.

All that day, she spent making sure Riviera had ice packs for her face and all the little treats she liked to eat. She even made grilled cheese and bacon sandwiches, one of Riviera's favorites. The three of them played board games and even watched soap operas together. As she sat between them on the couch, she realized it had been some time since they'd had a day like this, just the three of them talking and spending time together. Did she really work so hard that she slighted the girls? Ever since she'd been left with them on her own, she'd obsessed about having enough money to remain independent, to take care of her girls, and she'd devoted herself to that goal. Working in the office till six or later, bringing files home, delegating "family time" to her parents, she'd absorbed herself in her work.

And now my work has come back to haunt me.

She'd have to do better. She couldn't let the girls get so far out of her sphere of influence that something like this could happen. Not again.

Once the shock of the incident with Riviera wore off, Nick's predicament crept back into her thoughts, too. While she hadn't contacted him about what had happened, she tried to call him just to check in. He didn't answer his phone. *Ha! He's probably doing the same thing I am, protecting me from the troubles he's going through. Aren't we a pair?*

She didn't hear from him till the next day. Making chocolate chip cookies with the girls, she grabbed the phone when it rang, her sticky fingers leaving a glob of dough on the receiver. "Hello?"

"Hey."

"Nick?" A smile came to her unbidden. She wiped her hands on the worn yellow dishtowel and ducked into the other room. "How are you doing?"

A hesitation. "I'm fine. I was just calling you back. Everything all right with you?"

"Sure! We're all good."

"Well, that's good."

A silence fell on the line. *My God, we're both bad liars.* She tried to fill the awkward moment. "Any news?"

"No, not really."

"Oh." Another long pause. "Have you talked to Roy?"

"I did."

When he didn't go on, she prompted, "And?"

He sighed. "Not much he can do till IA is finished with their investigation. He said he hasn't seen one go on this long. Ever."

"Did you tell him you thought Morgan was behind it?"

Conversation in the kitchen behind her had stopped. She glanced around the corner to see both girls watching her.

Nick replied, "I did, but he discounted it as too hard to prove."

"Yeah, I know what you mean."

Riviera gestured to the phone. "Ask him to come to dinner."

Hope chimed in. "Yeah. We need a man around here."

Suzanne made a face, and both girls smiled. "Hey, I've got an idea. The girls want you to come for dinner tonight. We're making cookies this afternoon. They're delicious. Can't resist them, I promise."

He didn't answer right away. "I don't know, Suzanne. Maybe it's not a good idea."

She hated the despair in his voice and resolved to chase it away. "We insist."

"I'm not very good company."

The girls hung on her every word, making puppy-dog eyes. Suzanne grimaced with mock exasperation. "I don't think they care. You'd better come or they're going to hound me." That broke the girls into giggles.

He didn't answer, and Suzanne added, "Pretty please?"

She didn't take offense at his hesitation. Sometimes people just needed to deal with things in their own way. All the same, she was a lawyer. Lawyers lived to solve problems. It was the pinnacle and result of all their education and training. Why wouldn't he let her help?

"You don't understand the implications of my situation, Suzanne. This could be just someone at IA yanking my chain, or this could get serious. If some *pistolino* gets it in his head to bring me down, the district attorney could file a sexual assault charge like that." He snapped his fingers next to the phone receiver. "The press gets hold of it, it'll be in all the papers, and you'll start hearing the whispers, see the fingers pointing. Then that taints everyone around me. You're better off being as far away as you can be. You and especially your girls."

"That's bull," she shot back. "I know you didn't do this—"

"Oh, counselor. Come now. We both know that the justice system has very little to do with truth."

Suzanne struggled a few seconds for a

comeback, then chose the line he'd used on her that very first time. "Come on, Nick. No hassles. Just dinner."

"I'll think about it. Thanks for making the effort." She heard the line go dead.

The sound burned her like a hot match. What more could she do? She'd tried everything. He clearly didn't want her help. It sounded almost like he didn't want her, either.

That realization brought her up short.

All along she'd been trying to convince herself that she didn't need him, that she didn't want him in any serious way. But now that he was pushing her away, it hurt.

The girls studied her, her expression apparently giving her away. "He's not coming, is he?" Riviera asked.

"He's got a lot on his mind with work," Suzanne said. She hadn't explained the situation to them. Anticipating that it would be handled quickly, she'd never guessed this investigation would tie up all their lives for three weeks. "Maybe next week."

"Yeah, that'd be good," Hope said, going back to spooning cookie dough onto the metal sheets. But something in the way she looked at her mother made Suzanne think she knew there was more to it than work. "We'll be fine, babe. Don't you worry," she said, slipping an arm around her daughter's shoulder for a hug. Riviera insisted on being included, and she hugged them both.

She meant what she said. How many times had she insisted she was just fine on her own? She could take care of herself. She'd cared for Hope and Riviera for all their lives. If Nick felt like he didn't want them to be part of his life, she'd just have to adapt. What could she possibly need from him that she couldn't get herself?

****

Christmas came and went with Nick still playing the martyred hermit. Suzanne and the girls had a warm family weekend at her parents' house, where all of them were duly spoiled. She hadn't told her parents about Riviera's injuries. The girls had stayed home the first weekend after the incident, and the bruises faded by the time they'd visited again. Riviera didn't want them to know, ashamed she'd been taken in by Joshua Morgan, and Suzanne could understand that. So far there was no hint of danger to her parents from this web of fear that seemed to be closing in on Suzanne and Nick.

And it better stay that way.

When she hadn't heard from Nick for a few days, it was time to be pushy. She called Roy White and asked him if they could have a strategy session. She mowed down his objections that he couldn't discuss his clients with her and just set a time and place, an open-all-night greasy spoon in Millvale, on the city's north side. Suzanne invited T.R. Fries, a longtime friend and reporter at the Pittsburgh Press, who'd done a little informal research and digging around at the department, at her request. She'd even overcome the criminal defense attorney's natural suspicion of news reporters, since T.R. was a pretty stand-up guy.

The only point on which they all agreed was that the situation was out of control.

"It's a tough break, Nick," the scrawny, balding reporter said, after they'd looked through all the paper Roy had been able to get out of IA, which wasn't much. He pushed up the nosepiece of his wire-rim glasses for the tenth time. "Who'd you piss off?"

"I'm not sure," Nick said. He and Roy exchanged glances.

Suzanne frowned at her colleague, a compact package of intense energy, his wiry frame not appearing any more relaxed in his jeans and sweatshirt than he did in his suit at court. They must have decided to keep the Morgan connection quiet for now. *No sense in stirring up more trouble.*

T.R. stared into the screen of his laptop. "There's a story here, that's for sure. I just don't think it's the one they're trying to sell me at the station house."

"What does it sound like to you?" Roy asked T.R.

"I'm not sure yet," the reporter said. He kept staring at his screen. Suzanne wondered if he was trying to draw them out, to get more information for his own story. Or was he hiding something?

"Come on, T.R.," Nick said. "I can take it."

"It's not that. The stories are too slick. Everyone gives the same details. The *exact* same details."

"Hmm," Roy said, raising an eyebrow.

"Right. If you have ten cops involved in the same bust, a couple of them will know the background, some know the perps' histories, others have information about the consequences and follow-up. As far as Sansone goes, from public information officer to sergeant to street cop, they all know *exactly* the same thing."

Suzanne absorbed his opinion and took a sip of cooling coffee. "Do you get any feeling for how far they're willing to go? Are they pursuing this to the bitter end?"

"No one's making commitments," T.R. answered. "But the distinct dark tone to the comments convinced me they're really serious."

That silenced the group. Each fidgeted with the detritus of the coffee and munchies on their respective plates. Concentrating on possible new directions to take, Suzanne jumped when T.R.'s cell went off. He read his message, then started packing his things away.

"Gotta go. Dead body in East Liberty." he said.

Roy smirked. "Another hot Thursday night in

the big city."

"If I hear anything else, Suz, I'll call you."

"Thanks, T.R." She watched him walk out, feeling like every road in this case would end up a dead end. The three of them sat in silence until her patience finally snapped. "Damn it, there's got to be something we can do!"

Roy shook his head. "Nick's in the best position to gather the dirt from his brothers in blue. He's had three interviews. Haven't you been able to dig up anything or even figure out where they're going?"

"I really haven't pressed them," Nick said with a shrug. "The instigator could be one of several people. If it's inside, someone who steps up to help would be in the line of fire. I don't want to jeopardize anyone else."

The lawyer frowned. "I usually hear bits and pieces, and there are a couple officers who tell me things." At Nick's surprised look, Roy said, "Even lawyers get the lowdown somewhere." He waved at the waitress to bring more coffee. "But even those officers are shut tight."

"What are we going to do?" Suzanne said, more downcast with each moment. "You can't just sit around and wait until the magic fairy pops in and takes care of the problem!" She turned to Nick. "Whether those sergeants set you up or even if it was Gr—"

Nick's hand covered her mouth before she could say the councilman's name. "This isn't any different than any undercover operation. If you're going to catch the big man, you have to let the scenario play out."

"And in the meantime? What? Everything goes to hell?"

Her words floated in a thick pool of silence. The two men brooded and didn't look up from their cups. Her frustration with self-appointed domestic terrorist Greg Morgan bubbled up to the boiling point and just ran over.

"That's it then? We just concede to the bad guys?"

Roy took a deep breath, then eyed her. "When is the last time you slept a full night?"

Where did that come from? "I don't need you to be my mother," she snapped.

"Of course not, Suz," Nick interceded. "But you do need to *be* a good mother. You're really stressed out here. How can you take care of the girls if you're not taking care of yourself?"

"So you're ganging up on me?" Suzanne looked from one to the other, realizing she was being "handled." The recognition annoyed the hell out of her. She was a big girl; she didn't need them to tell her what to do.

"We're not 'ganging up' on you, Suzanne. There's a lot going on, and we need each member of the team to be at his or her best," Roy said. "You and I both know the legal system has flaws. If we're going to get to the bottom of this, we'll have to be ready to investigate any possibility, however unexpected."

Irritated, despite the knowledge their concern was sincere, she looked at her watch. It was late. She didn't want to leave the girls alone too long. "Fine, I'll go home."

"Want me to walk you out?" Nick asked.

"No, I'm just right outside. Call me tomorrow?" To Roy she added, "If there's anything I can do, let me know." He nodded.

She got into her car, watching them through the diner's wide front window. The two of them began an intense conversation as soon as she turned the ignition key. There *was* something she wasn't privy to. Nick must be "protecting" her again...

She growled and fought the tiny voices of exasperation which crept into her head by placing a

Doobie Brother's greatest hits CD in the slot and turning it up. "China Grove" started to play and she sang along, slightly off-key, as loud as she wanted. *Screw them both.* She had her own network of contacts. Someone would have the information she needed. She'd find a way to help Nick, even if she had to sneak behind his back, just to spite him.

Chapter Twenty-Two

The holidays passed, and the children returned to school as if their lives hadn't been turned upside down. While Suzanne was preparing red beans and rice for the family dinner one evening the first week of January, Hope brought her a plain white envelope with no return address, just a carefully-inked "Attorney Taylor" on the front.

"I almost forgot to give this to you. Some guy gave it to me in the parking lot at school. Said he was one of your clients, and he didn't have time to get to your office today."

"Really? Thanks, honey." Hope headed upstairs to her homework, and Suzanne just studied the envelope. *Odd.* She couldn't remember ever getting something via her kids before. And who would know she had a child at the high school?

She knew who.

Better see what's inside.

She gingerly opened the envelope and drew out the dog-eared piece of notebook paper inside. At the top of the paper was a blotch of red, inartfully drawn to represent a bloodstain. The writing underneath was bold, black, and terrifying.

I've been busy, bitch, but I haven't forgotten about you. I can get this close to your children. If you love them, you'd better leave my children alone!

The words echoed in her head like a chanting locomotive, speeding faster along its inevitable track. *Close to your children, close to your children, close to your children.*

Her heart racing, she set the paper and envelope on the counter, jerking her hand back like they had been a pair of cobras. Several people might have held these sentiments—Jack Wachowski, who'd confronted her on the courthouse steps, several others in various stages of family disintegration. No clue in the writing or the words who might have done this, but gut instinct gave her a prime suspect. *Gregory Morgan.*

The threat was beginning to sink in. She felt vulnerable. Despite her income, she hadn't put the children in private school or taken any special precautions, wanting them to grow up as normal as possible. Even after what had happened to Riviera. If nothing else, this example demonstrated to her that she couldn't possibly protect them every day, everywhere. They were at risk. What if the man had handed her an envelope full of anthrax instead of paper? What if he'd had a knife instead of the envelope?

The progression of evil thoughts scared the hell out of her. She desperately needed a moment. She folded the letter and shoved it into her pocket, then turned off the stove and hurried down the hall to the office, closing and locking the door. She leaned against the door as if to keep out all the bad things in the world, half expecting a huge axe to come slicing through the door panels after her.

What should she do?

The police hadn't taken the last incident seriously. In the end, they'd reduced the charge to harassment and cited Joshua. His dad had paid the fine, probably with a cocky smile. It wouldn't serve much purpose to call them again, now, would it?

Besides, she couldn't prove who'd sent this. This note was handwritten. The one she'd received outside the Benedum had been typed. No way to tell if they were from the same person. Or the emails Riviera had received from that "jonboy." She'd never verified who those had come from. Maybe Joshua Morgan, now that she thought about it. Would there be a way to prove it? She didn't know. Maybe it was time to involve the professionals after all. Maybe she could make them believe her.

She picked up the phone to call the police, but then hesitated before she dialed 911. She'd tried to get Nick distracted over the last weeks and hadn't been able to do it. If anything would grab his attention, this would be it. He had practically begged her to let him go after the bad guys last go-round. Maybe this would help them both—and give her a way back into his heart.

She dialed Nick's number.

"Sansone."

"Nick, I need your help. Please come over to the house. Please."

"Suz? Are you all right? Is someone there?" Nick demanded.

She told him only about the note she'd received tonight. "I think Morgan's back in the picture."

"I'll be there in twenty minutes."

His sudden click and absence gave her the impetus to wipe her face and collect herself. She checked on the girls. They were upstairs, each of them, chatting on their computers. She double-checked the doors, making sure they were locked. Morgan would have known the letter would strike inside her defenses. She envisioned him at his wide councilman's desk, slashing the words onto the paper with that angry script.

She stopped abruptly in front of an open curtain. He could be there right now, watching her, waiting for her reaction, wanting to see how much he'd hurt her. Her heart thumping like a loose tire in her chest, Suzanne went from room to room, closing the curtains. Hope came out of her bedroom, stopping to study her mother with a peculiar look.

"Mom? What's the matter?"

"I'd like you to stay away from the windows, would you?" Suzanne finished the upstairs curtains and hurried to the lower floor to do the same.

"Can I help?" Hope followed her, graceful arms reaching for the wide curtain across the picture window in the living room.

"Sure. Let's get this done quickly." They moved through the downstairs, closing curtains, and Suzanne confirmed the doors were locked again.

"Is someone out there, Mom?" Hope hung back from the window, as her mother had instructed, but her eyes were wide with fear. "Are the police coming?"

"I've handled it, I think." Suzanne's smile was shaky. Her fingers were, too. She moved into the foyer and crossed her arms tight.

"It's that letter, isn't it? Was it from that Morgan guy?"

"I don't know, hon. I don't know." It sucked to feel helpless. She hated it more with each passing minute.

"Do you think he sent those emails that Riv got?"

Something in Hope's demeanor set off a parental alert. What had Hope kept from her? "Is there something else I should know?"

"I've had a couple of scary emails too. I didn't want to give you more to worry about. But I saved them. Come on." With a defeated air, she led her mother upstairs to her room.

****

Some indefinable tremble in Suzanne's tone struck at Nick's heart. She didn't get rattled often, but she was now. That warning note allowed him to shrug off his self-imposed exile long enough to find his weapon and an extra clip of ammunition. Tucking those inside his jacket, he jumped in his truck and gunned the motor, leaving a black stripe of rubber in his driveway in his haste to depart.

I'm coming, babe.

She hadn't asked him for a thing until now. In fact, he had to fight to get her to admit even minor vulnerabilities. If she'd called him for help, that note must be worse than she'd let on. Which meant the danger was very real. As he drove, he whipped the police light onto his dashboard and plugged it into his cigarette lighter. People zipped out of his way as they spotted the red flashing in their rear-view mirrors. Belatedly, he remembered he was suspended, and probably not authorized to use any police power. *They can call my mama...*

"Come on, come on, get out of the way!" he shouted as he swung wide to pass an elderly couple out in the family station wagon.

He made the usual twenty-minute trip in thirteen, anxious thoughts wondering what he'd find at her house. Had Morgan struck at them? If anyone hurt Hope and Riviera, he would personally choke that person's heart out.

Nick squealed into the driveway, throwing rocks right and left under his tires as he barreled toward the house. He jammed on the brakes and grabbed his pistol, checking to make sure the extra clip was in his pocket. Making a 360-degree scan, he found nothing that didn't belong. No other car here besides Suzanne's sedan. His gun at the ready, he moved, cat-like, toward the house, watching behind him for an ambush.

At the front step, Nick surveyed the area once again and prayed that when he opened the door, he wouldn't be greeted by a tragic scene. He took a deep breath and twisted the handle. It didn't turn, so he knocked.

Several long seconds passed before the door opened, during which he imagined a dozen bloody scenes he could find inside. As the door swung inward, movement caught his eye; someone on the stairs. He registered that it was Riviera at just about the second she shouted, "Mom, Nick's here, with a gun!" Instinct spun him to face her. She eyed his gun with a frightened peep and ran back upstairs.

Nick pointed the weapon toward the ceiling, annoyed he'd scared the girl. "Suzanne!"

Suzanne stepped out, Hope half hidden behind her, both their faces pale and drawn. Their eyes, too, were on the gun.

"Is anyone here?" he asked.

"No. I checked and locked it up." Suzanne's hands were clenched into fists. Hope patted her shoulder. Nick found it odd that the child was doing the comforting, but he could see the emergency, if any, had passed. Nothing else looked amiss.

He tucked the gun back into his jacket, and all of them seemed a bit relieved. "Let me see the letter."

Suzanne pulled an envelope from the pocket of her sweater. "Sorry about fingerprints. We all touched it."

Nick shrugged. "It happens." All the same, he held the paper as little as possible, just by the corners, while he read it. The heavy black letters and the red splotch alarmed him, just as they had Suzanne. He was no handwriting expert, but the person who'd created this was angry, at a minimum, and perhaps unhinged as well.

He folded it again and returned it to the envelope, stepping close enough to put an arm around Suzanne's shoulders. A split second later,

Hope slipped under his other arm, seeking comfort. He held both of them, feeling them tremble inside the safety of his embrace. No matter how disgraced he might be, they still counted on him. *That means so much...*

"I think I scared Riviera," he said, with a gesture toward the steps. "I didn't mean to."

"I'll talk to her," Hope said, and she gently detached herself. "Thanks for coming, Nick." She ran lightly up the stairs after her sister.

"I don't want them to be frightened," Suzanne said. "It's not fair. No one should take out what happens in a legal case on a lawyer's family."

"Some fear is healthy, Suzanne. If they aren't scared enough, they can be hurt. Or dead. That's not a better choice. It's unfortunate, but the world isn't made up of nice people. They need to be aware."

She nodded. "You know I trust you with our lives."

"Then we'll do this by the book." Nick took his cell phone and reported the threat to the police. It galled him to have to call in like an average citizen, but his name still carried enough clout to get the call noticed, since the dispatcher agreed to send someone immediately.

"The situation's a little more complicated than you know," Suzanne said.

He knew her well enough to guess what she meant. "Something you haven't told me."

She sighed. "A couple of somethings." When his frustration came up to the level of his eyes, she took a step back, her hands spread in a gesture of surrender. "I know. I probably should have told you. But you've had so much to deal with, I wasn't going to bother you with any of this. But it's getting too close and too big for comfort."

Torn between scolding her and holding her safe in his arms, he opted for neither. "Tell me."

"Hope's computer may be compromised." She explained a little about the emails that both girls had received, all anonymous, but with the same threatening bent. Then she told him about the episode with Morgan's son. By the time she was finished, she was in tears and he was livid.

"The guy is digging himself a hole. I swear to God I'm going to bury him in it!"

Pacing to release some of the murderous energy circulating inside him, he calmed enough to think like a detective. "Okay. Here's what we'll do. We'll get it documented the right way, so we can nail him. Let me talk to the girls before the police get here, to see what else might be important to let them know."

The two went up to Hope's room, where the girls had composed themselves and were in what appeared to be careless attitudes across Hope's twin bed with its lilac chenille spread. Their frightened eyes, however, betrayed them as they looked immediately at Nick's right hand to see if he were carrying his weapon.

"I put it up," he said, hands in the air to show they were empty, as if he were in a police action movie. "Sorry I scared you. When your mom called, I thought the worst."

"Exactly how bad is it, Mom?" Hope asked. Her tone suggested she thought her mother had previously withheld information from them.

"It's Joss's dad, isn't it?"

"We don't know, Riv. Maybe."

Nick interrupted. "If it is, this just shows how dangerous he is. He's injured his own wife and children, and clearly he won't hesitate to hurt you if he felt it would get him what he wants." When Suzanne bristled, he cut her off. "I'm not bound by your rules of confidentiality, Suz. I need to know. Hope, can you describe the man for me? The one who gave you the letter?"

"He looked pretty normal. Taller than me. He had a long coat, like a raincoat, and it was..." Her face scrunched up as she tried to remember. "Black, or gray or something. I couldn't see his hair—he had a black pull-on hat. He wore boots. And his eyes were blue."

"Did he look familiar?" Suzanne asked.

She thought a moment. "I might have seen him before. But I have no idea where, or who he was."

"Wait," Riviera said, seeing a silver lining in the making. "Does this mean we don't have to go to school anymore?"

Suzanne hardly missed a beat. "Um, let me think about that. NO."

"I can pick you up and drive you," Nick volunteered. His general duty to protect and serve the public could be fulfilled on a small scale. After all, in his eyes, this family was a particularly important segment of the public. No matter what his predicament, he didn't intend to let them down.

Suzanne said, "You don't have to do that."

"Of course I do. I'm not letting my girls deal with this alone." There. He'd said it. She could protest all she liked about how Hope and Riviera were her responsibility and she could take care of them, but when the worst had happened, she'd called him. He was ready. "Besides, it gives me something to do."

Her eyes widened in understanding, and she nodded.

"So, valet service," Hope murmured, eyes narrowed. He could almost see her weighing the benefits and disadvantages.

"Police escort," Riviera added. "Like that reality-show family with an undercover identity from the FBI."

"You won't do anything embarrassing like turn on the siren, will you?" Hope asked.

"Not unless you deserve it," Nick replied. They were taking this much better than he'd hoped. *Which probably meant they weren't scared enough yet.* He thought about what Suzanne had said, the bruises on this young girl's face and arms, and rage bounced around inside him like a silver ball in a pinball machine. This had to stop. It *would* stop. One way. Or another.

Suzanne still looked nervous. "But make sure if you're home before me, that you keep the doors locked, and call me or Nick with any suspicious thing that happens, okay?"

"Of course, Mom. We're not idiots." Riviera rolled her eyes.

Just then, the doorbell rang. Suzanne stiffened. Nick crossed to the window. A police cruiser had parked in the driveway behind his car. "Come on down and talk to the officer," he said.

Suzanne opened the door, and let in a young, sandy-haired officer in a Pennsylvania State Police uniform. He smiled when he saw her and introduced himself as Tim Jennings. When he saw Nick in the foyer behind his complainant, his brow furrowed in surprise.

"Lieutenant, I didn't know you were on this case." It seemed like the young man's voice climbed half an octave.

Nick remembered this kid—well, not such a kid anymore. He'd served his first six months under Nick's command on the city's force, then when an opening presented itself, had transferred to the State Police. Jennings had started out fresh-faced and a little gullible, but some time on the streets had polished him well, if what Nick saw before him was any indication.

Nick smiled to reassure the young man. "I'm not, Jennings. I just happened to be here. This is my good friend, Suzanne Taylor. Let me catch you up on the situation."

As the officer took notes, Nick gave him a condensed version of the story, withholding Greg Morgan's name, as they had no proof of his guilt. *Yet.* Nick took the letter from Suzanne. The officer slipped it into a plastic bag as evidence. When Nick had finished, Jennings asked Suzanne a series of questions about her practice, about any potential persons who might have done this.

She tiptoed around many of the confidential issues, which irritated Nick. He did his best to pull back. So damn frustrating that he couldn't just handle the matter himself. He couldn't even go after Morgan, if that's who it was, as a private citizen. While he was being investigated, any actions he took would be examined under a microscope. The most he could do was orchestrate others' interventions. This galled him to his depths.

Jennings also interviewed the girls, who handled the situation with a little wide-eyed caution and a bit of flirtation on Hope's part. When Jennings finished, he put his notebook away. "Now the computer intrusions—"

Nick spoke up. "I've got that under control, Jennings. An expert's ready to look over the computers and tell us what we need to know. If we find something of note, I'll be sure to forward you a copy of the report. But the sooner we get a definite ID on the letter, the better. You understand me?"

"Yes, sir. I'll take care of it." The officer replaced his broad-brimmed hat and returned to his car. "Expert?" Suzanne asked.

Nick nodded. "I've got a friend who's the best at this kind of investigation. We'll get the computer analyzed. Maybe all of the computers in the house, just to be safe, since they have the same line in."

"All the computers? I never opened any suspicious emails!"

"It may not matter. If they've infected one of the girls' computers with some sort of Trojan horse, they might be able to tap into any other computer on the network."

Suzanne's face froze. "Oh, my God."

"Just the sort of thing that our prime suspect would be aiming for."

Hope frowned. "That's outrageous. Will your expert be able to find out who sent the mail?"

Riviera chimed in, "How do they do that?"

"Well, they'll look at the email headers for the sender's address, and the message ID generated by the email client that sent the message. The server chain shows the return path of sender to receiver, and the last bit will give us the IP address—the exact Internet point from which the email was sent. Then we should be able to get a warrant to find out from the company that provides Internet service exactly what computer it came from."

Suzanne sighed. "So you have to take our computers to the lab?"

"Not at all. Charley can come download the messages, or make a copy of the hard drive so he can analyze it more thoroughly back at the lab. But we'll leave them untouched till then." He read all the furrowed brows around him and put an easy smile on his face. No use in upsetting them more than they were already. "It won't be hard on you at all. I'll have Charley do a full overhaul when he comes out."

"All right." Suzanne included all of them in her relieved expression. "So we'll leave that to the experts."

"Mom, when's dinner?" Riviera asked.

"Oh, any time, I guess. The rice should be long done by now." She turned toward the kitchen, then turned back, looking fetchingly over her shoulder. "Nick, you'll stay?"

When he hesitated, the girls started in on him.

"Come on, Nick, please! You haven't been over for so long! We missed you!" They each grabbed a hand and pulled him into the kitchen.

"I guess I'll stay," he said wryly.

While the girls set the table, Nick couldn't help but notice how often Suzanne's gaze stole up to the window, suspiciously probing the shadows. He didn't have to worry about her being sufficiently aware of the danger. She'd dealt with enough lunatics to know what they were capable of. The real question was how well did she know Greg Morgan?

Chapter Twenty-Three

Dinner was a remarkably cheerful and bubbly occasion, despite the afternoon's events. Each of them seemed determined to put their worries aside. The girls scarcely stopped talking, filling Nick in on all the new twists and turns of their lives. Hope roundly reminded the detective that her beloved Steelers were headed for the playoffs, and Riviera rambled on about her role in the community theatre show. Suzanne was grateful she didn't have to say much. Her mind was occupied in solving the mysteries.

Could they absolutely blame Morgan for the letter?

The author could be a dozen people she could think of. Any of the mothers or fathers in one of her cases could be upset enough to lash out at her. But something about the malice in the words, even the tortured penmanship, told her it was Morgan.

She moved, almost robot-like, to clear the table after dinner, suggesting ice cream for dessert. Nick helped Riviera select bowls and set out nuts and syrup toppings. Suzanne passed, hovering by the stove awaiting the whistle of the teakettle while the others laughed and teased, scooping rocky road ice cream. Nick's frequent stolen looks, though, told her he knew what preoccupied her. No doubt his mind was on the same thing.

After the girls went upstairs, as unhappy as

she'd predicted at the computer prohibition, she and Nick took their steaming cups of tea to her office. She closed the door. "So?" she asked, sitting on one end of the loveseat.

He eyed the small sofa, then pulled a chair over close to it. "What are we going to do about Morgan? Why the hell didn't you get a restraining order against him after what happened to Riviera?"

"When the police wouldn't follow through, I didn't see the point. It would just have given him the chance to grandstand, because I didn't have concrete evidence." She eyed him. "That's what your expert's going to get us, right?"

Nick nodded. "He'd better. Where are you on Maddie's case? Did you finally win the restraining order?"

"That's the odd thing. He gave in. He caved. I thought we were past the worst of it." She held the cup close to her mouth, taking a moment to let the cinnamon scent clear her mind. "He did make a threat after the hearing."

"I hope you called him on it. Maddie has the right to—"

"Not to Maddie. To me."

His face hardened into rock. "You didn't think it was important enough to mention? Or that I might care?"

She reached out to pat his knee. "I thought he was bluffing. Like I said, I thought he'd moved on. I'm not going to make excuses. You know what they say about hindsight."

He sighed. "I know, love. I want to help. That's all." He fidgeted in silence for a moment. "What did he say?"

"He said he'd get me, and mine, for what I was doing." She couldn't help a flashback to that courtroom, how close he was to her, how threatened she'd actually felt. The heat of his hatred. She'd been so sure he was just spouting off, that someone in his public position wouldn't dare lash out the way he had. "Guess he meant it after all."

"See, that fits in with a theory of mine," Nick said, pulling her back to the present. "I think it's more than a coincidence that I've been accused and suspended right after Morgan became aware that we were together."

Suzanne blinked. What? We're together?"

"I—well. Yeah. I mean, aren't we?" He suddenly looked very vulnerable.

Were they? They'd been off and on, asserting their independence at times and then coming together for warm comfort. She'd at least considered the possibility of long term. And she'd called him on purpose, to reinforce that connection. "I guess…I guess neither one of us has actually said it." A little nervous laugh escaped her.

"Okay. Now I have." He reached out to pat her knee possessively.

So now they were together and he was her…boyfriend? "Boyfriend" did seem like such a stupid term for a grown man. So what then? Going steady? Another ridiculous term.

"Yeah, okay." The smile still on her face, she returned to the rest of what he'd said. "You were suspended after Morgan knew we were t—together." She hated that she stumbled over the word. She cleared her throat and went on. "So you think the allegations have something to do with Morgan? And me?"

"Once Reickert made that appeal to me, to stay away from you, I knew something was seriously wrong in the department. Morgan holds too much sway there. He's got quite the political influence, and not all of it above the table." He leaned back in the hard wooden chair and took a drink from his cup.

"But I'd figured what's happened to you trickled from Washington and the others."

"That could be. Back to Morgan and Maddie. What's next? What's he stand to lose here?"

"The lawyers are negotiating the property division. Slowly. Very slowly."

"So Morgan is under the gun."

"Yes." She sipped her tea, her mind ticking along in the background of their conversation. Would Morgan cave on the property as he had on the protection order? Now that he had stolen his son from Maddie? Maybe that would be enough for him. But she had to be fair. "We have to keep the possibility open that this particular threat isn't him. People do crazy things when they're going through a divorce. You learn to ignore them after awhile."

"My gut says that this is just escalating menace, designed to throw you off. Get you off Maddie's case. Based on that, I'd say Morgan isn't the kind of guy who likes to be ignored."

That theory made the most sense. No one had been so persistently aggressive before she'd taken this case. They knew for sure the Morgans were involved in the one incident. The likely choice was that he was involved in all of them. "So what do we do now?"

"We'll see what CSI finds on the letter. We'll go over these computers with the tech equivalent of a microscope. We'll find out exactly what Morgan's up to."

She felt better knowing he had a plan. "I appreciate you offering to take the girls to school. That's one thing off my mind."

"Happy to do it." He shifted over to the love seat next to her. She snuggled into the curve of his arm. "Wish you'd let me protect you, too."

"And give up this exciting, dangerous life? Never." She smiled to let him know she was teasing.

"I didn't mean to keep this from you, not in a mean way. I actually thought I was helping. You've got enough to—"

"Hush," he said, putting a finger to her lips. "I'm the one who saw that Maddie needed help and sent her to you. I'm in this with you."

They sighed almost simultaneously, and Suzanne hoped he was comforted by her as much as she was by him after their long separation. "I'll be more careful, Nick."

"That's all I can ask."

She leaned against him, thinking. "You know, if we can nail him with either of these things, his case will be shot to hell. Even his own attorneys won't be able to take him seriously after this. I wouldn't be surprised if the divorce just moved ahead quietly to its natural conclusion."

"I hope you're right, babe."

Babe. That was a new one. She'd have to work a bit to get used to that. She'd also have to get used to her own lies. She had no reason at all to believe that Morgan was finished. Even an animal would fight like hell to protect its territory when wounded and desperate. Maddie had wounded her husband by escaping his control. Desperation was only a deposition away.

Chapter Twenty-Four

Suzanne tried to get back into the swing at work, and still keep her days short enough to spend more time at home. After all that had happened, she hated leaving the girls home alone. When she asked him to, Nick would stay till she got home, and occasionally even had dinner ready when she arrived—a treat she hadn't expected. They became almost domestic. What surprised her the most was how much she liked it.

If balancing her concern for Nick and for her children's safety wasn't difficult enough, Maddie Morgan appeared at the office the following week. Her black eye showed Greg hadn't changed his *modus operandi*.

Suzanne stared for a moment, then drew the slender woman into her office. "How did this happen? You have a protection order. He shouldn't have been anywhere near you!"

Pathetic in a worn cotton jumper and blouse, Maddie wouldn't look at her. She slumped on the love seat as if even her spine was ashamed. "I know I shouldn't have listened to him, but he was just being so nice, and he sent flowers, with a card that said he was sorry. When he came last night to drop the kids off, I said he could stay for dinner. That was all. But then he wouldn't leave."

"When did *that* happen?" Suzanne asked, pointing to Maddie's mottled face.

"After the children went to bed, he wanted to make love." A tear rolled down her cheek. "I kind of wanted to—I've been real lonely, Suzanne, I couldn't help it! But he started to scare me, so I asked him to leave."

"He wouldn't?" Suzanne sat at her desk to make notes, since she'd have to file a petition asking that Greg be held in contempt of the court's order.

Maddie shook her head. "He started getting angry when I wouldn't sleep with him, and asked if I didn't want to make love because my boyfriend was coming over later. I told him there was no one else, but he escalated right out of control."

"Did you call the police to report he'd violated the restraining order?"

"I tried to. But he tore the cord out of the wall and threw the phone at me." She grimaced. "That's when this happened."

"All right. I can file contempt charges, since he broke the order. The court can punish him with jail time—"

"I can't do that! Joshua already hates me. If I put his father in jail, I'll lose him for good. Isn't there something else we can do?"

Suzanne considered jail might be a real good place for both Joshua and his father. She hadn't told Maddie about what happened between her son and Suzanne's daughter. She'd thought Greg might tell her, since they had to appear before the magistrate to deal with the charges, but Maddie hadn't said a word. Suzanne guessed Greg had taken care of it all in secret, in the dark, the way so many of his deals were made. "You know, I didn't tell you what Joshua has been up to. I knew you were upset that he moved back with Greg. But maybe this is something you should hear."

Suzanne told Maddie about the night Riviera came home with the awful bruises, and Maddie's face slowly drained of color.

"Oh, my sweet Jesus," she whispered. "Oh, Suzanne, I never knew…I never thought Greg would stoop so low. My Joss, doing something like that?" Her eyes teared up.

"That's what happens when the sons identify with the abuser. They go out of their way to try to be just like him. Even if they've suffered from the abuse."

"I've got to get him out of there."

"I'm not sure he'll come. Right now, we'd be better off to focus on some of these other issues. Like keeping you safe." Sizing up the woman before her, she wondered how long Maddie could hold out before she invited Greg back in permanently. It was difficult to watch abused women falling back into the same track, but Suzanne had handled enough of these cases to know they sometimes struggled through a number of separations before they could make the final break.

Maddie shrugged and wiped her eyes. "The only thing he really cares about is his money."

Suzanne wanted the court to come down hard on Morgan, anything to shake him out of his self-satisfied smugness. "I can call his attorney to let him know what happened. I'll tell him if Greg does it again, we'll prosecute the contempt citation for a maximum penalty." Her desire for revenge burned inside, and she shut the lid on it yet again. *This wasn't the time.* "But he'll keep on until something gets his attention."

"I know. I've got to stand tough." Maddie's hands twisted nervously in her lap.

"Have you kept meeting with the support group at Womanspace?"

"I was going for awhile, and the kids had group, too, but they didn't like it." She sounded defensive. "I couldn't leave them with Greg because of the custody order, and they didn't want a baby-sitter." She must have detected Suzanne's disappointment, because she quickly added, "I know, I'm making excuses."

Suzanne nodded. "It's difficult. I do understand. Once the psychological evaluations are done, you can get back into a custody hearing and maybe solve those issues. You've met with the doctor, right? You and the kids?" Maddie nodded. "Greg will have to go, and the longer he puts it off, the more difficult it will be to convince the evaluator he's being aboveboard."

"What does that mean?"

"What I hope it means is that Greg will eventually give in and make a settlement on the property rather than give us an opportunity to demonstrate his mental problems in court. Wouldn't look good to the electorate, you know."

Maddie smiled wanly. "Appearances do mean so much."

"You should still go to the doctor and document your injuries, in case we need to go to court. What's your position on getting this thing finished up? The less ties he has to you, the more likely he is to move on."

"I'm done. I know now I can't trust him."

Suzanne agreed. "I'll put together a final proposal and draft a settlement agreement. His lawyer will go over it with him, and all we'll need is a couple of signatures."

Maddie hugged her. "Thanks, Suzanne. I'm sorry for dropping in, but I wasn't sure what to do."

"That's what I'm here for." Suzanne walked her to the door. "The day will come, you know, when this will all be over."

"If we live that long." Maddie smiled, but there was fear in her eyes.

"Don't worry. We'll outlast him." Suzanne wished she could feel as confident as she sounded.

****

Two weeks into January, and the IA investigation still hadn't closed on Nick. Roy White was beside himself, and Nick was beginning to flake out. Suzanne had had enough frustration over the lies crucifying Nick.

One of the reasons she'd gone to law school was to right the wrongs, help those in need. She could stand by no longer and watch this injustice occur, no matter what Nick said. He might think he was handling everything well, but his usual professional demeanor had begun to crack. From what she knew of police department politics, and the odd vibrations T.R. had reported, there was more at work here than a simple mistake. Someone had to find out what.

Maybe Nick didn't feel he could put anyone else from the department in a bad position, but Suzanne didn't have any such reservations. Hank Ferguson had to be able to help. Nick trusted him like a brother, and he certainly had been warm to Suzanne at the Sandoval banquet. She and Nick would never be able to move forward on the road to a permanent relationship as long as this hung over their heads. She had to do something.

First, she had to get in the station.

She pinned up her hair, tucking it under a stocking cap, so it wasn't so readily noticeable. Red hair always seemed to attract attention. A pair of old jeans and Hope's Steelers warm-up jacket transformed her from successful attorney to potential delivery girl. She stopped at Tony's to buy a couple of meatball subs and a bag of chips. All the way to the station, she prayed her disguise would get her through the front door and into Hank's office, long enough to get the information she needed.

All she wanted was the name and address of Nick's accuser. She'd find the girl herself and talk to her, find out why she was saying these things about Nick, and see if she could convince her to come forward and tell the truth.

She slouched into the lobby, chewing a wad of gum, pausing at the front desk to announce she had a delivery for Hank Ferguson. The desk sergeant hardly looked up as she waited, staring at the floor, hoping no one would recognize her. He made a quick phone call and told her to have a seat, Hank would be down.

Too nervous to sit in the well-worn leather furniture in the lobby, Suzanne paced, noting the contrast of the well-polished floors and the cobwebbed ceiling corners. The first floor of the police central administration building had been restored to its appearance a century before by some well-meaning supporters. The details along the ceiling and walls were now a cream color, the walls burgundy, and the weathered frescoes had been retouched to bring the colors to full brilliance. Taken as a whole, Suzanne decided it had been a much more baroque era. She preferred her airy flowers.

"Miss, I didn't—"

At the first sound of Hank's voice, Suzanne turned to reveal her face, warning him with a look not to give her away. He visibly reassessed his response, giving a quick glance around the lobby. Apparently he saw no one who alarmed him, so he came closer.

"It's five-fifty, and I don't have change, man," Suzanne said. "Maybe you got exact change in your jacket?"

Take the hint, damn it.

Hank seemed to catch on slowly. "Yeah, c'mon upstairs and I'll get your money." He pulled her along with him past the frowning desk officer and his feeble protests about a visitor's pass. As soon as they were out of sight, Hank's demeanor changed, and he gave her a quick hug."Golly! I'm happy to see you. How are you?" He hesitated as blue eyes softened, and asked, “How’s Nick?”

“I swear, you are the only person in the universe who can still say ‘Golly’ and not sound like a total goofball,” she said. On his heels all the way, she avoided eye contact with anyone else between the top of the stairs and the detectives’ offices. She noticed Washington, but he lounged on a female officer’s desk, cracking jokes. They gave her a scant look, then returned to their self-appreciation.

“Well?” Hank asked after he’d closed his door safely behind them. “How’s my boy?”

“He’s not good,” she said, her anger evidencing in a tart reply. “Pretty despondent. The investigation doesn’t seem to be moving, hmm? Bogged down in IA?”

Hank nodded. “Have a seat?”

She shook her head. “Not in character, sorry.” She handed him the bag, peeking to see if anyone in the big room through the glass windows was watching what was going on in Hank’s cluttered office. “This place is a catastrophe!”

The detective shuffled some papers on his desk, and shifted half a pile, looking for some money. Suzanne guessed Hank worked like she did, creating stacks of work in progress, probably cases in different stages of investigation. His tedious search through the morass was telling on her strained nerves. She didn’t know how much time she could spend here before she aroused suspicion.

“You know this case against Nick is bogus,” she said.

“Of course I do,” he growled. “I wish there was something I could do.”

She eyed him, an implied challenge hanging between them like fall wood smoke. “Isn’t there?”

“Like what? Look, kid, we’re all stepping carefully around here at the moment. What happened to Nick went much too smooth, and those higher up didn't have his back. What we hear doesn't make anyone anxious to intervene."

What a bunch of cowards, she thought. "I see. Let me rephrase that for you. What you're saying is that you and the rest of his so-called friends are too scared to lose your fat pensions to stick your necks out for him."

"That's not fair!"

Suzanne bit her lip. No reason she should take her frustration out on one old man a year away from retirement. "I'm sorry, Hank, I know it's not your fault. It's so frustrating to have to stand by and watch. Not even knowing who the enemy is."

Hank glanced out his office window at the squad room. "The enemy is probably closer than you think. You're right to worry about being here too long." As she started to turn around, he barked, "Hold still!" The tone caused her immediate obedience. "They may not know I know. But I do. And now so do you." His smile was grim.

They stood in silence a minute, and he visibly handed her some money, which she managed to drop back on his desk, concealed by one of the leaning stacks. "Thanks, Hank. Listen, I have this crazy idea..."

"Anything might work at this point."

"I need the name and address of the girl."

"The girl? What for? You're....oh, no you're not." He stared at her. "You're right, that's a crazy idea. It's damned insane!"

"I'll go see her. See what she'll tell me, woman to woman." Suzanne turned and moved toward the door. "Come on, Hank, it can't be slower than Internal Affairs."

He stopped her as she went out the door. He spoke, louder, for the benefit of the others. "Hey, you can't just walk downstairs unescorted. Don't they tell you anything down at Tony's? Jesus!"

As they got to the stairwell, they found themselves alone and unobserved. "All right, I'll see what I can do. But if you find that information in your hands, I never gave it to you, you got it?"

"Gave what?" She smiled to seal their pact. Her heartbeat quickened as she realized he'd actually agreed to her request. Maybe now, at last, she'd be able to do something useful.

His eyes narrowed and he stopped about halfway down the stairs, taking her elbow. "Nick know you're doing this?"

She shook her head. "He'd kill me. Don't you tell him, either. If it works, he'll know soon enough. Then you can come to the wake."

He laughed at last, and let her continue her descent. "If it works, I'll spring for the funeral myself."

"You're on." Before they came out in the lobby, she leaned over and gave him a quick peck on the cheek. "Thanks, Hank. I knew we could count on you. "

As she stepped away from him into the lobby, his face became gruff. "And you tell Tony if he doesn't start sending you guys out with change, I'm gonna quit ordering from there!"

"Yadda, yadda, yadda," Suzanne said, walking away quickly. Her head down, she passed by Reickert in the doorway, and hurried down the street to her car.

Not until she was inside with the doors locked did she take a minute to give thanks to the fates at large that Hank was willing to help her. *Now if only the girl was willing to listen to reason…*

Chapter Twenty-Five

Four days later, a courier delivered an envelope bearing the printed return address of the precinct where Nick worked, marked "personal and confidential." Suzanne took it from a puzzled Donna's hands and carried it into her own office. As she'd hoped, it was a name and address on plain white paper: Cassandra Trujillo, 920 Kincaid Street.

Thank you, Hank.

She'd put together a loose plan, not really sure how to go about this kind of spy business. Most of her work was done in the open, either in court or in legal offices. Skulking around the back streets of Pittsburgh was not her style, as a rule. Whoever had gotten to this girl to convince her to accuse Nick probably had something to hold over her in return for her testimony. Suzanne had to have some coin, some counter-offer, to make the girl tell the truth.

If she'd even listen...

Nick had said the girl was a prostitute, maybe not even eighteen years old. What were her concerns? Would she take Suzanne's word? Would she need protection? Suzanne was discouraged just thinking about the possibilities.

But she had a name.

With all Nick had done for her, she knew she had to try. He'd stuck with her through all her own emotional twists and turns, and he'd come to mean a lot not just to her, but to her daughters, too. She worried that if something didn't break soon, *he* would.

When she got home that night, she typed the address into an Internet mapping site, searching for the unfamiliar street. It turned up off Penn Avenue out toward East Liberty. Well, there it was. *All I've got to do is go there and tell her... Tell her what?*

That, Suzanne couldn't guess just yet. Money? Suzanne had money. She could pay the girl, if that's what it took. But she preferred something more...what was the word? Moral? She didn't want to bribe her to say anything. What Suzanne would rather do was something to change the girl's life, to show her that something existed in the world besides pain and lies. Suzanne would wait until she met the girl, take some clues from her environment, to determine how to make her see the damage she was doing to a good man.

Even as the thoughts passed through her mind, her cynical side mocked her Pollyanna attitude. *Oh, yes, with the right words and a big smile, we can change everyone's world into sweetness and light, turn their frowns upside down, make it all perfect...*

It was ridiculous to even hope for something so out of reach.

Who could ignore the fact that poverty, accidents of birth, economics, drugs and bad decisions in general set the path to the place each person would find themselves in life? Cops and dirty politicians could take advantage of those whose fortunes had fallen so far they had little to lose. Cassandra Trujillo might well be one of those unlucky people. Suzanne didn't want to be just one more in a line of users, who took this girl for all she was worth, then kicked her aside. She intended to make Cassandra's life better, if it could be done.

The second ticking clock in Suzanne's focus was her need to make her move soon. The longer she waited, the more chance she'd let something slip to Nick, and he'd forbid her to go. He still believed in the system. If they would just be patient long enough, the innocent would be vindicated, he'd said. She knew better. The courts were full of liars and cheats using the system to their own benefit. Nice guys finished last.

Not if I can help it.

When Donna informed her a few days later that a custody matter scheduled for hearing had settled, suddenly giving Suzanne several free hours, she knew that was the time. *Show time.*

She'd decided the best approach would be to appeal to this girl as a woman, find out what happened, learn the girl's story. Originally, Suzanne had thought to tape their conversation, but she didn't know if Chief Reickert would accept the recording as legitimate evidence. After all, she could certainly be perceived as having a bias. The only undeniable plan would be to have Reickert speak to the girl directly, to hear the exculpating words from her lips.

But first, Suzanne would have to find her, and second, convince her to come forward.

When the time came, Suzanne worried about every detail, right down to how she was dressed. She didn't want the "social worker" look, because people in that neighborhood would probably distrust government intrusion, and she might not get in the door. If Nick's co-workers had threatened her, she had plenty to fear from the authorities. On the other hand, she didn't want to dress down too much, because then she'd lose whatever advantage her position might bring her.

She chose office casual at last, navy blue wool blazer and slacks and a flat-toned blouse. *No jewelry,* she decided, knowing the character of the neighborhood. Then she relented and stuck in some cheap butterfly-shaped earrings. *If they mug me for those, they're in worse shape than I am.*

At the end of the morning's work, Suzanne stopped by Donna's desk, slipping Hope's stadium jacket over her blazer. She'd thought of wearing the blazer alone, but the wind was whipping snow crystals like cut diamonds against her window, and she knew it wouldn't be enough.

"I'm taking a long lunch. I'm not sure when I'll be back."

"All right," Donna said. "If you're not here when I'm finished, I'll just lock up."

Suzanne nodded. "Thanks," she said, and she headed out to her car.

****

Like most northern cities Pittsburgh in mid-winter was not an attractive place, all browns and grays, snow blending them into a neutral environment. But some sections of town, Suzanne thought, were even uglier because of their lack of amenities. The area that housed Kincaid Street was one of them.

The block where Cassandra Trujillo lived was lined with tiny row houses, built close together, most in bad repair. The house across the street had black holes for windows, gaping frames rimmed with shards of glass. On either side of Cassandra's address, the homes' peeling paint topped damaged porch supports. The Trujillo house was one of the smallest, couldn't be more than three or four rooms, Suzanne thought, white paint fading past gray. Thick beige curtains covered every front window. No signs of life. She wondered if the girl had already left town.

With a sigh, Suzanne locked her doors, taking her purse, and started to walk up the cracked sidewalk to the door. Then she became aware of all the eyes.

She felt she was being watched, and a surreptitious glance around showed her the thin black man, walking down the street toward her, the old Spanish woman with a bandanna around her hair sweeping the porch across the street, and half a dozen other people peeking out from behind curtains or doors to see what stranger—what trouble—had come to their neighborhood.

Not wanting to draw attention to herself and her mission, both for her own safety and the girl's, Suzanne pulled her coat closer and hurried to the door of Cassandra's house without acknowledging the watchers. She rapped sharply on the door with her knuckles. There was no answer. She thought she heard music playing, so she knocked again, harder. *Come on, Cassandra, be here!* she appealed silently.

No one came to the door.

Suzanne was torn. She'd pushed herself to the bounds of her courage to make herself come here. She couldn't leave without accomplishing her goal. Shivering, she muttered, "Can't just barge in."

Then she wondered why not.

"What the hell... here goes." She tested the tarnished door handle. It turned without impediment. *I could just say I thought she said to come in.* With a quick look behind to make sure no one was sneaking up on her, Suzanne turned the handle and stepped into the hall, where she was met with a melange of odors. The first whiff smelled like backed-up sewage, succeeded closely by a burnt-egg aroma. Shuddering, she noticed piles of clothes on the floor in the room off to her right, near a folded-out sofa bed covered with worn blankets. She heard a tinkle of silverware straight ahead in what might be the kitchen, followed by a string of Spanish words.

"Hello?" Suzanne called.

"Who's there?" came a suspicious female voice,

and the music cut off abruptly. Before Suzanne could answer, a young woman moved into the doorway, silhouetted from behind by the light from the kitchen window. She wore a long cotton gown or bathrobe in a pale blue. "What do you want?" she demanded.

Suzanne found herself struck dumb for a moment, now that she was where she wanted to be. *What now?* "Cassandra?" she asked.

"Who want to know?" The girl's face was soft in shadow, but her accented voice was hard. "What you doing in my house?"

She kept her voice at a warm pitch, and took a step forward, allowing the light to shine on her face. "My name is Suzanne Taylor. I wanted to talk to you about the police department."

The girl didn't move. "You got a warrant or something?"

Suzanne shook her head. "I'm not a cop."

"Who are you then?"

"Someone with a reason not to trust the police."

"What business I got with the police?" The girl shifted slightly in the doorway, and as she turned to an angle, Suzanne saw the gently-rounded belly of a pregnancy. *Now that's an interesting development...*

"I hear you're under pressure to testify against a cop," Suzanne said, hoping the girl wouldn't panic. Because the voice sounded so weary, she'd thought at first that Cassandra was grown-up, but as the light caught the edges of her face under her long hair, Suzanne noted the huge dark eyes and soft skin of a teenager.

"I think you better go," the girl said, taking a step forward.

Suzanne saw no threat in the girl's stance. No one else had appeared. She took a deep breath. This was her chance, and she had to take it. "I know that cop, Cassandra, and I know he would never do the things they're saying he did." She moved forward, too, hands at her sides, trying to show she had no intention of harm. "I think he's being set up by some other officers who want to screw him over."

"I don't want to talk about that!" Cassandra said, scooting back to the kitchen. "Get out!"

"Nick Sansone is a good man." Suzanne followed her, slowly, hoping the girl was still listening. "He told me he was worried about you, out on the street alone. That's why he picked you up."

A long silence, then a thud of something falling. "Who asked him?" the girl muttered.

Concerned the girl had been hurt, Suzanne hurried around the corner. When she came into the kitchen she saw some cereal boxes had tumbled from the cupboard. Paint hung in peeled strips from the wooden cupboards. The linoleum was cracked and torn, but cheerful yellow curtains hung at every window. "Are you okay?"

"I told you, get out!" Cassandra's eyes blazed. She turned to face Suzanne, her hand twitching on the counter near a large butcher knife.

Briefly, Suzanne's insides froze. Would the girl really do something so desperate as to stab her? She'd be within her legal rights, since Suzanne had entered without invitation. But that little thing didn't look capable of murder. Swallowing back the fear, she said, "Cassandra, I just need to know what happened." Suzanne stopped where she was, her mind clicking ahead along a new path. "That officer is my fiancé. He told me he loved me, that he'd never be with another woman." She managed to choke a tear into her voice. "If he cheated on me, I deserve to know the truth."

The Hispanic girl stared at her for a minute, then burst out laughing. "You came here to see if your man step out?" she asked, derision dripping from her tongue. "Why should I keep track of some cop's sex trips?"

"No, you're right. It's not your responsibility," Suzanne said, capitulating suddenly, trying a new tactic. "I shouldn't have come." She turned away, just a little.

"Got that right." Cassandra moved away from the counter, bending down to scrape some pet food from a can into a dish on the floor. Suzanne noticed for the first time a scrawny kitten rubbing against the girl's ankles. It sprang to the dish and gobbled the food down as if it were starving.

"I'm just a single mother, you know, and my kids really love the guy. This whole thing has really torn us all up. And him, too." Suzanne couldn't tell, under lowered lashes, whether anything she said was having an effect on the girl. "I could help you."

"You think so?" The girl eyed her with suspicion.

"What is it you need?"

"That's it, huh? Just 'what I need,' and you fix everything up all nice? Hah!" She tossed the can into the trash. "That's what screwed me in the first place."

"What do you mean?"

The girl stood a little straighter, sizing her up. "What make you think you can help me? You a social worker?"

So much for her attempt at disguise. "No, actually I'm a lawyer."

"Huh." The girl didn't sound impressed. She was as painfully thin as the cat, except for the bulge in her mid-section.

"When are you due?"

"None of your business." The girl's hand went to her abdomen, as if to hide her secret. Suzanne waited, not moving, hardly breathing, and was gratified to hear Cassandra say at last, "June third."

"I have a client whose baby is due in June," Suzanne said, trying to build a bridge again with the girl. "She's having a boy. Do you know if yours is a boy or a girl?"

Cassandra shrugged. "Don't matter."

Suzanne tried to read her face. "Being a single mother's not easy." The kitten had finished eating and had come to Suzanne's feet, purring loudly. She bent down to scratch its bony back, watching the girl to see if anything she said made an impression.

"Not like I chose it," the girl said, plopping down into a rickety chair at the tiny, two-seat table.

"I have two daughters, one about your age," Suzanne said. "Their dad took off when they were little girls and never had anything to do with them again."

"So?"

The girl's tone was flat, and Suzanne could see she was losing ground. *Had she tried every possible connection they could have?* She had to establish trust through some bond, and soon, before Cassandra Trujillo really threw her out of the house. But the girl flashed warm and cold, which gave Suzanne hope she could still connect. Somehow. *But what was the key?*

Silence fell between them, Cassandra staring out the window and Suzanne crouched down with the kitten. She could think of nothing else. Finally the girl spoke, without moving, in a near-whisper.

"He was really nice to me." The girl's bottom lip quivered. "Stopped and bought me hot chocolate on the way to the station."

Suzanne smiled, wonder filling her as she realized who Cassandra meant. "He's like that," she said. Her leg beginning to cramp, she stood up, taking the cat into her arms.

Another silence. Suzanne didn't want to push, now that the girl had started to open up, but finally she said, "So you remember Nick?"

Cassandra nodded. "He wasn't in a police car. I

think he was on his way home."

"He told me he didn't want to see you on the street. He thought you could get hurt."

"None of his business, either." She frowned, and Suzanne could see the beginnings of tears in the girl's eyes, which she brushed angrily away.

"I keep telling him he sticks his nose in where it's not wanted." She took a step toward the other chair, and the girl didn't move to stop her. When she didn't respond, Suzanne continued, "He's always trying to tell me what's good for me, even if I don't think he has a right."

"Damn cops, always messing with stuff."

"Got that right." Suzanne made her way to the chair and slid into it, grabbing the edge of the table as the rickety chair teetered. The girl was pretty, in a waif-like way. Probably a big favorite with the pedophiles in the red-light district. "He never touched you, did he?"

Suddenly confronted with her proximity, the girl looked into Suzanne's eyes. Something there must have appealed to her, because she shook her head.

"Thank God," Suzanne said, relief flowing over her, making her droop, not realizing until that moment that she might have heard any number of possible answers. She was just grateful to have heard the one she believed in.

The girl reached for the cat, setting it on the hump of her stomach to pet it, where it purred its way to sleep. Water dripped steadily from the faucet, creating a background rhythm. A car without a muffler passed by the front of the house, creating another momentary distraction.

"If he didn't do anything...why did you say so?" Suzanne asked, without accusation.

Cassandra looked at her, and the hard edge flicked back to her eyes, but faded a moment later. "I had to," she said.

"Someone threatened you?"

She hesitated, then looked away. "I—no, it wasn't like that. He promised… but I had to—" Her erratic speech drifted off.

"Who?" Now that the words were coming, she tried to rein in her eagerness, before she cut off the source of information. She found it difficult. *Very difficult.*

"Jojo. He said he'd take care of me," Cassandra said. She seemed to retreat into herself as she picked at her thin clothing.

Jojo...that name was familiar. Yes. Washington. The man who had danced with her at Sandoval's retirement banquet, who thought he was such hot stuff. Jojo Washington. "He framed Nick to get the lieutenant's slot," she whispered, horrified that someone entrusted with the public good could be so underhanded. And this girl had helped him. *But let's not blame her. She's got enough strikes against her.* Suzanne gestured toward Cassandra's womb. "Is he the father?"

The girl shook her head. "No, he just come around for awhile before all this happen. After, he said if I say this man molested me, that he would take care of me, give me money for the months I'll be off the street cause of the baby."

"My God." Suzanne wanted to reach out, shake the girl, punish her for what she'd done to Nick, to all of them. *What was the modern equivalent of thirty pieces of silver, anyway?* But that wouldn't get Suzanne where she wanted to be. She had to be able to prove to Reickert that it was all a lie. And who was really responsible.

Still speaking as if she were in a dream, soft and unfocused, the girl went on. "But he hasn't been around for awhile."

Suzanne wondered if this distancing, this altered state, was the girl's way of releasing control, being able to speak to Suzanne. Perhaps Suzanne could take advantage of that state to plant some strong ideas about right and wrong.

"What if he doesn't come back?"

"He will. He promised!"

"You just said he hasn't been around. I think he's got what he wants, with Nick about to be fried by the police department. He won't need you for anything."

The expression on the girl's face let Suzanne know the thought had already occurred to her. "Fuck him. I don't need his money."

"Cassandra, don't you have family to take you in?" Suzanne asked. "There must be someone, somewhere, who cares about what happens to you."

"If that was true, don't you think I'd be there? They could care less." Her eyes had turned to black marble. "Why I should trust you? You just trying to twist me to save him. Everyone's always just trying to rip everyone off. I just got there first this time."

Suzanne wanted to wipe the proud look off the girl's face. "So what is it you want? Money?"

"I gotta take care of my baby." She shrugged. "Don't want to be a welfare momma. That's why I work the streets, to have a better life. I'm not in the projects. I got my own place. It isn't much, but it's all mine." She stared at Suzanne. "I don't have no pimp running my life. No one tells me what to do."

"Except Jojo." Suzanne tempered the sarcasm, but it still came through.

Cassandra looked away. "So what's new? The world goes round, mama."

"Sooner or later, this will all come out. Do you know they can charge you with perjury for your part in it? You want to have your baby in jail?" Suzanne asked. The quick gasp of breath was answer enough. "I can intercede for you and promise you won't have to face charges if you tell the truth, and clear Nick."

I hope those aren't empty words, she thought. Reickert would probably go along with her, as long as she could deliver a full confession.

I hope.

"I don't know." The girl's sudden discontent must have disturbed the kitten, who woke and jumped down with a yowl. Cassandra got to her feet and paced across the kitchen and back. She murmured vague phrases Suzanne couldn't catch. Finally she stopped before Suzanne and looked her in the eye. "You telling me, straight up, I'll walk? No charges on the streetwalking count or lying to the cops?" Her chin firmed up as she moved into negotiating mode. "Your word?"

Suzanne nodded. "I'll take you straight to the police chief myself so you can get the word from him."

The girl considered the offer, and agreed at last. "I must be *loco*. We got to meet somewhere Jojo won't know, and I'll need protection from him, too." She smiled for the first time. "But you're a crazy bitch, too, to come here, to ask me this." She looked sad. "No one ever cared about me the way you love him."

Suzanne stood up, legs shaky with relief. "You're young yet. Give yourself some time, Cassandra." *Now what?* "Can I call the chief?" Cassandra nodded, and Suzanne dialed the number for the station, then actually got through to Reickert himself, using the pretext of a legal emergency.

"Chief, it's Suzanne Taylor. I'm sure you remember me."

A shocked pause preceded his choked response."Yes, I remember. What can I do for you?"

"Can you meet me at the Point in an hour?" Suzanne glanced over to Cassandra. "I have a witness who can tell you the truth about what happened, as long as she can be protected. Up till now, she's been threatened and, shall we say, 'persuaded' by your officers."

Reickert said nothing at first. After a long pause, he spoke, voice thick with emotion. "Is that so? I think I could fit that into my schedule."

"I thought you might. But I'm serious about this conspiracy. Don't tell anyone you're coming," she said. "Anyone."

"Now look here, Miz Taylor—

"No, you look here. I'm not letting anything happen to this girl. Or to Nick. Either you're interested in the truth, or I'll find someone higher up who will be. Someone who's not beholden to a certain city councilman."

Another pause, then a cough. "All right, then. The Point in an hour."

"You crazy, girl," Cassandra said as Suzanne clicked her phone off.

Suzanne smiled. "Maybe so. We'll see what he does."

She hated the thought of being at the Point, the state park located at the meeting place of the Allegheny and Monongahela rivers, where it formed the Ohio, especially this time of year. The wind off the water would be freezing. But she'd promised this girl she'd be safe. At the Point, they'd have a clear view all around, and they would be out of range of possible snipers on Mount Washington. Surely she couldn't represent this girl because she had a blatant conflict of interest, but there was no reason she couldn't watch out for her, at least for now.

"This isn't the end, Cassandra. We'll get you help with the baby. You're sticking your neck out, and I know it. I promise you'll come out of this okay."

"We'll see." The thin girl didn't sound optimistic. "I'll get dressed."

She pushed off the chair and went into the other room. For a moment, Suzanne wondered whether she would call Jojo, to warn him, set them all up. Then she spied a cell phone lying on the kitchen counter. She hadn't taken it with her. Maybe they'd be all right. As the saying went, the truth might set them free.

Chapter Twenty-Six

Fifteen minutes later, they were heading west on Penn Avenue toward the city. Cassandra was quiet on the way, lost in her thoughts as she stared out the passenger window, one hand on her belly. Traffic was light through the Strip, since it was a weekday afternoon. They'd be at the Point on time.

Suzanne glanced at her companion every so often, not sure exactly what to say. Small talk seemed out of place. She didn't know the girl, didn't know her background, didn't know what had brought her to this particular place in these circumstances. Cassandra's history was none of her business, and she had no right to pry. The future, however—that was a place where Suzanne could have some impact.

They pulled into the parking lot on the Mon side, Suzanne's eyes searching out potential trouble. No police cars in sight. Just the usual lone walkers this time of year. In summer, whole families came down to stroll the waterfront sidewalks, especially when the fountain was operational. She and her girls had enjoyed many picnics on the park grounds. But this was no picnic.

"We'll walk up to the pool," Suzanne said, then she opened the door. "We're under the bridge there. If anyone's coming, we'll see them."

She didn't move in her seat. "Look, *chica,* I don't know whether this is gonna fly. I've got to take care of my baby. Maybe it's better if..."

"We've got to stick together on this. I'm backing you one hundred percent. I'm going to walk right up there with you." Suzanne studied her, praying she wouldn't give in to fear. "Come on. We're clear."

The girl reluctantly climbed out of the car, walking with Suzanne, who matched her step to the girl's slower one. They crossed the space past the Fort Pitt Museum, and moved on to the area of the reflecting pool. Suzanne took a look around the park, not seeing anyone suspicious. Cassandra took a seat on a bench, pulling her thin coat close around her thickened body to protect her from the cold wind.

Suzanne, more nervous as the minutes passed, was grateful to finally spy Reickert walking toward them. He was alone.

As he approached her, he scanned the area, perhaps looking for a trap as well. That was the atmosphere they all lived in. "Miz Taylor," he said by way of greeting.

"Chief." She shoved her hands into her pockets, the wind blowing right through her.

"Let's hear the girl."

"Let's talk terms first." She placed herself between the chief and Cassandra. "This poor child is pregnant. One of your officers used that against her to persuade her to give false evidence. She needs the department's help. I've promised her she'll get it."

His eyebrow ratcheted up. "You're generous with my department's money."

"The department can pay her in other ways besides cash, and you know it. She's got charges, and you've got some pull there. But cash is good, too. Better to pay for the truth than pay for a lie, isn't that so, chief?" She eyed him, thinking of the way he'd handled Nick. "People do an awful lot of things for money."

He gave her a grudging shrug. "Haven't heard

what she has to say."

"Cassandra, come here, honey." Suzanne beckoned the shivering girl forward.

The young woman came closer, several inches shorter than either of them and clearly more vulnerable. She took a shuddering breath and kept her arms crossed against the onslaught of the wind. "You're gonna make sure my baby's taken care of, right?" she asked Reickert.

"You know what you're talking about, sweet thing?"

She only nodded, brown eyes wide and suddenly innocent. She shivered as if she would dissolve in the cold. Suzanne wanted to put her arm around the girl for support, but wasn't sure she'd accept it. "My baby?" she insisted.

"The chief will do everything he can, Cassandra. I will too," Suzanne promised.

Reickert moved so he stood between the young woman and the wind. Suzanne approved. "Give me your name, your address, and tell me what you know about this."

The words came hesitantly at first, but then they tumbled loose faster, lighter by the minute, as the burden of the lie was lifted from her shoulders. Suzanne listened, praying Reickert would credit the girl with the truth of what she said. He'd have some money he could give her. He could also waive her charges and deal with a potential perjury situation over her testimony on the incident. He had to. He just had to.

"You'll say this down at the station?" he asked gruffly. "Then testify against Washington? And any of the others?"

She nodded, still trembling. "That Lieutenant done nothing to me. He was a nice guy."

Reickert coughed and eyed Suzanne. "Maybe those bozos in Internal Affairs need a little shaking up, too," he added. He shook her hand. "Will you ladies come back downtown so we can put this on the record?"

Cassandra looked frightened. Suzanne took the risk this time, and put her arm around the girl's shoulder. Cassandra didn't pull away. "I'll be there with you," Suzanne promised.

As they reached the parking lot, Reickert asked, "Does Nick know?"

Suzanne shook her head. "We came straight from Cassandra's house."

"I think he ought to be told. You want to do it?"

"No, I don't think I'd better. He'll be angry I interfered. God knows I complain about him meddling in my life often enough."

"Damn fool ought to be grateful," Reickert muttered. "All right, I'll notify him later this afternoon, after we get a full statement from the girl." Reickert looked at Suzanne as though she'd given him the best Christmas present ever. "I knew in my heart it couldn't be true. You've done one hell of a public service."

"I had to do it," she said, over and over, breathing a deep sigh of relief. Nick would get his life back, and that was worth whatever it cost.

****

Suzanne stayed with Cassandra Trujillo as she'd promised, through the sworn testimony Chief Reickert wanted on the record. He asked the questions himself, until he seemed satisfied he had what he needed. He gave the girl a hundred dollars out of a witness fund, then Suzanne took her to one of the pregnancy assistance agencies, to arrange some income and care for the girl while she was awaiting the birth of her child. Once she'd given her statement, the girl seemed reluctant to return to her small house, as much as she'd bragged about it before.

In her bright, cheerful office decorated with photos of mothers and children, the agency worker, Mrs. Johnson, said, "We have a house where some girls stay. Did you bring your things?" Cassandra shook her head. The woman patted her shoulder. "Don't worry. We have someone who can take you over to pick up what you need."

Suzanne smiled at the girl. "You've done the right thing. These women will help you prepare for the next step—becoming a mother." When the girl's worried face didn't change, she added, "I expect Jojo and the others will be off the streets very soon."

The girl shrugged. "Probably best I leave, too," she said morosely. "Start over again in a new town."

Suzanne nodded. "I'm sure Mrs. Johnson here can help you decide about that." She dug in her purse for a business card. "I really appreciate what you've done. I hope you'll stay in touch. Let me know about the baby?"

"Sure, whatever," the girl said. At Mrs. Johnson's urging, she turned and went into the back, taking the first steps toward a new life.

Suzanne stared after her, praying she hadn't sacrificed Cassandra's life to improve her own. Certainly the girl's life could be different with a fresh start through the agency. Maybe she'd even stay off the street after the baby was born. Suzanne had no illusions about the life of a prostitute. If the girl was hooking that young, it was because she felt she had no other options. Suzanne had sent clients to this particular agency before, and knew they did good work. All she could do was hope Cassandra discovered a better life.

The clock on the wall chimed six o'clock. The afternoon had moved so fast. In the parking lot, Suzanne called home and Hope answered. Suzanne explained she was still downtown. "I'm leaving now, so I should be home in half an hour or so. Is everything okay?"

"Just fine, Mom."

"If you girls are hungry, go ahead and make some mac and cheese or something."

"Okay. See you soon."

As she turned the key to start the car, Suzanne wondered whether Nick had heard the good news yet. Her adrenaline fading, chunks of reality began to fall into her mind. *What was I thinking to go to that neighborhood alone? What if the girl had a pimp there? Or a group of drug dealers? What if Jojo had come while I was still there?* She shuddered, thinking of the alternate outcomes. Good thing she hadn't put too much thought into her decision—too many reasons she could have talked herself out of going to see Cassandra.

And only one to make herself go.

She smiled, an inner warmth filling her as she thought about Nick's future, now rescued from dishonor. She couldn't wait to see him again.

Chapter Twenty-Seven

Nick heard the doorbell and ruefully checked his worn sweats and stocking feet, not exactly dressed for company. He'd been hanging around the house most of that week, except for his regular run to take Suzanne's girls to school in the morning. After school they had so many different activities, it had proven difficult to catch up with them. So he'd called them as agreed about five p.m., just to make sure they were both home.

The bell rang again, and he regretted the cluttered end table and other signs of disorderly housekeeping, but he clicked off the mindless talk show. He'd only had it on for noise, so he didn't feel quite so alone. It was dark out. He picked up his pistol and held it in his hand, ready, just in case, as he pulled the door open.

On the doorstep under the light, he found Hank Ferguson, his pudgy face split ear to ear with a huge grin, a six-pack of beer in one hand and a white bag from Tony's in the other. Totally unexpected, the appearance of his friend confused him.

"What's up, Hank?" Nick asked.

"What's up? You mean you haven't heard?" Hank pushed past Nick into the house, and Nick caught a whiff of Italian spices. "What the hell happened in here?"

Nick followed him into the living room, where his former partner was surveying the disaster.

Seeing it through someone else's eyes really demonstrated how much he'd let it slip. "Oh, that. Haven't had much need to take care of it, I guess."

Hank eyed the gun. "Don't think you need that, pal."

"Huh? Oh, probably not." Nick set the pistol on the counter and went back to the first question. "Heard what?"

Hank set his packages down and grabbed Nick by both shoulders. "You're clear, man! Washington set you up, but Reickert shut down the investigation today. You're back on as of eight a.m. tomorrow!"

Nick shook his head, wondering if this was another of the dreams he'd been having. It just seemed too miraculous. "Washington? Says who?"

"The girl came clean with Reickert, told him everything!" Hank was clearly amazed at Nick's good fortune. "I thought for sure Suzanne would have called you."

"Suzanne? Why?"

Hank froze. "Hey, these beers are getting warm. Want one?" he asked in a clear attempt at diversion.

No, no, something was up there. "Why Suzanne?" Nick demanded. "What did she do?" He moved around in front of Hank, who had just popped his can open. Foam rose through the hole, then settled back in.

"Maybe I'd better let her—"

"Too late. You already said it." *If she went behind my back...*

Hank took a step away. "Now, Nick, there's no need to blow a gasket here. She asked me for—"

"*You* let her get involved in this? What the hell were you thinking? These people aren't just playing around!" Nick rubbed his face with his hands, trying to keep his temper under control.

"She was going to try something anyway," Hank said. "Wasn't it better that I could help?"

"What did she ask you for?"

Hank took another step back.

"Stop that! I'm not going to hit you. I'm not going to hit *her*. I just can't believe you'd do something while there was an investigation going on through Internal Affairs!" He glared at Hank, then took a breath and forced his face into a smile. He wanted Hank to come clean. "Now, what did she ask you for?"

"The girl's name and address."

"And you gave it to her?" Nick counted to ten, then changed his mind and took a beer. He drank about half the can, then looked back at his partner. "Did you know what she was going to do with it?"

Hank nodded, and took another pull from his can. "She said she'd go talk to her, see if she could find out the truth."

Nick was torn between astonishment that Hank would jeopardize an ongoing investigation by stealing information from a police file, and awe that Suzanne would go to such an extent to try to rescue him. Were they all crazy? Speechless, he shuffled around the room, trying to make sense of what he'd heard. *But it worked,* a tiny voice repeated in the back of his mind. He ignored it.

Hank hung back till Nick relaxed and allowed a small smile. "It might have been crazy, son, but I had to let her try. If there was anything else I could have done to help her, I would have." He chuckled. "You should have seen her, Nick. She came barreling into my office, all over me for not doing more. She demanded the information so she could take care of things, since we men couldn't seem to handle the situation." He shook his head. "She's a real tiger, and she loves you an awful lot."

Nick collapsed into his recliner. His head buzzing with the revelations which confronted him, he suddenly remembered there was a beer in his hand. He stared at it for a minute, then drank it and set the can down.

"So she got the girl to confess?"

"Reickert said you'd been completely cleared and that Washington, along with Malron and Vasquez, had been implicated in fabricating her original testimony. They're gone." Hank came closer and sat in the chair next to Nick's. "Have you had anything to eat today? Man, if you're going to drink beer like that, you'd better eat something." He took sandwiches out of the bag and set one in Nick's hand.

Gone? The Three Amigos, removed from his squad room? A ripple of pure relief ran through him. He absentmindedly took a bite from the sandwich, then set it down on the table. He couldn't believe it.

"Suzanne went, herself, to talk to this girl? What did she say?"

"How should I know? Whatever it was, it worked!" He bit happily into the other sandwich.

Nick knew the general area where the girl lived, since he'd filled out the papers when he first booked her for soliciting him. It was not the kind of place a female professional ought to be, even by daylight. *How could Suzanne take such a risk?* Then heard Hank's words: "She loves you an awful lot."

All along, Nick had felt he was fighting an uphill battle with Suzanne. Every time he got close, she always managed to set him apart again. He knew she was only protecting herself. No matter what he'd tried, he couldn't seem to convince her he was not John Taylor and had no intention of hurting her. But this crazy stunt showed she had real feelings for him. The impact of this revelation overshadowed even the news of his miraculous exoneration.

"She loves me," he said to Hank.

"No kidding." He chuckled and went on with his dinner.

"I should call her." As Nick stood up, he swayed a little, partly because he'd had a beer on an empty stomach, partly because he'd been presented with too much earth-shattering information at once. Hank immediately set him back down in the chair.

"Eat." Hank gave him back the sandwich. "You can call her later. First, get hold of yourself."

"But—"

"No buts. Eat."

Nick complied without further argument, realizing it wouldn't be of much use anyway. He went on with his thoughts about Suzanne and the wonder of his new understanding. *What would he say to her? How did you thank someone for restoring your dream, your life?*

Hank finished eating and drank some more of his beer. "So you want to go out and celebrate?"

"Yes, I think I do."

"You want I should call some of the guys?"

Nick smiled. "No, I think I'll call Suzanne and take the opportunity to thank her for what she's done."

"What? You're going out with the girls instead of us?" Hank half-whined, all-teasing.

"Just one girl," Nick said. "One very special girl." He punched Hank playfully on the shoulder. "But thanks for the sandwiches, and the help. It was good to hear the news from you."

"My pleasure," Hank said. "I've been pretty worried about you with all that claptrap going on. Glad it's over." He stood up and stretched. "Guess I'll go home and spend the night with my wife."

I wish I could say that, Nick thought. *Maybe someday soon...* "Good night, old man. See you at the office tomorrow." He laughed. "Hey, that sounds real good. See you at the office tomorrow!"

"Thank her for me, too." Hank picked up his jacket and ambled out the door, tipping his hat.

Nick waited until he drove away before he picked up the phone. Conscience stinging him, he called his buddy Charley. He should have heard back about the computer trace by now. After what Suzanne had done, he owed her an answer about those emails.

He got his friend on the second ring. “Hey, Charley, it’s Nick Sansone. Checking up on the—”

“Oh, man, your friend definitely has stepped in something,” Charley said without any introduction. “Yesterday afternoon, we finally deciphered the last piece. You’re not gonna believe this.”

“Try me.”

“The emails came from a cell phone that belongs to Councilman Morgan’s kid. What the hell’s going on?”

Nick gave him the briefest of explanations, all the while his nerves burned hot at the thought of Morgan putting his boy up to these tactics. The man just didn’t learn. Bad enough to send paid goons out to deliver his messages. Suborning his own son should be a crime in itself.

After he got Charley off the phone, he dialed Suzanne’s number. One of the girls answered, Riviera maybe. “Is your mom home?”

“Sure, just a minute.”

In the background, he heard the girl calling for Suzanne, who picked up an extension, probably in her office. The original connection cut off as Suzanne answered. “Hello?”

“What have you been up to?” Nick said, trying to sound angry. He would never have asked her to put herself at such risk, especially not on his account. He didn’t intend to let her off the hook easy.

“Up to? Now what’s happened? More trouble?”

“Where you’re concerned, there’s always trouble.”

“Funny, that’s what I always say about cops,”

she said. He heard the smile in her voice.

"Don't even try to put me off, Suzanne. I can't believe you'd..." He sighed. She obviously knew why he'd called. "Hank was just here. He told me everything."

"Oh." An awkward silence followed.

"Can you get away tonight for awhile? We can go out somewhere to talk. You can explain what the hell you thought you were doing, you crazy woman!"

"You're the second or third person to call me crazy today," Suzanne said. "I'm going to start believing it pretty soon."

"Well, can you?"

"Of course. Let me make sure the girls have everything they need, then I'll meet you...at Frederick's?"

"Sounds good. See you in an hour?"

"Fine."

Nick hurriedly showered and dressed, wearing what he knew was her favorite aftershave, and debated stopping by the grocery store to buy some roses. Nah. He'd leave that for later. Right now, he just wanted to get his hands on her. In every possible way. She'd managed to redeem him, single-handedly.

The conversation they'd had with that Pittsburgh Press reporter must have ignited something in her. He'd seen the fire in her eyes when he insisted on waiting until the investigation had run its course. He'd assumed everything would turn out fine. Maybe it would have. But maybe it wouldn't.

She'd changed it all.

He arrived at Frederick's before she did and chose an isolated corner booth, so they'd have a chance to talk without interruption. The place was a neighborhood bar along Route 19, quiet and casual, mostly inhabited by regular patrons who liked the simple red vinyl booths and the bartender's pretty wife Beverly, who waitressed most nights. Bev came over as soon as he was seated. "What can I get you, handsome?"

"A beer. No. Make that an orange juice," he said. *Better keep my head clear.*

"Straight?" As he nodded, Beverly made little clucking sounds and went over to pass Fred the order. She was back with a tall, icy glass of orange juice almost immediately.

Several minutes later, Suzanne came in the door, wearing dark narrow pants and a black turtleneck, wrapped in a large puffy knitted shawl of multicolored earth tones. Nick slid out of the booth and came across the room to take her in his arms. She returned his embrace, pressing up against him. He could tell she didn't want to let go any more than he did.

"It's good to see you," she whispered near his ear. Her warm breath stirred him in a way he knew they couldn't act on in public.

He reluctantly released her, but left his arm around her shoulder while they walked over to the booth. "Zinfandel?" he asked.

"What's that?" She peered at his glass. "Orange juice?" She shrugged. "That sounds good."

"Bev, another?" Nick called, and the woman nodded in reply. He slid close to Suzanne, leaving his arm where it was. "So."

She smiled mysteriously. He waited, just enjoying the feel of her next to him, until the server brought the second glass of juice. "So."

"I heard today we were right. Charley traced those emails to Morgan's son's cell. So either the kid sent them, or his dad used the phone. Either way, I'll pass on that information to the local department. They'll be pressing charges against him."

Suzanne's smile faded into shadows. "Morgan is

an idiot. I can't believe he'd set his kid up like this. Maddie's brokenhearted about him."

"I agree. But he's not the only idiot I know." He studied her, thinking he'd never seen anything so beautiful. "Hank tells me the Three Amigos are history, because you went out to East Liberty to find this girl. That could have had very bad consequences."

"Why can't you just say thanks without nagging me about taking risks? Just once, Sansone, it would be awfully refreshing."

His fingers squeezed her shoulder. "No, babe, I meant to say that I'm just amazed. You never fail to surprise me, counselor."

The way her face lit up showed him that pleased her. "I hope not, Detective. I don't want to be boring."

"I don't think you'll bore me for some time to come, dear Suzanne." He kissed her, then held her tightly. "I will never be able to thank you enough."

When he released her, she wiped a tear from her cheek. "I'm the one who should thank you, for all you've done for my girls, and for me."

"You all mean the world to me."

She smiled. "Back at you." Her eyes sparkled, and he cut off her next words in the most pleasant way he could think of. That kiss led to another, and soon they left Frederick's and retired to Suzanne's house to hold each other close through the night.

****

The next morning, Nick marched into the stationhouse, his head held high. He personally watched with satisfaction as Washington, Malron and Vasquez emptied their personal belongings into boxes, then were escorted from the police headquarters building. Still uneasy that the matter was really over and done with, he felt out of place in his office, worried he'd somehow changed in the weeks he'd been away.

Chief Reickert had been so guilty about his lack of support that he'd offered Nick an upcoming plum assignment: escorting an extradited prisoner to California. The trip would take a week, and all his airfare and hotels would be paid by the city. "You deserve to get away," Reickert had said.

Nick was looking forward to the trip. It would be a good chance to wipe the slate clean, get all the lingering depression and frustration out of his system, and start fresh with Suzanne when he returned. Too bad she couldn't go with him, but this was business. From now on, he intended to keep business and his private life separate.

****

The girls had gone to a Saturday afternoon basketball game, and Suzanne paced through the empty house restlessly. She'd run laundry, shaken the rugs, and even emptied the clogged trap under the bathroom sink. The only office work she was interested in was a pending call from Greg Morgan's attorney approving the settlement she'd proposed. Under the gun with the criminal charges for stalking and threatening her, as well as the harassment by communication charges, she guessed he'd have to accept. But she didn't think any news would come through until Monday, when the corporate attorney-types returned to work.

In quiet desperation, she broke her own resolve to leave the dishes for the girls to do when they returned, and washed them, setting them in a wooden rack to dry. She looked out the window across the yard as she worked, the snow piled a foot deep waiting for next week's January thaw. She couldn't wait until the tulips she and Nick had planted in the fall would stick up their bright, cheery heads.

How long ago that was! The winter had been

shot through with drama, thanks to Nick's personnel problem and her own dealings with the Morgans. But both those matters were concluded, and it was time to face the future.

Nick's commandeering style still irritated Suzanne from time to time, but he'd done much to scale it back. She'd begun listening to second thoughts she had during her intake interviews, and refusing to take some potentially dangerous cases, now that she'd seen how vulnerable she could be. So there was hope.

Hope also defined her relationship with Nick. Still wary of commitment, their time together over the past months had convinced her his love was sincere. She'd found hers was, too. He'd become a part of her life. Now that he was gone, she missed him.

He'd been on his assignment only a week, yet it had seemed so much longer. Ten times a day she wondered when he would call, or wished he were there during an empty hour. What had she done before they'd met? She must have had other activities which filled those moments, because she surely had never spent so much time staring off into space as she had these last few days...

A click of a door latch closing somewhere in the house brought her daydream to a standstill. She turned and dried her hands quickly, listening for a greeting or footsteps, but heard neither. Her heart skipped a beat as she realized she was alone, miles out in the country, and her gun was...where?

In her home office, out of reach. Looking around, she realized she had no real place to hide in the kitchen, though she could run out the back door, if she could only make herself move. But she couldn't. A sharp knife was in reach. She grabbed it, holding it in front of her, watching the doorway in horror.

Nick's head suddenly popped around the corner.

As he spotted the knife, he stiffened. "What's happened?"

"What's happened? An idiot's entered my house, apparently. Holy mother, Nick. If I'd been armed, I could have killed you!" She dropped the knife to the counter and he crossed the room to wrap his arms around her. Suzanne wanted to punch him, but his arms felt wonderful around her. She slipped hers around him, familiarity guiding her hands, and buried her head in his broad chest.

"I didn't think," he said. "Has there been more trouble? Have you heard anything from Morgan?"

Suzanne shook her head, her cheek feeling the texture of his flannel shirt. Nick's hands moved on her back, massaging her, releasing pockets of tension. Deep sounds of pleasure escaped her throat as he worked. Her neck received the same treatment, and as it let go its tightness, her head eased back against his shoulder. Nick tipped her chin up and kissed her, a kiss born of a week's frustration and need, and relief of coming through the fire.

Feeling the emotion echoing through her, Suzanne was possessed by an overwhelming urge to take Nick to bed on the spot. She unbuttoned his shirt slowly, slipping her hands inside to brush through the dark hair of his chest. He shivered and stopped kissing her long enough to ask, in a thick voice, "What about the girls?"

"They're not here," she whispered. "Won't be back for hours." She took his hand and pulled him toward the stairs. Feeling wanton, she led him up to her peach-toned bedroom, where they undressed each other at a pace like pouring honey, and slipped into her bed, letting their suppressed emotion and fear and anger transform itself into steamy passion. Afterward, they held each other, heat radiating from their bodies, all thought chased from their minds, gradually drowsing into blissful sleep.

Sometime later, the door slammed downstairs and woke Suzanne. She heard her daughters' excited voices and footsteps coming toward the stairs and started to get up, but Nick reached out sleepily to pull her back under the covers.

"It's too late," he murmured. "You'll never get dressed before they get here."

Embarrassed, she realized he was right. The footsteps headed straight for her door.

Riviera burst in, pigtails flying, calling, "Mom! Where's Nick?" As she surveyed the room, she diagnosed the situation and blushed beet red. "Oh, look. There he is," she said, and disappeared. Hope passed by, looked in quickly, said, "Hey, Nick," then giggled and mercifully shut the door.

"Oh, my God," Suzanne said, burying her face in the pillow. Nick chuckled, and she smacked him on the arm. "How can you laugh?"

"Because your face is hilarious. Not like they haven't figured out the score between us, my darling. Now come on, let's get dressed. I missed my girls."

A few minutes later, they came downstairs to join the girls in the kitchen. Hope poured some cola into two glasses. Riviera opened a bag of chips. When the adults appeared, she poured the contents into a bowl so they could all share, and they came to be enfolded in his arms, one on each side. Nick broke into a huge smile.

"I think they missed you, too." Suzanne said. She took some fruit juice from the refrigerator.

"Aren't you going to ask what I brought you?"

"You brought us something?" Riviera asked. "What is it? Where is it?" She took his hand and pulled him back toward the front door. Hope smiled at her mother, then followed the others to the truck, not wanting to look too eager. They returned in a matter of minutes with new T-shirts sporting

California designs. Nick had chosen one for each girl in her favorite colors and with her particular causes in mind, with a Hollywood logo for Riviera and an environmental issue for Hope. How did he remember all these things?

"And for you, my lady?" Nick said, handing Suzanne a small jewelry box.

Alarms went off in her head as she guessed it was an engagement ring of some sort. *No! It's not time for that yet!* But he winked as she looked up at him. He'd read her panic. "It's an awesome California thing, dude," he said.

She smiled and opened the box to find a mood ring. "Wow. I haven't had one of these since high school," she said.

"Put it on, Mom. Let's see what kind of mood you're in," Hope said.

"Should have done that half an hour ago," Riviera said in a stage whisper. Hope, standing next to her, quelled her sister's enthusiasm with a controlled elbow to the ribs.

Suzanne placed the ring on her right hand ring finger, and they all waited, watching, as the ring changed from black to amber to green, and finally blue. "What does blue mean?"

Hope read from the card in the box. "'Content and happy.'"

"Well, then, it's right." She gave Nick a hug and kiss, and the girls joined in for a group hug.

"Me, too," Nick said. "I really missed all of you."

Once they finally let go of each other, they sat around the table, sharing stories of the time they'd spent apart. As the evening wore on, Suzanne realized she was perfectly content. Her objections to a permanent relationship with Nick receded to a place far back in her mind. For tonight, at least, she didn't intend to be separated from her lover and friend.

Chapter Twenty-Eight

Two weeks later, Suzanne stood on the doorstep of Maddie Morgan's home, impatiently tapping her foot, the signed divorce decree in an envelope in her hand. The nightmare had ended, saved by the agreement of her husband's lawyer to bifurcate the divorce. That meant they could put off the contested division of the property and proceed with the legal divorce immediately. Maddie had jumped at the chance to finally terminate her relationship with Greg Morgan, who'd been acting even more erratic of late. She'd even called that morning to invite Suzanne for a cup of coffee to celebrate after Katie had gone to school.

But if Maddie was expecting her, what was the hold-up? Suzanne looked at her watch. She had appointments scheduled with clients just after noon, and she couldn't be out here all day. Maybe Maddie was upstairs and hadn't heard the bell. She pushed the amber-lit button twice more.

Suddenly the door opened and someone grabbed Suzanne's wrist. She dropped her purse and the papers she was holding as she was yanked inside the darkened house and unceremoniously thrown to the couch.

"Well, look what we have here," said a caustic male voice Suzanne recognized immediately as that of Greg Morgan. "If it isn't Miz Taylor, attorney extraordinaire. Come to celebrate with my dear ex-wife?"

Suzanne's eyes, blinded at first, took some time adjusting to the difference in light levels from the sunlit street to the Morgan living room, with its heavy drapes pulled closed. The shadowy figure pacing before the coffee table had to be Greg. A survey of her surroundings gradually showed her Maddie and her daughter on the loveseat six feet away, wrapped tight in each other's arms. Maddie's dress was torn, and the little girl's hair was unkempt. She still wore her pajamas.

"Suzanne, I'm so sorry," Maddie said quickly. "He made me call, then pulled the phone out of the wall—"

"Shut up!" Greg shouted. He moved his arm to point at Maddie, and Suzanne caught a glint of light off a handgun with a long barrel similar in appearance to Nick's .357. Maddie whimpered and clutched her child closer.

"Mr. Morgan, this isn't the answer to your situation," Suzanne said as calmly as she could.

"Oh, yeah? What do you know about 'my situation'? Hmmm?" The man came close to her, leaning over her shoulder from behind. The smell of alcohol was almost overpowered by his body odor. He was sweating up a storm. "You think I can just go on about my business, now that you've helped my wife—my *ex*-wife—steal half of everything I own?"

He staggered around to sit next to her on the couch. Suzanne fought every impulse not to pull away from him as he brought the gun up close to her head. "I'll lose my council seat, you know. Divorce doesn't appeal to the voters." What light there was showed her the fire in his eyes which never failed to frighten her. He stared at her for a long few moments, then he shoved himself to his feet, stumbling across the room.

"All she had to do was take care of the house

and raise the children. I didn't ask her for a Goddamned dime. I paid for everything." He gestured broadly around the room, almost falling as he waved his arm. "I worked ten hours a day, sometimes fourteen, to keep her in our nice house. And she left it! For this piece of crap! Did you think we had a bad house?" he demanded of Suzanne, the gun vaguely pointing in her direction.

"It was a wonderful house," she said, sharply aware of Maddie crying behind her. Funny how law school never taught some of the skills that might really be useful. Investigating police conspiracies. How to get out of hostage situations. Ridding one's life of a crazy man...

"See, Maddie, even the bitch thinks the house is great. So I hit you a couple of times. I got a temper. So I'm sorry." He lurched forward in a mock bow, nearly fell. Maddie burst into tears. "That's it!" Morgan yelled. "I'm so tired of listening to all the whining and crying. It's going to stop now!" He stalked over to where Maddie sat.

Is he going to kill her? Suzanne wondered, heart racing. *Would he kill his child? What was he up to before she came in? Had her arrival changed his plan?* She strained to see what he was doing, trying to guess if she could do anything to stop him. She was fifteen feet from the door. In his present frame of mind, Morgan wouldn't hesitate to shoot her if she ran. Or Maddie and her child. Or all of the above. *Keep thinking, Suzanne...*

"Where's Joshua?" she asked. Maybe a new train of thought would divert him from whatever plan he had. "Figured you'd bring him along to show him how clever you are."

"What do you care?" Morgan sneered. A slow grin came to him. "Did you like his little messages? He thought your girls were real hot chicks, you know. Too bad the one was as stubborn as her mother. She needs to be taught a lesson in how to treat her man."

Suzanne growled and got to her feet."Yeah? I should teach you a lesson in—"

Drunk as he was, Greg was across the distance between them in a split second. He backhanded her, knocking her onto the couch. Her face felt like it had exploded, from her cheek right up into her eye. She moaned as the pain echoed through the nerves and rattled back.

"He's at school," Greg said. "Thanks for your concern. Now shut the hell up."

Maddie gasped. "Greg, please, don't do this."

"I don't take orders from you!" Morgan set the gun down behind him, still well within reach. He picked up a roll of duct tape from the coffee table. Maddie's eyes widened and she whimpered as he came closer to her. He grabbed his daughter's arm and yanked her away from her mother. "Go sit over there with the bitch lawyer."

Katie ducked away from her father and came to sit in Suzanne's lap. She was trembling so hard she could barely sit still. Greg pulled a length of tape from the roll and ripped it off, using it to cover the lower half of Maddie's face. He added two more pieces, securing them on top of the first, then ripped another long piece he used to secure her wrists behind her.

Nursing her swelling face, Suzanne realized Morgan had moved out of range of his weapon. It might be their only chance. "Katie," she whispered breathlessly in the child's ear, "can you run to the door and get out? I can keep him from getting the gun before you get there. Run fast like a jackrabbit to the neighbor's house. Ask your neighbor to call the police, so someone will come help us."

The child continued to tremble, but she finally nodded.

"Okay. One, two, three-go!" Suzanne pushed the child off her lap and heard the pattering feet run to the door. As Morgan realized the child was moving, he started to turn, but Suzanne stood up, blocking his line of sight. She was on the wrong side of him, so there was no way she could get between him and the gun, but she could delay him in reaching it.

"You little whore! Katherine Marie, you get back here now, or I'm going to shoot your mother!"

"Katie, keep going!" Suzanne called to her, reaching out toward Morgan. "Run fast! Get help!" She heard the lock turn and the door flew open, flooding the room with light. She was face to face with a madman. Morgan was livid. His eyes had taken on such a burning intensity she thought they'd explode. He grabbed her shoulders and shook her, snapping her neck back and forward, then threw her to the couch and leapt for the gun. In the few moments before he'd closed the door again, Suzanne had seen Maddie's terror-filled eyes watching Greg's every move.

We're going to die.

Morgan went to the window, peering out from behind the drape in search of his daughter. He was cursing and tapping the gun barrel on the windowsill. Suzanne ached from the tip of her head to the kneecap that had hit the coffee table when he tossed her down. Only the knowledge that he could shoot her if she didn't pay close attention forced her to sit up. The act of coming upright set her head spinning. She saw him out of the corner of her eye, as he turned slowly toward her.

His voice was devoid of emotion. "You just can't leave well enough alone, can you? You always gotta meddle in other people's plans." He took a couple of steps forward, stopping unsteadily halfway between Suzanne and the door. "We don't have much time, now, thanks to your damned heroics." He looked back and forth between Maddie and her attorney. "So, who gets it first?"

Maddie shook her head and moaned, but she was helpless in her tape bonds.

"Now if I really loved you," he said to his former wife, crossing to sit beside her, "I'd shoot you first and put you out of your misery." Greg smoothed her hair like he would a child's, then cuddled her to his side with his left arm. "Come on, honey, you know we had sixteen good years together. Don't I owe you something?"

The guy was truly sick, and had nothing left to lose. Suzanne prayed that Katie would get help soon. She felt a trickle of liquid run down the side of her face. Could it be blood? Even if she'd been tricked into coming here, she couldn't accept that this was the end for her. *Come on, Suzanne. Stay focused.*

Even as she chastised herself, her vision faded, and her girls' faces rose up in her mind's eye, smiling and happy. A stab of pain ran through her at the thought she might never see them again.

And Nick...

The depth of loss that poured into her at the idea that she had been in his arms for the last time overwhelmed her. All the denial she'd carried with her for these past months washed away, leaving only the knowledge that her love and need for him was deep and everlasting. She'd tell him so the next time she saw him, and she'd do everything in her power to make them all a family, together.

If she got the chance.

Please let me have that chance...

Suzanne twitched at the click of a locked gun hammer. Greg Morgan had cocked the weapon and aimed it at Maddie, who he held tightly around the neck.

"This is harder than I thought it would be," he said, abruptly dropping the barrel of the gun to his lap. "Maybe it just takes practice."

Suzanne strained to see what he was doing. The closed curtains kept the room drenched in shadows. She rolled just a little sideways, trying to present the narrowest target possible. *What did he mean, "practice?"*

The meaning became all too clear as she saw his arm come up and point at her. "Thanks for everything," he said in a chilling tone. "I really mean that." There was a click and a flash. A bang reverberated through the room as he pulled the trigger.

****

Nick Sansone, in his office filling out duty assignments for his unit for the next two weeks, stopped when something coming over the police radio in his office caught his attention. The dispatcher gave the code for a hostage situation and sent the negotiating team to an address in an exclusive gated community, and gave the suspect's name as Morgan.

Say what? I don't think I heard that right.

He stepped away from his desk and turned up the radio. The dispatcher was sending more units. "Two known hostages, suspect is armed and considered dangerous," she added in her monotone voice. *Two hostages? Wonder if Suzanne knows...* He was about to pick up the phone and call Suzanne's office to tell her when there was a knock at his door.

"Nick?" It was Hank, the lines in his face deep as canyons.

Nick had never seen him look so old. He got to his feet slowly. "What is it?"

Hank stepped just inside the door, refusing the seat Nick offered him. "You heard the call to the Morgans' house?"

"Yeah. Who's the gunman? The councilman?" He was only half serious, but from the look on Hank's face as Nick came around his desk, he realized he'd guessed correctly. "Morgan? Really?"

"Nick, about the hostages." Hank looked at the floor, and Nick could see Hank's Adam's apple move as he swallowed several times. Horror washed over him, an icy bath, as he realized what Hank had come to tell him.

"Suzanne's there, isn't she?" As Hank nodded, his eyes full of compassion, Nick felt a huge void open around him and a rushing in his ears. *This can't be happening.*

"Hey, Nick? Nick!" In a blur, Hank was next to him, arm around his shoulders. Pain on his cheek told him Hank had slapped him. "Nick, man, get a grip on yourself!"

Nick shook off the dizziness and sat heavily on his desk, taking deep breaths. He put his arm out and grasped Hank's. "I'm okay. It just wasn't what I expected to hear." *Dear God, protect her,* he prayed, the faith of his grandparents and his parents coming to buoy him with a small bit of hope. "All right, let's go."

"Go? Nick, I think you'd better take it easy a minute," Hank said, trying to hold Nick down in his chair.

No way Hank was going to keep him from this. "I'm fine. I'm going. Are you coming?" He looked at his old partner, forcing a faint smile. "I'm not sure I'd be a very safe driver at the moment."

"I just came so you'd hear it from a friend, Nicky." He glanced at the door. "Reichert'll have my ass for this. All right. Let's go." Hank shouted to the office secretary they were leaving, and they grabbed their jackets and headed down the stairs before anyone could stop them.

All the way through Oakland, past the universities, Nick's mind raced through the possibilities. He was sure Suzanne had not expected

Morgan to be at Maddie's house. Maddie had a restraining order. She must have walked into some unexpected scene, which meant she wouldn't be armed. Hell, she probably wouldn't have been prepared at all. That meant she was as vulnerable as Maddie herself. It wasn't fair, after everything she'd done, saved Nick's whole career, to lose her now. He loved her more than anything in the world.

"How did they discover Suzanne was there, anyway?"

Hank swerved to avoid someone pulling out. "Apparently Morgan had his wife and daughter at gunpoint when Suzanne came to the house. The daughter escaped and went to the neighbor's house, and the neighbor called 911. The little girl picked up Suzanne's pocketbook from the front step on her way out, so they had all her ID." Hank smiled sadly. "She told the neighbor Suzanne told her to run for help, then kept her father from coming after her. Suzanne saved that little girl's life."

Nick leaned back in the seat, trying to relax, trying to keep himself from getting worked up. Suzanne always did have a soft spot for kids. He wanted some assurance that Suzanne could be saved. If Morgan had been pushed far enough to terrorize his family, then he'd crossed that line between safety and insanity. He'd have nothing to lose. Suzanne was in real danger.

"What about the son? Is he there too?"

"Don't know. I haven't heard that."

It was slow going on the Morgans' street, even though the department badge let them past the protective gate and the subsequent barriers. "Just park anywhere," Nick barked at last, frustrated. "We'll walk."

Hank pulled over immediately, then chased after Nick, who bailed out as soon as the car stopped. "Hey, wait up!"

Nick heard Hank puff up behind him, but he couldn't stop till he reached Maddie's new house, the one Greg was barred from, police cars parked at varying angles in front of it. Uniformed officers restrained curious neighbors and encouraged them to return to their homes for their own safety. Surveying the scene, Nick eventually spotted the captain in charge of the negotiating team and made his way to the command post.

"Sansone?" the short, bulky captain said in surprise. Jack Higham had graduated a few classes before Nick at the Academy, and they'd always been on good terms. He lifted his dark glasses at peer at Nick. "This isn't a downtown case."

Nick nodded and leaned close. "My—girlfriend—is one of your hostages," he said quietly, so all the officers wouldn't hear. Officers were normally discouraged from being involved in cases with family members, and Nick knew by all rights Higham could have him thrown off the scene.

"Son of a bitch." The words reeked of emotion. "I'm sorry."

"Me too." Nick tried to smile, and almost succeeded. He looked up at the house. Suzanne's car was parked in the driveway. The closed curtains hid all signs of life. "What's happening? Where's the Morgans' daughter?"

He could see Higham debating whether to fill him in, protocol forbidding it, but at last the captain let his humanity override the rules. "She's over there in the van, talking to Sergeant Fuller. Best we can determine, her father showed up this morning before she went to school. He went nuts, ranted most of the morning until the attorney arrived, then he grabbed her. It wasn't long after that the girl managed to escape, when the lawyer managed to create some kind of diversion."

Nick nodded, clenching his teeth to keep his

chin firm. He couldn't show how close he was to having his heart torn in half. Higham would boot him for sure, then. "Are we sure the women are unharmed at this time?" he said, when he could get the words out without betraying himself.

The captain's steely eyes stared directly into Nick's. "We don't know. The neighbor reported a gunshot about ten minutes ago." As another officer called the captain to the telephone, he excused himself. "We'll do the best we can," he said.

Nick turned away, cold fear in the pit of his stomach. Hank finally caught up with him as the news media vans started pulling up on either side of the barricades. Nick shared with Hank what the captain had told him.

"So what now?"

"Now we wait," Nick said, staring at the brick residence.

****

Suzanne felt a thud behind her right shoulder into the frame of the couch. By some miracle, Morgan had missed, even at this close range. *Was he that drunk, or is it just too dark to tell?* The noise of the shot echoed in her ears. If he couldn't see her well enough to fire accurately, then he probably couldn't determine if he'd hit her without turning on the light. So she'd just play possum. If he thought she was dead, surely he wouldn't try to shoot her again.

Or at least she hoped so.

She let out one, long, ragged breath, then tried to make her breathing as shallow as possible, so Morgan wouldn't realize she was alive. She heard Maddie whimper.

"Now that wasn't so hard," Morgan muttered.

From her position on the couch, Suzanne could make out the two of them on the loveseat. Maddie shook her head, begging with her eyes.

He must have put the gun down, because his right hand was empty so he could caress Maddie's face, just as if there weren't three layers of duct tape there. "Don't you see, I'll have to kill you now. I'm a murderer, Maddie. See what you've made me do?" He kissed her forehead gently. "You should have stood by me. That's what women are supposed to do. Women are supposed to be sweet and obedient, not ball busting bitches like her. But I guess she learned her lesson now. With all the trouble that woman caused us, she still couldn't stand up to good, old-fashioned Smith and Wesson justice." He snickered, then burst into a whoop of hysterical laughter. He stood up and grabbed the gun, firing it into the ceiling twice. "Smith and Wesson justice! Makes all men equal!" Chunks of ceiling plaster rained down on them.

Suzanne tried not to flinch. Her ears still rang from the reverberation of the prior shot, and now every sound felt like it came from the depths of a tunnel. He kept giggling, just a little, every so often, and then fell to his knees before his helpless ex-wife.

"You always said you thought I should treat you with respect, dollface. Let you try something first. It's finally your chance. You'll be dead, and I'll be free. Able to start over again, far away from here. All that money I had squirreled away—oh!" His tone changed to pure treacle. "Did your attorney fail to find my hidden treasures? Oh. Yes she did. But, see, now you won't have to bother to have her disbarred. I've disbarred her for you." He kissed her again. "You're welcome."

Then the phone rang.

The noise penetrated Suzanne's ears with a pang. The bell apparently did the same for Morgan, because he leapt to his feet and whirled toward the offending sound, gun drawn. *I thought Maddie said he'd pulled the phone from the wall,* she thought dreamily, trying to focus on Morgan despite the ache in her head.

"It's my damn cellphone," he mumbled. "Who'd be calling me now?" He paced back and forth as the ringing continued from the coat tree by the front door. "Maybe it's the store. If they've got a problem, I can handle it and be back to you in just a minute, my love." The phone continued to summon him, twelve, thirteen, fourteen rings... He lurched across the floor to dig in his pocket for the phone.

"Morgan," he said. "Who's this? You're where?" A long pause was followed by a string of curses as he dropped the phone. He went to the front picture window and pulled the curtain aside ever so slightly. "Motherfucker." Ducking away from the window, he went back to pacing, then finally retrieved the phone.

A ray of hope lit in Suzanne. It had to be the police. If they were outside, the house would be surrounded, with the SWAT team ready to come in and rescue them. *Good girl, Katie,* she thought, relief threatening to overwhelm her. It was difficult not to move. Her position cut off the circulation in her hand, and the pins-and-needles feeling in it was becoming painful. Only a little while longer...

"Yeah, so what do you want?" Morgan barked. "Everything's fine in here. Me and the old lady are just having a little disagreement, that's all. Nothing we need cops to handle for us." He listened for a minute, then laughed his cocky laugh. "She's crazy! You know kids. They don't understand that mothers and fathers fight over nothing at all. Why don't you send her back in here, and she can see her mother is just fine."

Maddie shook her head violently, moaning through the tape. Morgan moved away from her, into the kitchen. Suzanne heard the clink of ice cubes into a glass and took the opportunity to move just a little, so her hand would regain feeling. She wasn't tied up. So if she had the chance, she'd do what she could to save herself and Maddie.

Listening, she couldn't believe Morgan was going to stop for a drink, right now. Not that getting ready to face down the whole police department wouldn't call for a little extra courage, even the liquid kind... The whole police department? she thought with a jolt. Would Nick be there? Cops hung on every word of those dispatchers on the radio. If he'd been there, he must have heard. Would he know she was there? Her lover could be going through the same agony as she, wondering if she'd survive this. She hoped he'd been busy, distracted—that he'd somehow be oblivious to what had happened. One of them, at least, could be spared this pain.

Morgan lambasted whoever was on the phone, someone obviously insisting on coming in to check on their welfare. Suzanne seized the chance to speak to the bound woman.

"Maddie, I'm all right," Suzanne whispered as quietly as she could. "Just hang on."

The woman slumped back in her chair, limp with relief. Suzanne relaxed into her "possum" position.

Morgan's voice was getting louder. "Who gives a damn if I shoot a gun into my wall? It's my wall! I paid for it, you bet I did, one way or another!" Another shot. "See, it's none of your fucking business!" He moved back into the living room rather suddenly, and Suzanne was grateful her timing had been perfect. He'd shoved the gun into the front of his waistband. "You can't come in and arrest me for shooting my house." He swirled the ice cubes around in his tall glass, and took a deep gulp of whatever was in it. "No, she can't come to the phone right now. She's laying down, resting. My daughter's disappearance upset her quite a bit." He listened for a moment, then said, "Yes, I *would* mind if you came in to check on her. This is still America, last time I heard. You have no business here."

Obviously agitated, Morgan resumed his pacing. "No, she can't come to the phone, either. What am I, a Goddamned message service? Well, I don't really care how that makes you feel. I'm a Pittsburgh city councilman. I'll have your job if you don't go away and leave me the hell alone!"

Suzanne watched the man, agonies of nerves grabbing her stomach. What would he do now? Would he get more desperate? Would the pressure of the police outside force his hand, so he'd shoot Maddie? The police evidently wanted proof that she and Maddie were uninjured. If they didn't get it, what would they do next? She tried to remember news reports she'd seen about hostage situations. Something about loud rock music and tear gas... Or sharpshooters? With dawning understanding, she guessed why Morgan had moved out of the kitchen. He'd been a visible target without the curtains drawn, as they were here. They wouldn't be able to get a bead on him in this room.

"What protection order?" he snarled. "That's a bunch of crap, that is... There's nothing to talk about. All I want is for you all to get the hell away from here. If you don't...well, maybe then someone *is* going to get hurt." He slapped the phone and shoved it in his shirt pocket.

"I should have killed the little bitch first." Morgan glared at Maddie, then returned to his erratic pacing, walking the length of the living room, muttering to himself.

Suzanne caught snatches of his monologue as he passed by her. He seemed to grasp the reality of his situation, because he was concerned for his own safety. He was trying to work out a plan whereby he could kill Maddie and still escape with his life, but his options had been severely limited by his daughter's betrayal. Morgan had probably figured he could kill Suzanne, his ex-wife and his child and be long gone before anyone discovered them. At least Katie's life had been saved.

His mumbled self-argument internal discussion continued for what seemed an eternity. Suzanne breathed shallowly through her discomfort. She couldn't risk even the twitch of a finger, or he'd take another shot at her. With the adrenaline that must be pumping through his system right now, the effect of the alcohol might be neutralized. The next bullet might kill her.

"Morgan!" The voice boomed from outside, amplified by a bullhorn. "This is Captain Higham. I'm giving you one final chance to release your hostages and come out with your hands up." There was a pause. "You have thirty seconds."

"Thirty seconds?" he said, sounding like a little boy caught setting off firecrackers in his grandmother's back alley. "I can't decide anything in thirty seconds." He pulled the cell phone from his pocket, then pushed some buttons. It must have been redial, because he started in on Higham as soon as the call was answered.

"Look here, you idiot. Do you want to get everyone killed? Do you know what that will do to your career?"

He listened, pacing, then burst into a shower of obscenities as he kicked the coffee table. The low table didn't weigh much, but the corner of it crashed into Suzanne's leg. She couldn't hide a moan as the point pierced her skin, but thankfully he was distracted by his argument. She lay there fighting to stay silent.

Hey, maybe I'll tell him I'd be in less pain if he'd just shoot me.

It was a joke, a bad one, and not funny to

anyone else since she couldn't even breathe it aloud. But the black humor helped her hang on.

"Get me someone with some balls, huh? I can't negotiate with you."

Oh sure you can, Suzanne begged silently. *Someone needs to get us out of here.*

But the truth was, Greg Morgan was right in front of her, off his last nut. Maddie was helpless in every way. The police were all on the far side of a locked door. She was the one with the best chance of making a difference.

Could that happen without her losing her life?

"Yeah, well, here's the thing," Morgan said. "You just don't seem to believe me. So let me show you what I've got up my sleeve." A nervous laugh. "Or down my pants." He cut the phone off again and set the glass, now empty, on a table. He pulled the gun out of his waistband and studied it a moment, taking a long breath. "I've got to do something." He cocked it and pointed it at his former wife. "Maddie, I wish there was another way. I know you wouldn't want to live without me, my darling. Guess we're both going, now. Don't see much other way to go. See you on the other side."

That was it, Suzanne realized. He'd put together the final picture that he wasn't going to survive this. That meant he had nothing to lose. If someone didn't intervene right now, they were all dead.

A flashback to those headlines, those phone calls when she'd lost that client years before filled her mind. She'd promised herself she wouldn't lose Maddie, and she wouldn't. She wouldn't.

"No, damn you!" she yelled, shoving herself upward, throwing herself at Morgan. Her leg was half asleep and she stumbled over the table sitting askew between them. His mouth dropped open, and he staggered back as she fell into him. The gun went off once, twice, close to her head, but she didn't think she was hit. She was deafened, though, the ringing in her ears blocking all other sound. Morgan reeked of sweat and spoiled alcohol. He tried to wriggle out from under her, but she couldn't move.

Moments later, the front window exploded inward, and the room filled with a bright light. Her ears popped. Suzanne rolled off of the heavy-set councilman and hit the floor, the contact sending waves of pain through her. The floor shook with the pounding of heavy feet, motion all around her, men in uniform, men with guns, but she couldn't focus. Had he hit her? What had happened? Was Maddie all right? The confusion overwhelmed her, and she faded from consciousness, still trying to put together her situation.

"Suzanne?"

The voice penetrated the fog that had swallowed her up, consumed her. She struggled to follow it.

"Suz, come on, honey, open your eyes."

That was Nick's voice. She knew it. Her breath caught and she fought to open her eyes. When she finally got control, she looked up briefly, blinking in the bright light. The air was cold. She was outdoors. She was...in an ambulance. *What?* A paramedic swabbed her forehead. Her arms were bandaged. Her lips battled to get words out.

"That's my girl. Come on. You're going to be all right."

Someone squeezed her hand and she forced herself to keep her eyes open. It was Nick, looking worried, kneeling next to her, on her right side, while the paramedic worked on the left. "Maddie?" she whispered.

"She's good. She's fine." He grinned. "You saved them both."

"Hope I'm getting hazardous duty pay." She coughed, and tried to move. At first, she felt rising panic as she couldn't move her shoulders or sit up, but Nick tapped the stretcher's restraining straps.

"Just relax, all right? Everyone's out of the house, you're safe. Jim here says you're in one piece, just banged up a bit. They're getting you ready to go to the hospital for a thorough check."

"Don't want the hospital," she murmured. Something she wasn't asking. What else did she need to know? Something nagged at her.

"You're going. Period. None of your usual legalese or stalling or technical excuses. I nearly lost you and I'm going to make sure you're all right. I'm not letting you slip away again. No argument on this one, woman. "

She knew that tone. *Not like there's much you can do about it now.* Wait. Morgan. That was it. "What happened to Greg?"

Nick glanced up at the paramedic, who shook his head. "Pity," he muttered. To Suzanne, he said, "Suicide by cop. They said when they went in, he still had the gun in his hand. He wouldn't put it down, and actually tried to take a shot at a couple of the guys. They didn't have much of a choice." He frowned. "Guess it'll save the city the expense of a trial."

She sighed with relief. "It's over."

He leaned down and kissed her lips, a soft, warm reminder of all they'd shared and all those days yet to come. "To the contrary, my love. Everything is just beginning."

A word about the author...

Alana Lorens dreamed for many years of being an astronaut, maybe even President, but settled instead for inspired excursions into fictional places with fascinating imaginary companions that she likes to share with others. She has been a published writer for over thirty years, including seven years as a reporter and editor at a newspaper in Homestead, Florida. Her list of publications is eclectic, from science fiction to romance to horror, from tech reporting to television reviews. This is her second novel with The Wild Rose Press; the first, SECRETS IN THE SAND, was released in April 2011. Alana is married to an absent-minded computer geek. Together, they have a dozen computers, seven children and a full house in northwestern Pennsylvania.

Find out more at http://alanalorens.com

Thank you for purchasing
this Wild Rose Press publication.
For other wonderful stories of romance,
please visit our on-line bookstore at
www.thewildrosepress.com.

For questions or more information
contact us at
info@thewildrosepress.com.

The Wild Rose Press, Inc.
www.TheWildRosePress.com

To visit with authors of The Wild Rose Press
join our yahoo loop at
http://groups.yahoo.com/group/thewildrosepress/

www.ingramcontent.com/pod-product-compliance
Lightning Source LLC
Chambersburg PA
CBHW070834280626
47161CB00015B/596

* 9 7 8 1 6 1 2 1 7 2 5 1 4 *